THE CON

NICOLE MARSH

The Con Blurb

My name is McKenzie and I'm broke. Like eating a single dented can of SpaghettiO's for two days in a row, broke.

When my shady neighbor, Derek, proposes an idea for some easy money, I make a difficult decision and turn him down. You see, he wants to rob someone from the nice part of town and even though I'm desperate, I don't know that I'll ever be THAT desperate.

Until, a few days pass and suddenly I am THAT desperate. Honestly, the whole idea is a bit like Robin Hood... steal from the rich to feed the poor (myself). Robin Hood is a legend so it shouldn't be too hard to follow in his footsteps, right?

Unless the family you're trying to con has a son your age. A golden-boy quarterback with certified swoon-worthy abs... er manners, type son. To rob his family, I'll have to get close to him without revealing all my secrets, or allowing him to steal my heart. Which should be easy, because he'd never be interested in a girl like me... right?

Contents

I shuffle the pile of small bills, counting the ones and fives a second time and sighing when I come to the same amount.

$52.50.

After a full day filling in, last–minute, for the local catering company, I didn't even break a hundred dollars in tips. My aching arms and feet begin pulsing even harder, upon learning their efforts were for a meager fifty bucks.

I try to placate myself; any money is better than no money. In time, this town will be behind me. Once I scrape together enough cash from working these odd jobs, in addition to my regular shifts at the motel.

Unfortunately, that day is not today. Although, it's looming closer, along with my eighteenth birthday and high school graduation.

With determination, I heave my weary body off my rickety kitchen chair. Shuffling towards the counter, I move to open the ancient, silver coffee tin sitting there.

I'm not old enough to establish a bank account, yet. So, for now I make do with hiding my small savings in plain sight. Placing the money inside, I pull out the old, folded, lined piece of paper from between the small rolls of bills. I cross a line through the previous amount and write in the new.

Goodbye $253.83.

Hello $306.33.

My life savings. A measly three-hundred bucks.

Sighing, I open one of my cupboards and swipe my hand around until it hits a dented can of SpaghettiOs. Almost all the food I buy is in packaging that's a little damaged. The imperfections lead to discounted prices, even though there isn't a change in the taste. Maybe someday I'll be the type of person that cares how the outside of my food looks but starving stomachs don't care if packaging is pretty. Right now, I'm too broke to be picky, so all the canned and frozen food in my house is a little banged up.

I inspect the pot on the stove and determine it's clean enough to use again without washing it, then plop the contents of the can inside. Twisting the knob for the burner until the clicking sound turns into flames, I rest against the opposite counter, a mere eight inches away. Tapping my foot, I eye the pot as I wait for it to heat up my dinner.

A knock startles me as I watch the thick, red liquid dotted with yellow circles in the pot begin to bubble. Cautiously parting the curtains, I peer through the tiny, rectangular window placed over the kitchen sink.

Outside, on the dry, patchy grass, stands my hulking,

tattooed neighbor, Derek. His eyes jump from my door, locking onto my face peering through the dirty glass. He mimes opening a door, jabbing at the one before him pointedly.

I guess there's no way I can avoid him, since he's clearly seen me. Exhaling heavily, I force myself to open my door, yanking on the flimsy tin, but leaving the old, holey screen between us. I address him politely, "Why are you here, Derek?"

Well, that's polite from me.

He smirks, his sharp incisors flashing in the light of the setting sun, and the dimple on his left cheek makes an appearance. "Is that any way to greet an old friend, Kenzie-girl?"

I shrug, hoping he'll just get on with it. We both know he's not an old friend, but I'm tired and hungry, and don't have time for his bullshit. So, I let it slide.

"Can I come in?" He says, his tone low and secretive.

I don't move, allowing the silence to linger for a moment and his smirk starts to drop from his face. His dimple slowly disappears, and his dark eyes narrow the longer I stand with the screen between us, unmoving and unspeaking. I finally realize he's not going to leave without specific prompting from me. Annoyed, I respond, my tone completely flat as I force the word past my lips. "No."

He glances to his left and runs a hand through his thick, dark hair like this already isn't going how he expected. I'm sure it isn't. Derek has that bad boy, motorcycle gang vibe going for him. His head is shaved on the sides with a length of dark, floppy hair across the top. He's tall and well-muscled, since he spends most of his days lifting cement bags or whatever it is construction workers do. Tattoos cover the visible skin on his arms and chest, winding down into his shirt beyond sight.

I bet I'm the first girl he's spoken to, in at least three years, that hasn't swooned when he used his bedroom voice and dimpled grin to try and get what he wants. But unlike those other girls, I've grown up in the same neighborhood as him and I know Derek is Trouble--with a capital T. The kind of guy that you want to keep close enough to watch, but far enough you can walk away unscathed when the shit finally hits the fan for him. I know he couldn't afford his car, motorcycle, and the piles of electronics he's always moving in and out of his trailer, on the salary of a construction worker. So, shit will hit the fan for him, eventually.

His voice is exasperated, and his eyes are hard when he finally speaks again. "Look, I don't know how to tell you this, but everyone around the park thinks you've been acting uppity. Almost as if you're too good for this place. I think you should come to my party tomorrow night so your old friends don't become enemies."

I scan his serious face while I consider his words. Lately I have noticed some of my neighbors stopped greeting me whenever I ride past on my bike. I hadn't given it much thought before now. Nevertheless, being labeled as uppity when living in a trailer park is never a good thing. Derek is definitely bad news, but his words surprisingly sound like a warning from an "old friend", as he had put it.

Reluctantly, I nod my head at him. "I'll think about it."

Derek's dark eyes give me another hard stare. "You wanna be careful Kenz. Anything could happen to someone out here alone." The 'like you' belonging at the end of his sentence is silent, but we both know his implication. He continues after a brief pause, "It's better for people to have your back, than to have people coming after it." The serious expression falls from his face and he takes a step closer to my screen door. His gaze slides up and down my body clad in a pair of grimy black pants and a stained white blouse, the clothes I wore to my catering job. A salacious look enters his eyes and his lips turn up at the corners. "You sure you don't want some company, Kenzie-girl?"

With a roll of my eyes, I slam the door shut and turn the measly lock in the handle. "Goodnight, Derek." I shout through the thin material. His veiled threats have my heart racing, but I shake off his words and the residual fear, stepping away from the door without waiting to see if he responds.

A weird gurgle coming from the stove quickly distracts me from our interaction. I rush to check on my dinner, having forgotten about it during my conversation with Derek.

"Shit, shit, shit."

The pot bubbled over, spilling a coat of red sauce over the blotchy metal sides. During my distraction, the liquid spread across the stovetop to drip down onto my cracked linoleum floor. Eyeing the scene for half a second, I rush to open the closest drawer and grab an oven mitt. I frantically lift the pot, placing it into the sink before turning off the burner.

Pausing for a second to regroup, I push away the stray strands of raven hair that escaped my ponytail and dig under the sink for a spare roll of paper towels and some cleaner. Armed with the only tools I have, I return to the stove and carefully wipe up the spill, avoiding the hot portions of metal near the burner the best I can. My stomach grumbles in protest as I use the entire roll of paper towels to wipe up over half of my dinner.

When I'm finally finished, I plop the rest of the SpaghettiOs into a bowl and sit at the table. They're now cold and barely edible, a slightly congealed mass of red sauce and tiny circular noodles, but I devour them anyways.

After cleaning up my meal, I take the world's quickest shower before falling into bed. Despite my bone-deep weariness and throbbing limbs, I lay awake for hours. My mind continues to drift back to Derek's words, replaying them over and over. The repetition of his message causes me to become slightly paranoid and I force myself not to jump at every howl of the wind and slam of a trailer door.

In an attempt at reassurance, I create a little mantra and continue saying the words to myself as I lay in the dark. At some point, I finally drift into a fitful sleep.

Chapter 2

I jam my feet into the hideous black shoes that are part of my work uniform and hustle out my front door. This morning, I slept through my first alarm and now I'm running late for an extra shift I picked up at the motel. Even though I went to bed at a decent time, I tossed and turned all night, and I feel like I barely closed my eyes before it was time to wake up.

Outside, I peel my bike off the rusted side of the trailer and hop on, immediately spinning the pedals as rapidly as possible—in hopes of making up for lost time due to my late rising. I alternate between sitting and standing, as I pump my legs aggressively, flying down the street. As I'm rounding the corner to my destination, a car honks loudly and someone catcalls me. Startled, I whip my head in the direction of the noise. The movement throws me off kilter and I barely make the turn without falling over. After regaining my balance, I flip off whoever it was, knowing they can't see me, but committing to the motion to soothe my soul, regardless.

I arrive at work with two minutes to spare. Throwing my chain around the bike rack out front, I fan myself with my shirt a few times before walking into the motel. The air conditioning inside hits my sticky skin, cooling the sweat generated from pedaling in the Alabama summer air. It feels good now, but I know I'll be sweating again soon, once I begin cleaning rooms.

My boss, Mr. Mouchard comes strolling out of his office as the sensor sends a dinging noise through the lobby, alerting him someone has entered. When he sees it's me, his upper lip tweaks into a grin. "Ahh the beautiful McKenzie. I didn't realize you were working today."

Mr. Mouchard looks like a rat, with his buck teeth, creepy pencil mustache, and skinny hunched frame. He tries to hide the fact that he's bald by growing out the few wispy strands of hair he has left and combing them over the top of his head.

I act polite, but distant towards him, even though he creeps me the fuck out with all his innuendos and his inclination to stand too close. Just over a year ago, he was the only person in town willing to hire a sixteen-year-old with no work experience. He also pays cash, under the table, so I don't have to file taxes by myself or pay a check cashing fee to have access to my money. I may not like the guy, but I need him.

For now.

"Took over Jenna's shift," I call over my shoulder, continuing through the front lobby to the custodial closet. I open it quickly, stamping down my timecard simply labeled MC. I'm sure it's illegal to pay minors under the table, but I guess keeping my name off everything makes him less likely to get caught.

On the door inside the closet is a list of rooms that need to be cleaned. Giving it a brief glance, I make quick work of loading my cart with the fresh linens and cleaning supplies I need for the day, then wheel the cart out.

Mr. Mouchard lurks behind the front desk, stroking his left index finger across his thin, brown mustache. He's pretending to stare at something on the counter, but I can feel his eyes following my movements. Ignoring him and his creepy, beady eyes, I roll the cart outside towards the first vacant room on the list.

Room 103.

I do a courtesy knock and yell, "housekeeping." After a ten second pause with no response, I swipe the universal room key from the cart against the pad next to the door and push down the handle into the room.

A cursory glance confirms it's empty. I tug the cart in halfway behind me, enough to prop the door open, then take in the state of the room.

The sheets are tangled into a massive, twisted heap on the center of the bed, and the pillows are on the floor. A few dots of brown-red liquid are splattered across the bedding. A broken beer bottle lays on the floor in the far corner and one of the walls has an unidentifiable brown substance smeared across it. In the bathroom, the toilet is unflushed, and the towels are all jumbled on the floor, one entirely drenched with yellow liquid.

Not too bad.

At least not for this place.

I make quick work of donning my yellow rubber gloves and start with gathering all the discarded fabrics. Next, I pick up the large pieces of glass and vacuum over the smaller ones. I spray and scrub the wall, wipe down the bathroom, and replace the linens.

Within twenty minutes the place is as clean as it's going to get. Sliding my cart out, I move on to the next room, praying the rest are as clean as room 103.

They're not.

By the time my four-hour shift is over, I smell like rancid sewage.

A combination of miscellaneous substances, splashes of liquid from unclogging toilets, and sweat has completely overtaken the light, fresh scent of my deodorant. My hair has half fallen out of its ponytail; the dark strands falling around my face and sticking to my clammy neck. My pale blue work top is stained and damp.

With another sigh, probably my twentieth of the day so far, I wheel the cart back towards the lobby. Pausing outside the door, I take a bracing breath to prepare for my next interaction with Mr. Mouchard.

Steeling my spine, I enter, making a beeline for the custodial closet. Swinging open the door, I park the cart and stamp my timecard again, signifying the end of my shift. I turn to leave, reaching my hand to flip off the light switch, but stop dead in my tracks, stifling a quick inhale when Mr. Mouchard appears in the doorframe.

He smirks at me, holding his hand out. Resting in his palm is a small stack of bills. "Payday," he rasps out. His breath hits my face, due to his unnecessary closeness. I'm forced to flatten my expression against a flinch when I inhale his used air that smells of bologna and coffee.

My face remains neutral while I reach out to snatch the money, careful to avoid touching his moist palms. I've made that mistake in the past and I never will again. It took me half an hour of scrubbing to remove his salami-scented sweat from my body.

Quickly flipping through the stack to assess the amount, I shove the money deep into the pocket of my black jeans and raise an eyebrow, waiting for him to move out of the way. Mr. Mouchard tries to hold out, hoping I'll slide myself against him to exit. I widen my stance and cross my arms over my chest, settling into the closet, refusing to be forced to touch my creepy, middle-aged boss.

He finally backs down once he realizes I'm not going to brush past him to leave. He slinks away, retreating to the counter in the lobby. I wait until he's fully ensconced behind the desk before turning off the light in the closet and striding to the front door.

"See you tomorrow, Mr. Mouchard," I call out in a polite, but flippant tone. Then exit into the summer heat without waiting to hear his response.

Outside, I hop back onto my bike and pedal the mile and a half worth of asphalt separating me from my trailer. Prior to returning home, I stop at the administrative office for the park, needing to pay my lot rent. Propping my bike against the side of the building, I take a deep sniff near my underarms to see if the wind has cleared any of my unpleasant odor.

The deep breath ends on a gag.

Nope.

Still stink.

I force myself to go into the office anyways, being smelly doesn't make it so my rent isn't due. Inside, I stand by the front counter, waiting for the manager to acknowledge me. Dragging my money from my pocket, I count out $40 from the $47 I made today, between my hourly wage and weekly tips at the motel.

When Mildred finally glances up from her computer, I offer her a shy smile. "Hey Mildred, I brought the first half of my lot rent." I hold out the small stack of hard-earned money, even though parting with it feels like handing away a piece of my soul. At least the office manager allows me to pay half the lot rent on the first and the other half on the fifteenth. And living in the trailer park in our tiny town is dirt cheap.

Mildred shuffles the bills between her hands, counting, then recounting again. "You're twenty dollars short," she states in her gravelly voice, without glancing up from the money on her desk.

"No, no." I stammer, protesting. "I just counted it, that's forty dollars."

"Lot rent went up to one-twenty. Didn't you get the notice? We sent it to the email address on file." After her words, she finally moves her eyes to my face, raising a single, questioning brow in my direction.

Shit.

It's my mom's email address on file. Meaning I didn't get the notice my lot rent would be increased by fifty percent, because my mom is technically the one renting the lot.

My stomach clenches over the thought of paying more to live here. One-hundred and twenty bucks a month for this place is a total scam. The roads are dirt, the grounds unkempt, and at least twice a month our water gets shut off without notice.

"I didn't. I mean, we didn't get the notice or maybe my mom forgot. Let me run home and grab another twenty!" I exclaim, inching backwards to the door.

Mildred stares at my face for another second before her gaze drops back to her computer. A silent dismissal, as if she doubts my ability to pay and is already planning on a vacant lot in the near future.

Scrambling, I exit the office and frantically pedal the short distance to my trailer. I guess I'll have to pull money from my savings jar to cover the rest of rent due today.

Unfortunately, this isn't the first time I've had to do this, and I groan at the thought of my savings dwindling, just to keep living in a shitty trailer. There's been times when it couldn't be helped, like when I had the flu last year and when I needed time off to study for the PSAT, then later, my finals.

I refuse to fail out of high school and give up my dreams of college; to work more so I can stay afloat in this crap hole. Dreaming of a better future is one of the only things that keeps me going.

Short-term, I'll pull a twenty out of my jar to cover rent.

Long-term, I'll need to see about picking up more shifts at the motel.

Or maybe find another job, a steady one, not odds and ends like the catering gig.

On top of everything else, my senior year of high school is starting in a week, which will limit my availability, making it more difficult to find work, and pick up extra shifts.

By the time I reach my trailer, I'm a mess of stress and anxiety. The minute I feel like I'm finally climbing uphill, an avalanche falls on top of me, eliminating all the progress I've made. Clambering inside, I firmly shut the door behind me so no one can see what I'm doing. I open my canister and pull out a small roll of bills, count out a few to make $20, then carefully replace the lid, and slide the container back into its place.

I decide to walk back to the front office. It's only a quarter mile away and I'm not particularly eager to part with my money, anyways. The distance passes quickly, with the summer sun beating down on my already sweaty skin. I open the door and step back inside, feeling grimier and poorer than before.

Mildred silently holds out her palm and I place the bills into it, waiting to release my breath until she confirms I'm no longer short. "Alright, dear. You're good until next month."

My breath whooshes out of my body and she scribbles down a hand-written receipt for me. I snatch the paper, shoving it into my back pocket as I trudge home for a shower.

Chapter 3

With slow determination, I blow-dry my hair creating a straight sheet of midnight colored strands floating around my shoulders and down my back. Wandering from my bathroom to my closet, I consider all my options before choosing a pair of light wash jeans with holes in the knees and a thin strapped, flowy, floral tank top. After I slide into a pair of sneakers, I square my shoulders and take a deep breath, then step out of my trailer.

Usually I avoid the other residents of the trailer park, as much as possible. Connections with these people will inevitably suck me into staying here after I graduate, which is not an option. The park is a temporary stay for me, not a permanent destination. My goal is to save up enough money and move away from this place. I want to grow roots in a bigger city, hopefully while attending college on a scholarship.

When I turn to lock the door behind me, I experience another bout of indecisiveness.

Do I really want to go to this party?

Of course, I don't, but I push away the thought of abandoning the party. Living here is not ideal, but while I do, I need to be friendly and fit in. Like Derek said, I'm alone out here and advertising my loner status will only add to my problems.

Following the sounds of music drifting down the dirt road, I pick my way across the patchy, grass "yards" towards Derek's trailer. Upon arriving, I take a few minutes to survey the small crowd. It's eight at night, but the sun hasn't fully set yet, leaving plenty of light for me to check out the scene.

A small fire has been built in the center, just a few logs thrown together on a patch of dirt, with camping chairs and blankets scattered about the grass. Some people are using them to sit, while others stand around in clusters. Seeing the other girls, half dressed in tiny summer dresses, I feel overdressed. Or at least over-covered, as in too much skin is covered by my ripped jeans and sneakers.

Derek glances up from his conversation with a few guys he rides motorcycles with, and his dark eyes instantly lock onto mine. "Kenzie-girl," he yells, accompanying my name with a "come here" motion.

His bellow has half the party focusing on me, probably wondering who Kenzie-girl is, since I barely recognize anyone here. Ignoring their looks, I weave between the blankets and chairs, slowly making my way towards Derek.

He smiles as I approach, stepping forward to drape a tattooed arm around my shoulders, firmly holding me against his side to introduce me to his friends. "Kenz, this is Zane and Kevin."

Derek's friend Zane nods his head at his name. He's a tall, skinny dude with spiked hair, clad in a wife beater and gym shorts. He's also wearing a pair of aviator sunglasses, at night, which he probably thinks makes him appear cool and mysterious. He kind of looks like a douchebag that's stuck in 2004, but I keep my opinion to myself.

The other guy in our semi-circle, Kevin, leers at me over the top of his beer. He's almost the exact opposite of Zane. He's short, coming only to my shoulders, when I stand at five-foot eight, with a paunch overhanging his too-tight cargo shorts.

I say my hellos, then crane my neck around, glancing longingly back at my trailer. I already regret letting Derek's warning convince me to come here. It doesn't even seem like this is a party for people our age that live at the park.

I'll stay for an hour. That's long enough.

One hour. I can do it.

I tug myself free from Derek's arm and wander over to the keg. After filling my plastic cup with beer, I situate myself at the fringe of a small group gathered nearby. I sip on the warm, bitter liquid in my red solo cup, while eavesdropping on them as they talk about their boring lives. I'm not actually participating in the conversation, but act like I am to keep Derek away.

A blonde-haired guy is in the middle of a story and I tune in, "This chick ordered like fifty-three cheeseburgers all with different toppings." He wildly gestures his hands in the air, making a big swirling circle.

I finish my beer while listening to him. He's kind of a maniac, making erratic motions that don't match his words, but I find myself laughing along with the rest of the group anyways. Distractedly, I finish two more cups full of the gross beer, back to back, as I watch him weave random tales and wave his arms around in the air to emphasize each point.

His antics and my slight buzz distract me, and I don't notice anyone approaching until a hand roughly grabs onto my arm. I'm dragged halfway around the trailer before I think to make a ruckus, to protest, to do anything to make someone notice what's happening to me.

Dropping my weight, I attempt to force the hand to release me, but the grip stays tight. I squirm around and see Kevin's chunky face leering at me.

"Dude, get the fuck off me," I demand, spitting the words out, angry over this guy's serious overstep of touching me without my permission.

He laughs at my vitriol, brushing it off as he continues hauling me towards some unknown destination. He's short, but outweighs me by at least fifty pounds and my struggles are ineffective at halting our progress forward. He finally stops when we're at the backside of Derek's trailer, facing the woods.

There are no lights on this side, and the sun has finally set, leaving us steeped in darkness. All the trailers are facing the opposite direction and a small trickle of fear runs down my spine. We are isolated, on the outskirts of a party. One I don't think anyone would notice or care I'm missing from.

Kevin increases the strength of his grip, while I survey our surroundings. The trailers blur as he twirls me to face him and adjusts his hands, moving further up my biceps. His hold on my skin feels tighter than a boa constrictor, and I already feel a bruise forming. He hasn't said anything yet, just firmly clutches my upper arms, while breathing heavily.

Out of the corner of my eye, I see the door to the trailer on my left begin to slide open. A hulking form exits, outlined by the porch light.

Hurriedly, I open my mouth and shout, "Help!" My voice is loud, but instantly muffled as Kevin places a sweaty palm against my face.

I open my mouth to bite his palm, eager to scream again. Hoping someone, maybe even the bulky stranger, will come to my rescue against this creepy drunk guy holding me hostage. My bite is futile, Kevin doesn't change his grip, he barely even grunts in response.

Attempting the tactic again, I open my mouth and... bite air. My eyebrows fly up my forehead in surprise as Kevin suddenly stumbles away from me. He half-falls back onto the dry grass, catching himself with his hands at the last second.

Stunned, I turn from my would-be assailant and come face-to-face with someone I never expected to see in my trailer park.

Collin Franzen.

"What is richy-rich doing in the trailer park?" My words are slightly slurred, and Collin narrows his eyes. I realize belatedly I spoke the thought out loud unintentionally.

His baritone is quiet, but firm and threatening when it floats through the air to reach my ears. "Back off."

My forehead scrunches in confusion, until I comprehend his words aren't directed at me. Twirling around, I find Kevin approaching again, from behind, invading my space as he strides forward. I take a step toward Collin, although I barely know him, my instincts tell me he is the lesser threat in this scenario.

Kevin stops to stare at the newcomer. "Who the hell are you?"

His question doesn't receive an answer.

Kevin takes another step forward, this time away from me and towards Collin. He puffs his chest out, as if that will make up for over a foot in height difference and a significant amount of muscle tone. "I asked you a question," he says to Collin, a scowl marring his face.

"And I chose not to answer." Collin's white teeth glint in the near dark as he smirks.

Kevin takes another menacing step forward and Collin's fist flies, hitting Kevin square in the nose. He drops like a sack of potatoes, hitting the ground with an impressive thud, a small flare of dust kicking up upon impact.

Collin turns to me; concern clear in his bright gaze. "Are you okay McKenzie?"

Stunned, my eyes widen at his words. "You...You know my name?"

"Yo, you crash my party throwing punches? What

the fuck dude?" Derek asks indignantly, cutting off Collin, as he rounds the corner into sight.

After another lingering, assessing look, Collin turns to Derek. "When he wakes up, ask what he planned to do with McKenzie when he started dragging her back here."

Derek's mouth drops open, but he quickly snaps it shut, lowering his fists from in front of his body. After a brief stare down, two pairs of eyes turn to me, one light and one dark. Their voices overlap as they both offer me their time.

Derek blurts out, "Come sit by the fire with me, Kenzie-girl."

While Collin offers, "Let me walk you home."

"I can walk home by myself, it's like fifteen feet away," I respond. Gesturing my hand in a circle to encompass the trailer park and Kevin still slumped on the ground. "Thanks for everything," I mutter, glancing at Collin then Derek.

"Anytime," Collin replies firmly, his gaze intensely focused on me.

When he finally walks away, I release a breath I hadn't realized I was holding. For the second time, I'm brought back to reality by a firm hand gripping my arm, but this time it's Derek, using his grasp to steer me home.

"You're straight trouble. I knew there was a reason I liked you, Kenzie-girl." He shoots me a wicked smirk as we walk, his face flashing in and out of sight from the porch lights we pass.

I stay silent, but Derek keeps chattering anyways. "I

always forget Golden Boy's grandma lives in the park. He doesn't usually waste his time with us though. Maybe he liiiikes you." He releases a cackle, like that last statement is too ridiculous to fathom, then we both fall into silence.

Our steps are the only noise, as we tread across the crunchy, dead grass. We finally reach my trailer and I fumble a few times before successfully opening my door. Derek leans in as if expecting a kiss when I pivot in the doorway to say goodnight.

Scoffing, I twirl back around and slam the door in his face. "Goodnight Derek," I call through the thin piece of tin before stomping towards the back of the trailer.

A muffled noise that sounds a lot like, "Someday, Kenz," comes through the door, but I ignore it to get ready for bed.

Chapter 4

"Mrp. Mrp. Mrp. Mrp" echoes through my brain before I've slept long enough to process the noise is my alarm. It's time to wake up for another shift at the motel.

In my groggy state, I slam my hand around to my left until the incessant noise ceases. Breathing out a sigh of relief at the silence, I shift to reacquaint myself with comfort, under my pile of blankets.

My brain is drifting back into a fuzzy dream state when a pounding noise begins at the front of my trailer. Groaning, I aim to ignore it and fall back asleep until a voice is added to the ruckus. Derek yells, "Kenzie-girl, open up, I need to talk to you."

Reluctantly, I drag myself out of my bed and trudge towards the door. Smoothing my hair into a slightly more respectable, but still tangled low ponytail, as I walk.

"What do you want?" I grit out while yanking the door open.

His gaze floats down my body, pausing on my chest briefly, then continuing all the way to my toes. I cross my arms and begin to tap my foot. "Derek you have ten seconds to tell me why you're waking me up before I shut this door in your face."

"I love it when you talk dirty to me," he purrs, his tone sultry to accompany the joking words.

"Ten, nine, eight…"

"Okay, okay." He holds his hands up in front of him, palms outward as a signal to pacify me. "I've been thinking about it all night. Golden Boy never interacts with anyone at the park, then he acts all knight in shining armor to save you from Kevin last night."

"He's not an asshole, like your friends. What's your point?" My words are each punctuated with a tap of my foot on the linoleum.

"Well, he seemed like maybe he actually feels… fondly towards you and his parents are super rich. They live in that brand-new development on the other side of town," Derek continues then shrugs, as if I'm going to fill in the blanks.

I throw my hands up, exasperated. "Did you come over here to play matchmaker? I don't have time for your shit, Derek."

"No, No," He waves his hands in the air, brushing my words aside. "I was thinking: what if you pretended to like him back, scoped out his parents place and then gave me the details? Zane and I would case the place and we could all split the profits."

I laugh and move to slam my door, but Derek's hand snakes out, whipping open the screen and gripping the thin piece of tin. I'm caught off-guard and my laughter dies in my throat as I narrow my eyes. Blatantly, I glare at his hand, still holding my door with the screen resting against the backside of his palm, then quirk a brow at him.

"Just think about it," he pleads.

"No." My tone is firm. I'm finished with this conversation, but Derek doesn't seem to get the hint.

"It's easy money."

"I prefer to work for my money," I counter.

Derek widens his eyes and pouts his lower lip. It's probably one of his usual seduction techniques which normally has girls swooning, but in my opinion, it makes him look like a child begging his mother for a cookie.

Not attractive.

"Kenzie," he whines, adding to the whole childlike vibe he's sending. "I'm taking all the risk. All you would do is be an informant and tell me the layout of the house, what valuables they keep in each room, and any security they have. Your part is way easier, with less risk involved, and you get an equal share in the profits. Aren't you saving up to leave this place? This will add to your funds. We could make a grand, each. Easy." Derek's tone is serious, and he allows silence to fill the space after his words.

Following the brief pause, I mutter, "I'll think about it."

I wish I could say my response was just to get Derek off my back, so I could close the door and prepare for work. However, he'd successfully put a bug in my ear like he'd intended.

A thousand dollars is a lot of money to someone like me. Dismissing the idea of adding such a large sum to my savings is difficult, even if I would have to commit a crime to earn it.

Derek's shoulders relax, making me realize how anxious he was for my response. "You do that Kenzie-girl. Let me know when you decide." Without having to slam my door on him, he leaves. I watch for a second as he drifts down my steps, back towards his trailer, our conversation repeating itself in my head.

A thousand dollars.

Sighing, I gently close the door and return to my bedroom. At least Derek kept me from being late. I slowly dig through my clothes until I find a clean uniform top, then begin the process of getting dressed.

By the time I'm ready for work, I've successfully talked myself down from Derek's offer and the potential money. Although it's tempting, I don't want to start down that path. I refuse to become the type of person that drags others down in order to climb up.

Deciding to tell Derek the next time I see him, it's a definite no from me, I lock my trailer as I leave, then pick up my bike. The heat is already scorching outside, and I waffle between grabbing a pair of shorts to ride in or not.

The thought of Mr. Mouchard eyeing my ass and legs in a pair of cutoffs, while I make my way to the lobby bathroom to change, makes the decision for me. No shorts today. I jump onto my bike and pedal in the direction of work, instantly beginning to sweat.

I arrive at the motel a few minutes earlier than usual.

Despite the sun beating down on me, I linger outside to kill the extra time, kicking pebbles on the cement, not wanting to spend a second longer with Mr. Mouchard than absolutely necessary.

When it's two minutes to my shift, I shove open the lobby door while sighing deeply. My steps falter, in surprise as my eyes find Mr. Mouchard and see he isn't standing alone. With him, behind the front counter, is a girl a couple inches shorter than my five-foot eight frame. She has cotton candy pink hair and huge doe eyes that take up a third of her face. Although the feature is extra-large, her small nose and plump lips make it work, and she's startlingly pretty.

"McKenzie, so glad you could join us," Mr. Mouchard oozes out, in his usual, slimy tone. He gestures to the girl standing next to him. "This is Candy, I hired her to take over some of your shifts, since you'll be starting school soon."

Fuck.

I needed to ask him for more hours to cover the raise in cost for my lot rent and he went and hired someone else?

Fuckity Fuck Fuck.

I'm forced to shake myself out of my inner dialogue, stepping forward to shake Candy's hand when she smiles and offers it to me. She leans across the counter to meet me halfway and her breasts instantly capture my attention. They're unnaturally large and threaten to spill out of her blouse at the slightest movement, straining the top button of her pale blue work shirt.

Dragging my eyes from Candy, I scope out Mr.

Mouchard. He doesn't even notice my suspicious glare, he's transfixed by Candy's bosom, creepily stroking a single finger across his mustache.

Well, crap.

Even if she sucks, there's no way he'll fire her. As long as she keeps the girls on display, her job here is safe. I glance down at my own, much flatter chest, briefly entertaining the idea of trying to show off my breasts to receive more hours on the schedule. I quickly brush aside the idea. Six dollars an hour isn't worth Mr. Mouchard's creepy attention.

No way.

Sighing, I resign myself to losing money and hours to Candy. Maybe if I'm lucky, she'll hate it here and decide to quit.

I paste on a smile and address the new girl. "Are we working together today?"

Mr. Mouchard shakes his head, answering my question for her. "No, you're on your own today. I'm going to show Candy here how to work the computer."

Work the computer?

I've been employed here for a year and a half and I've never been given more responsibility than cleaning the rooms and skimming the old, dirty pool. I want to rage at the unfairness of the situation, but I tamp it down and turn to the janitorial closet instead. With a fake smile plastered on my face, I check the list, then load up my cleaning cart as usual.

Just another day in the life.

Before I'm fully through the doors of the lobby, Mr. Mouchard stops me. "Oh, McKenzie?"

I pivot, facing the desk at the sound of my name, tilting my head in lieu of responding.

"You can have the rest of the week off. I'll show Candy the ropes and the two of us can handle it." I watch Mr. Mouchard as he watches Candy's tits. His gaze doesn't even acknowledge me as he cuts my shift.

"Great," I reply.

Fucking great.

Chapter 5

My thoughts wander as I pedal home after my shift. Where can I apply for a new position? I have two months until my eighteenth birthday, the day I can open a bank account.

That means, best case scenario, I'll find somewhere to pay me cash to help keep me afloat. Worst case scenario, somewhere will hire me and I'll stockpile a few checks, then deposit them the day I turn eighteen, or pay to have them cashed somewhere if I'm desperate for the money sooner. Either way, I really need to avoid the worst, worst case scenario which is anyone finding out my mom bailed months ago, leaving me in a trailer to fend for myself.

Freedom is so close; I can taste it. I can't have CPS sniffing around me sixty-five days before I'm legally allowed to be on my own.

As I'm mulling over my options a red "Now Hiring" poster catches the corner of my eye. Feeling like it's a sign from above, I quickly brake and drag my bike to the curb. Gently laying the rusted metal against the brick, I read the words painted on the awning of the building, "Pawnstar Plus".

It's never been my dream to work at a pawnshop, but beggars can't be choosers.

Opening the door, a tinkling bell rings across the shop. An older man with dark hair wearing a pair of khakis pops up from behind the counter. "Here to pawn something, dear?" he asks, in a jolly tone.

I shake my head. "No." Clearing my throat I continue, "I actually came to ask for an application. I saw the sign in the window."

"Ahhh, of course. Are you eighteen?" he follows up, while placing a sheet of paper on the counter.

"Not yet," I begin. "I will be in two months though."

A sympathetic frown appears on the man's face. "Ahh, bummer. I'm unable to have you here alone if you're under eighteen. Tell you what though, why don't you fill out the application anyway? I'll give you a call around your birthday, if we're still looking for someone."

I nod my head, even though I think this is a waste of time. I don't need a job in two months, I need one like yesterday. Disregarding the thought, I stride towards the counter, snatching up the pen placed against the glass for me and begin to scrawl down my first name.

Movement catches my eyes and I peer out from under my lashes. The pawnshop owner has drifted to the back wall and is placing merchandise onto shelves. A duster sits to the side, like I interrupted his cleaning tasks with my entrance.

Although I'll probably have to find something else in

the meantime, I already like this nameless man more than Mr. Mouchard. If he were to offer me an opportunity around my birthday, maybe I would leave the motel to work for someone that doesn't hover to stare down my shirt or at my ass, while I'm bent over.

Forcing myself to focus, I continue the application. Filling in the basic information and a small questionnaire. Quickly skimming through the questions on the backside, I check the appropriate boxes before signing my name with a flourish. Finished, I gently set the pen back onto the case and straighten up.

The man must have been watching me from afar, as he promptly returns to the portion of counter I'm posted at. He lifts my application and I can see his eyes dancing back and forth across the page as he takes in my information.

His previously jolly smile drops off his face as he reads, causing a nervous flare. "Is something wrong with my application?" I ask, attempting to maintain a light tone despite my concern.

He finally drags his eyes away from the page to meet my gaze, a crease formed between his brows and his lips turned downwards. "Are you any relation to Samantha Carslyle?" He asks, his tone much less friendly than before.

"Err, yes," I hedge. "She's my mother."

"I'm sorry, we're no longer hiring." The man says and I watch as he takes my application and tears it straight down the middle. Then tears those pieces in half again, sprinkling the quarters of the page into the garbage behind him when he's finished.

I nod once, even though I'm baffled by the man's bizarre behavior. Turning, I trudge back towards the door, feeling a strange sense of loss, even though nothing I had was actually taken away.

The second my hand reaches to push against the handle, the man's voice floats across the store. I pause, wondering if he's going to apologize for shredding the application he encouraged me to fill out. His words offer a different explanation for his actions. "McKenzie, if you could send your mom my way when you see her. Tell her Mack from Pawnstar Plus hasn't forgotten about the forty-five hundred bucks she owes him for the merchandise she stole last year."

My shoulders slump, and I nod without facing him. Resigned, I shove against the door and exit the shop.

My mom isn't even here anymore and she's still fucking me over.

I pull my bike off the ground and place my feet onto the pedals. Pumping a few times, I get myself into motion gliding down the road, and then defeat washes over me.

So much for a sign from above.

Not only do I have to find somewhere that will hire me when I'm not even eighteen, I also need to find a business my mom didn't screw over before she left our small town, and me, behind. With jaded eyes, I inspect each shop as I coast by.

The liquor store? Obviously not.

The grocery shoppette? Probably not.

The thrift store? No.

Each business I assess has me drooping even lower

over my handle bars, under the weight of my sudden despair. My thoughts drift as I reach the edge of downtown and make the first left to return to the trailer park. As hard as I try not to, I keep repeating Derek's words from earlier.

One thousand dollars.

What if I agreed to pull the con on Collin Franzen and his family?

Would it really hurt anyone?

The more I think about it, the less it sounds like a bad idea and the more it sounds like my salvation. His parents are rich. They're the type of people that could easily afford to replace a few electronics or pieces of jewelry. Anything Derek or Zane took would be a minor blip in the road for them, not a catastrophic loss.

The front tire of my bike hits the dirt path leading into the park. I pick up pace as my resolve strengthens, zipping past the office towards the trailers a few dozen yards ahead. Before I can talk myself out of it, I pedal across the pitted dirt, past my trailer. When I reach the end of the road, I skid to a halt, and throw my bike onto the patchy yellow grass in front of Derek's.

I muster up my confidence and raise my fist, hammering against the thin, wooden door. Pausing for a second, I perk my ears to listen for any sound inside.

"Hang on a second," Derek's voice hollers through the thin barrier, after a brief delay.

While I wait, I cross my arms over my chest to comfort myself, or maybe hold in the feeling that I'm doing the wrong thing. I know with a sense of certainty

I'm about to venture down a path I may not recover from, but I've run out of options.

My ancient coffee canister holds about two months' worth of savings. That's enough to keep me afloat until I turn eighteen, but just barely. If my shifts continue to get cut at the motel, I'm on the path to becoming a homeless teenager.

A thousand dollars is a lot to someone like me. In a literal sense, it's enough to change my life.

Derek's front door flies open, revealing his shirtless form in the doorway, his tattooed, muscular body on full display. I've seen the hodge podge of designs scattered across his arms, but never had a view of his entire upper body, prior to this moment. I keep my eyes focused on his face, despite the temptation to trace the myriad of designs inked into his skin.

If I did something like that, Derek would think I'm interested in him—which I'm not—and the result would be him bothering me more often than he already does. I'm here to create less problems for myself, not fully immerse myself into the Trouble that orbits around Derek, like the earth around the sun.

Derek quirks a brow, interrupting my inner turmoil.

I am a good person; I'm not like Derek. At least that's what I'm telling myself, despite my next words. Inhaling deeply, I release the breath slowly, delaying the inevitable for as long as possible with the lengthy exhale.

When the last ounce of air has passed my lips, I simply state, "I'm in."

His face transforms into a beautiful smile, his dimple fully popping into view. "Kenzie-girl. I knew you'd come around." Derek steps forward and wraps an arm around me, trying to pull me forward to join him in the trailer.

As quickly as I can, I wriggle free, brushing almost every inch of skin on his torso in the process. "I have some rules, first, Derek," I state sternly, re-crossing my arms and standing to my full height.

Derek is clearly fighting the urge to transition his friendly smile into a smirk, but he nods solemnly. "Would you like to come in, so we can sit and talk? I'll put a shirt on."

I squirm uncomfortably at the thought of entering Derek's trailer, I'm sure it's grimy and dingy.

"It's probably better if this conversation isn't over-heard," he adds on in a hushed tone, when I remain on his porch in silence, for a beat too long.

Reluctantly, I nod my head and brush past him as he holds the door open for me to enter. My eyes flit over the surfaces, which are all, surprisingly, pretty clean. His counters are cluttered with stacks of boxes and half of the table is unusable, hosting tubs of what looks like cell phones.

If Derek hadn't already approached me to help him rob the Franzen's, my suspicions of his extracurricular activities would have been confirmed by entering his trailer. It looks like he robbed a Best Buy.

I gingerly walk across the floor and perch on the edge of the clutter-free bench next to his table. I leave my legs extended into the center of the room, so Derek can't squeeze his way in to sit beside me.

His eyes dance, but he lounges against the counter and crosses his arms. "Okay, what are your terms?"

"I want half," I blurt out, immediately.

"Half of the money we make?" Derek asks, arching his brow.

I nod, once, vigorously. I've never negotiated before, but I feel like I've already started this wrong. I backtrack to make a point before laying out all my demands. "I mean, Zane doesn't even need to be involved and none of this would even be possible if I wasn't helping you. If we pull the con on the Franzen's, I want half of whatever money is made," I repeat in a firmer tone.

Derek scratches the underside of his chin, lost in thought. "I could just lie to you about how much we made. You wouldn't even know what half is."

"You wouldn't," I insist. "Because I'll have the information you and Zane were the ones to rob the house."

"You'd be taken in for facilitating the robbery if you ratted me out," he counters.

"All I did was talk about my friend's house, how was I supposed to know my neighbor was planning to rob his parents, officer?" I adopt an innocent tone and a scared frown as I make the statement.

He releases a deep belly laugh and relaxes his arms to his sides, lounging against the counter fully. "Fair enough," Derek finally says. "Anything else?"

His words allow my shoulders to relax, reducing some of their tension. If I decide to become this person, and commit to this plan, I need to make enough money that this is a one-time thing.

I eventually nod. "No one else gets to know I'm involved. Not even Zane if he helps you."

"Deal," Derek agrees without a second thought.

He pushes off the counter and tips forward, offering me his hand. I clasp my own around it, shaking firmly while his callouses scrape against me.

"What's next?" I ask when our palms have separated.

Derek smirks. "We seal the deal with a good ole fashioned fuck?"

I scoff and roll my eyes.

"Can't blame a guy for trying." Derek shrugs. "Now, Kenzie-Girl, you need to find a way to spend time with Franzen."

Chapter 6

The next morning, I wake up early and take my time dressing. I have all of ten outfits in my closet. Not by choice, of course. What girl doesn't wish she had a closet overflowing with the latest fashion?

But fashion requires money.

Since clothes can't be eaten when money gets tight, I've never splurged on buying nice things. Instead, I make do with the clothes my mom sporadically purchased for me from the thrift store or hand-me downs given by the school nurse, courtesy of unclaimed lost and found.

I change a dozen times, cycling through every combination of my few pieces, before settling on a sundress I rarely wear and a pair of strappy sandals. Examining my reflection in the mirror, I contemplate if my outfit is too fancy to go thank someone you barely know. My eyes return to the pile of clothes on my bed, flitting over the cut off shorts, tank tops, and halter tops.

Out of everything I own, this is probably closest to what people wear, on that side of town.

With my outfit decided, I exit into the early morning sun and pop my sunglasses on. Peeling my bike off the trailer, I carefully clamber onto the seat. I'm wearing a small pair of bike shorts under my dress to avoid flashing my neighbors, but use caution to avoid the greasy bike chain.

Once I'm settled, I push off the grass and pedal lazily. Even in our smallish town, riding to the Franzen house takes about forty minutes. They live all the way across the city, the furthest point from the trailer park possible.

I adopt a leisurely pace, not wanting to arrive a hot, sweaty mess. Thankfully, it's early enough the sun hasn't hit its highest peak and it's cooler than it will be midday.

Using the time to solidify my thoughts, I think over all the possible scenarios, trying to create a plan to get into Collin's house. Would it be weird to invite myself inside to use the bathroom?

I quickly dispel the thought, it wouldn't be possible to snoop, even if I gained access to the house today. There wouldn't be enough time.

I'm pulled from my plotting when I arrive at the entrance to the Franzen's neighborhood. Pedaling down the street, I take in the quietness of the area, appreciating how peaceful it is compared to the ruckus that's a typical occurrence at the park. Upon reaching Collin's house, I gently place my bike near the vast, green lawn, not wanting to disturb the quiet or the manicured yard.

He lives in the NICE part of town.

The part that has huge lawns, made of real, green grass with decorative shrubbery; the type of property other people are paid to maintain. The grass, although impressive in its liveliness in the middle of the Alabama summer, is just the foreground to massive, immaculate homes. They're all similar in size and distanced far apart, separated by clean fences. Each home has shiny, nice cars parked in the driveway, most of them screaming luxury.

Collin lives in the type of neighborhood where it's safe to play in the road and the families all have barbeques together that don't end in drunken brawls. The kind of place people probably imagine when they think of southern living.

I glance around in awe, before returning to face my destination.

Pausing a minute to survey the enormous, white, pillared house in front of me, I focus on tamping down my insecurities which flared up as soon as my tires passed the "Golden Oaks" sign posted outside the neighborhood.

I don't belong here, but I can do this.

Squaring my shoulders, I stride up to the front door and tap lightly, using the small, circular knocker attached to the forest green wood. Shuffling my feet, I wait for five minutes and begin to wonder if I should've rung the bell instead.

Unsure, I reach my hand out and lightly press the lit-up circle. Inside I hear an echoing chime, as loud as church bells. The chiming stops, but the door remains unanswered. I shift my weight from foot to foot, wondering if I should leave and come back later.

Is anyone even home?

Disappointed, I finally decide to leave, and return another day, despite the lengthy ride it took to get here. The longer I stand on the porch, the weirder it will seem to any neighbors that happen to look at the Franzen house.

As I place my right foot onto the clean, paved path down towards the main sidewalk—and my bike—I spot a figure running in the distance, feet pounding across the pavement with each long, determined stride.

The person looms closer, the sun glinting off a shirt-less chest and a head of golden-hued hair. I inhale sharply, as soon as I realize it's Collin. I remain rooted in place, watching his muscles flex as he sprints down the road, clad only in a pair of black gym shorts and bright blue sneakers.

I allow my eyes to roam his form as he finally jumps up the sidewalk and runs straight through his grass, stopping in front of me on the path leading to his house. His chest is heaving, with sweat running in rivulets down his defined pecs. My eyes follow the path, taking in his toned abdomen and ending at the drawstring of his athletic shorts.

Forcing myself to focus, I drag my eyes from Collin's body to his face. Scanning his features, I take in his sweaty, tousled blonde hair and thick brows. I examine his square jaw, Roman nose, and his plump lips. He's handsome, drool-worthy, even after his clearly intense run.

But I'm not here for that.

With my intentions set, my eyes finally land on his. The twin green orbs are staring at me inquisitively. He quirks a single brow, which somehow ups his attractive level by at least ten. "What are you doing here, McKenzie?" He drawls out the question, his perfect southern tone making the words gentle and charming.

My cheeks heat slightly as I realize he stood there silently, allowing me to check him out, before asking why I was here. Brushing aside my embarrassment, I focus on my end goal. Shrugging lightly, I say the words that will set my entire plan in motion, "I wanted to thank you for the other night. Could I, I don't know, buy you a coffee or something to show my appreciation?"

I watch as his entire face softens, a small smile tugging at his lips. "No thank you necessary. I was just doing what anyone else would do in the same situation."

"But no one else did. Just stop being so nice and let me buy you a coffee." My eyes flit down his body one more time. I tell myself it's to make a point, but my gaze drinks in every inch of skin as my eyes rove, directly contradicting the statement. I may never get to see shirtless Collin again, and I want to imprint my brain with this memory. "We can go another day though, since you just got done working out," I finally add, when my brain gets back on track.

"Do you have time to wait for me to shower?" he drawls out.

"Uhm, sure," I respond, with a furrowed brow, confused about the sudden change from a raincheck to Collin's showering habits.

His smile grows and his emerald eyes twinkle. "Why don't you come on in then? You can wait for me downstairs. I'll be real quick, then I can drive us downtown."

"Err, okay," I finally agree. Regaining my equilibrium after a pause, I quip back, "Sounds like a plan. Better for you to drive…. You'd probably throw off the balance of my bike if you stood on the back pegs."

My last comment makes him laugh, his small smile expanding into a full grin. His lighthearted happiness summons my own and I beam back at him for a minute. We both stand there grinning like dopes, until a dog barking nearby breaks the trance.

He steps past me, and I permit my eyes to check out his equally toned back while he moves. Collin's musculature is impressive and I wouldn't mind being a fly on the wall for any of his workouts. Dragging my eyes from his body, I focus on the ground, ensuring my feet carry me safely to the porch.

His house has one of those fancy, electronic keypad locks; he types in a code then swings the door inward. I try to catch the digits as he presses them, but the pad is partially blocked with his body and I don't want to be too obvious.

Collin steps inside, stopping in the entryway to beckon me forward with his hand. The open space visible behind him is larger than my entire trailer. This brief glimpse into his house fortifies me.

He's probably never struggled for anything.

"Why don't you come inside and wait in the kitchen?" Collin asks, interrupting my thoughts.

Using his parent's obvious wealth, I justify my future

actions; lying to and betraying someone I don't even know for my own personal gain. Settling my mind, I stride forward with a smile firmly fixed in place.

Stepping into the house is like being transported to a different world. The checkered floor, chandelier, and curved staircase in the entry belong in an Audrey Hepburn movie, not a small town in Alabama. My jaw drops as I drink in the opulence of the entry alone.

"You can follow me," Collin drawls and I realize he's left me behind, walking down the hall, likely in the direction of the kitchen.

I chase after him, noting the beautiful cream-colored walls peppered with paintings of scenery. The hallway has one of those long skinny tables with decorative candles on it and I admire how beautiful the functionless piece of furniture is.

We reach the kitchen which is made of white cabinets and dark granite. A small table with an L-shaped bench is tucked in the far corner and I wander over to it while Collin sticks his head in the fridge. He pops back out a second later, holding two bottles of water.

Ambling to my place at the table, he gently sets one in front of me, keeping the other for himself. "I'll be back down in a few minutes, make yourself at home," he states.

I nod, already overwhelmed by his gigantic, elegant home, even after barely seeing a portion of it. He abandons the kitchen, leaving the way we came, and I watch, admiring his fit form until he disappears from sight.

This place already has me all out of sorts. I'm surrounded by the most expensive furniture I've ever seen and drooling over the hot guy from school that's completely out of my league. I can count on one hand the number of interactions I've previously had with Collin and we've gone to the same school since second grade. The idea of the two of us becoming close is probably a joke, but I've come this far.

It's too late to back out now.

I pop the top on the water bottle and remain seated for about seventy seconds before I start wondering if I should be using this time to snoop. As soon as the thought crosses my mind, the front door to the house flies open.

"Collin?" A feminine voice shouts, the tone sounding polished despite the volume of the word.

Startled, I jump up from the table and take a few tentative steps into the hall. A swath of blonde hair comes into sight, as a woman wearing an elegant, blush pink dress and kitten heels strolls into the foyer carrying grocery bags.

Her eyes stop on my face and a polite smile crosses her lips. "Hello, dear. Do you know where Collin is?"

"Yes, he's upstairs. I'm his... friend McKenzie. Do you need some help?" I ask, watching her thin arms struggle to carry the five bags she has with her.

"Oh, yes dear." I move to grab one from her hands, but she waves me off. "There's more in the car, I have these few if you could start there."

Nodding, I leave the house and stop behind a beautiful, cherry red Mercedes. I gather four bags from the trunk, after a few seconds of admiring the shimmery paint. Bundling the bags together so I can use both hands, I lug them into the kitchen, wondering if they're filled with cans, based on their weight alone.

I'm on my second trip into the kitchen, when Collin suddenly appears at the bottom step. He snags the bags from my grasp and strides away, depositing them quickly before reappearing in the hall. "Is there anything else out there?" He asks.

I decline with a shake of my head, my eyes raking over his form clad in a simple t-shirt and jeans. How is it fair he looks as good in clothes as he does mostly naked?

Collins suddenly snatches my palm, the heat of his skin surprising me as he tugs me towards the door. I'm so startled by the action; I almost miss his next words. "Let's get out of here, before she corrals us into more chores," he mock whispers.

"I heard that," a feminine voice yells from the kitchen, her tone light with humor. "You kids get out of here. Go enjoy this nice weather."

Collin laughs a deep, rumbly sound that makes my stomach muscles clench. I release my own chuckle and force my feet to move alongside him as he hurriedly drags me through the house, away from the kitchen and towards coffee.

Less than half an hour with Collin and I'm crushing. Hard.

Boy am I in trouble.

Chapter 7

Collin leads me outside to escape his mom, popping open a portion of the three-car garage attached to his house. The bay reveals a massive, luxury SUV. My jaw drops to the floor as I observe the shiny, black paint and chrome rims, utterly in awe of a vehicle so fancy.

He heads to the driver's seat and opens the door, before realizing I'm no longer following directly behind him, rooted in place on the cement outside instead. "Are you coming?" He drawls out, his tone sounding mildly confused over my sudden stop.

"Is this yours?" I ask, disregarding his question while still stuck in place.

He shrugs his shoulders, looking slightly sheepish. "It was my sixteenth birthday present... The team has a lot of away games."

Of course, Collin would own a fancy SUV.

I scrape my jaw off the ground and force my feet to move, admiring the way my reflection shimmers against the dark colored paint and tinted windows as I walk by. Using the handle inside the door as leverage, I climb up, only to be awed all over again. I don't know enough about cars to know the type, but shiny paint, plush leather seats, and a sunroof all scream 'money' to me.

Trying to be subtle, I inhale deeply, hoping to catch a whiff of that new car smell everyone always brags about. Instead, I discover Collin's SUV smells like him… like warmth and sunshine. Prior to climbing in here, I would've never declared sunshine has a smell, but it's the perfect way to describe his scent. It's the smell of a warm summer day in an open field.

I perch on the edge of my seat, anxious to feel the car moving underneath me. Do luxury cars drive smoother than the beaters commonly found in the trailer park? I can only imagine the answer is a resounding "yes".

Collin eases his SUV out of the garage, slowly backing down the driveway before turning onto the road. My excitement over the vehicle quickly turns into fascination over the guy sitting beside me.

I surreptitiously watch him from underneath my lashes, my eyes drinking in his movements as he confidently maneuvers his car. His face is serious, and focused; the attractive features denoting his concentration. His movements remain confident and sure, providing me with comfort. Despite being in the vehicle with a near stranger, I find myself slowly relaxing further into the plush seat during the short drive to the coffee shop downtown.

When the car begins to slow, I tear my eyes away

from the mysterious Collin Franzen, shifting to the window to take in our surroundings. Collin drives his SUV close to the curb, and I use the side mirror to watch as he adeptly squeezes his large car into a tight spot, in two quick, sure movements. My gaze is drawn back to his face immediately, like the attraction of a magnetic force.

Who knew a hot guy that drives with confidence would be such a turn on?

A smirk grows as we sit there and he raises a thick brow, aiming it in my direction. "Ready?"

The movement makes me realize I was outright staring, drooling over his handsome face like a ninny. Shaking my head to clear it, I paste a smile on my face before opening my mouth to reply, "Uh, yes?"

Although I'm aiming to come across as a cool, collected, and equally confident girl, to match the effortless and daunting Collin Franzen, the unwanted words leave my mouth in place of something…. better. Not only that, but they sound like a question; higher pitched than usual and rising at the end.

My cheeks heat with embarrassment. Get it together Kenzie.

Thankfully, Collin doesn't comment on my weird behavior as we both unbuckle and exit the car. I mentally berate myself for my weird new Franzen fascination as I stay in place on the curb, hearing his door slam shut and his footsteps rounding the car.

Rather than continuing to stare at him, I focus my attention on the nearby area. I survey the portion of town we've arrived at. The entire block looks upscale, nicer than the road I normally bike down, on my path to the motel. The buildings are each unique, housing interesting and delicate-looking goods, slightly visible through their glass-front windows. I scan the street briefly, but my attention is quickly captured and held by the coffee shop a few steps past Collin's SUV.

It's a large, forest green building made of some sort of stucco material. Huge, streak-free windows cover the front, with a few bistro tables dotting the sidewalk preceding the entry. It seems trendy and cool, but also surprisingly inviting.

Until recently, I never spent much time thinking about Collin Franzen. Especially not how he passed the time outside of his glorious football career and reigning position in high school. For some reason, this calming green building suits him. I suddenly imagine him spending his free time here and I'm strangely glad he brought me.

With self-assurance I'm not one-hundred percent feeling, I stride up to the door. Imagining someday I'll be the kind of girl that fits in at a place like this, as I tug on the handle.

The interior of the coffee shop does not disappoint my expectations. I inhale deeply as I step inside, allowing the smell of deliciously well-roasted coffee beans to permeate my entire being before I continue to glance around.

A large, glass-front counter catches my eye. It begins a quarter of the way in, spanning almost the entire length of the wall across from us, displaying an array of mouth-watering pastries. A small, ancient looking register sits at the very end, making it clear this is the place to order. My eyes do a quick sweep of the rest of the shop, noting the chalkboard menu with scrawling script and the assortment of tables and chairs scattered about the floor.

This isn't my side of town, and I've never had the motivation, time, or really the money to visit a coffee shop. But, I wish I had visited here, before today. The realization of all I've been missing by never venturing out of my little bubble creates a pang of regret, deep in my chest.

The coffee shop looks like it belongs in a movie, yet feels quaint and homey like the rest of our small Alabama town.

I feel the heat of Collin's body against my back and I'm about to turn, to tell him how much I love this place and to thank him for bringing me here. Before I can complete the movement, a voice booms over the low, soothing music playing in the shop.

"I've missed you, sugar." The words carry across the room, spoken by a boisterous southern voice. One that pronounces the word sugar the southern way, "shugah."

My eyes scan the shop in search of its owner, until they finally land on a dark-skinned woman standing near a door to the far right. She's wearing a colorful scarf over her hair and a black half-apron covered in flour.

Collin brushes past me, a smile splitting his face as he approaches the counter. The woman meets him part way to give a firm squeeze over the top, holding him tightly in a motherly embrace.

"Hi Anna," Collin drawls when they finally break apart.

Her eyes inspect him for a second, then her focus transfers to me. "And who is your little lady friend?"

I felt like I was watching a movie, viewing the interaction as it unfolded before me. Now both sets of eyes become intent on me, with Collin using a hand to gesture me forward. I force my feet to move, creating a small clacking noise as I walk against the wooden floors in my heeled sandals.

It takes ages to reach the counter with both of them staring at me, but when I do, I offer a hand to Anna and introduce myself, "Hi, I'm Kenzie, McKenzie, Carslyle."

Anna enthusiastically shakes my hand, a warm smile still sitting on her face. "Nice to meet you, sugar. I'm Annabelle May Wright, but ya can call me Anna." She winks to punctuate the words as she releases my hand. "Now I know ya dint come all this way just to meet an old woman. What canna get ya two?"

I gesture for Collin to go first, tuning him out as he orders a drink without consulting the menu. Meanwhile, my eyes frantically scan the words, trying to find something I'm familiar with, besides "drip coffee". I'm unsure why, but for some reason I don't want Collin to know this is my first time in a coffee house, ordering expensive coffee.

Usually I brew my own caffeine, at home, in the old, finicky coffee maker I found at the local thrift shop. It isn't pretty, but it makes a mean cup of Folgers, which has always been enough for me.

Silence lingers, alerting me that Anna is awaiting my

order. Determined not to give myself away, I offer her a sweet smile, accompanied by equally sweet words. "Everything here just looks so delicious. I'm having a hard time deciding." She beams at my praise, confirming my suspicions that she's the owner of this quaint caffeine oasis. I continue, moving in for the kill, "What would you recommend? I was thinking something iced."

"How 'bout a blended drink instead? A Mocha Frappuccino? It's a hot one today. Something blended will keep ya cool."

I nod after I process her words, her drawl is much more pronounced than most, making her harder to understand. "Sounds delicious!" I reply, agreeing to her suggestion.

Taking a half step back, I wait beside Collin near the register. Together, our eyes follow Annabelle May as she dances behind the counter, transforming the act of making two coffees into an art form. It doesn't take her long to return and offer us our cups.

I examine both quickly, hoping to determine which one is mine without giving away that I've never had a mocha Frappuccino. I laugh when I notice Collin and I ordered the same thing. Each of Anna's hands holds the exact same drink, a giant cup of brown, slushy liquid, each topped with a pile of whip cream.

With trembling hands, I pull my wallet out of the tiny purse I strapped across my body this morning. I'm nervous what the total will be for two huge drinks looking this scrumptious. Pushing my trepidation aside, I inhale deeply and prepare to part with some of my hard-earned cash.

Collin places a warm hand over my two clammy ones, halting my movements as I unfold the battered leather to remove my money and I shoot him a questioning glance.

"I'll get this," he drawls, wallet already in hand.

My brow creases with my furious frown. "No," I respond adamantly. "This was supposed to be a thank you. How am I supposed to show my gratitude if you pay for our coffee?"

Eyes locked, we both square our shoulders, immersed in a staring contest that equates a battle of wills. Annabelle May stands behind the counter, watching our interaction. She presses a few buttons on the old-fashioned register and the total pops up on the tiny, customer-facing window. "It's $4.13." She tells me with a pointed look at Collin over my shoulder, her grin still happily in place.

I feel my shoulders draining of tension and Collin moves his hand away from mine, releasing his hold on me and my wallet. I count out six one-dollar bills and hand five of them to Annabelle May, placing the sixth into the Mason jar with "Tips" scrawled across the side in black script. She hands me back a few coins and I dump them into the jar as well.

Collin moves forward to touch me again, this time placing his free hand against my lower back and guiding me to a table in the far corner. I fight the urge to inspect the menu, wanting to calculate if Annabelle May gave me a discount or not. Four dollars seems awfully cheap for two huge coffees.

I may be poor, but I can't stand to be pitied. I don't want her to discount the price for me because she's worried, I can't pay. Although I would typically consider this an unnecessary expense, I can afford it.

Well, kind of.

A chair scrapes loudly against the tiled floor, interrupting my desire to defend my pride. Collin's expression is sheepish as I follow the line of his arms to the offending chair. He shrugs before plopping down and patting the seat beside him. I obey the silent instruction, comfortably settling into the table, next to him.

"Thank you for saving me." I hold my plastic cup up, waiting for Collin to clank his against mine, in a mock cheers motion. He does so rather dramatically and I laugh when he sticks his pinky out before taking his first sip. "So fancy."

"The fanciest," he agrees.

Excitedly, I take a long drink of my blended delicacy. The second the liquid slips down my throat, I bend over the table, clasping my head in both hands. "Ahhhh. Brain freeze," I exclaim as my body cramps in protest over the frozen beverage.

"Put your tongue against the roof of your mouth," Collin instructs after only a brief chuckle at my suffering.

I do as he says and almost instantly feel relief. As soon as I'm capable of speaking, I mutter, "You're a genius."

Silence reigns while I hold my head, allowing my

brain freeze to recede. "Do you want to play a game?" Collin eventually asks, ignoring my previous statement and pointing to a bookshelf situated against the opposite wall.

Gently pushing my chair away from the table, I wince as a scraping noise much worse than Collins cuts across the quiet music and peaceful ambience. His chuckle covers my embarrassment, providing a second for me to brush it off. I walk over to the bookcase and peruse their selection of games.

Out of all the ones on the shelves, there are only two I'm familiar with, Connect Four and Clue. Grabbing a game with each hand, I hold them up for Collin to check out. "Either of these suit your fancy?"

He taps his finger against his chin to pretend he's deeply contemplating the question. "Hmmm, I think I'm ready to solve a mystery."

With a giggle, I place Connect Four back onto the shelf and bring Clue to the table. We open the box and work together to set up the board with all the pieces. We each pick our pawns; Miss Scarlet for me and Professor Plum for Collin.

Shuffling the cards, we divvy things up and quickly get lost in the game. An indeterminate amount of time passes, as I lose myself to the simple pleasure of trying to outwit Collin. As I pick up the last clue to solve the game, I reach for my drink, placing the straw against my lips to slurp up more of the delicious chocolatey coffee, but nothing comes through the straw except air.

With a frown, I place the plastic cup back on the table. Simultaneously, Collin calls out, "Miss Scarlet in the ballroom with a candlestick!" He throws his cards down onto the table, preparing to take part in some victory gloating.

"No way," I shout, interrupting him. "It's Mrs. Peacock in the ballroom with the candlestick!" I throw down my own cards, pointing out how he's wrong. His grin falls into a frown, but I ignore him, celebrating my triumph. Throwing my hands in the air, I yell, "Winner!"

Collin chuckles, accepting his defeat with grace. He begins to return the pieces to the box and I move to help him. A pang of disappointment hits my chest when he returns the game to the open space on the bookshelf then remains standing next to the table instead of returning to his seat.

He glances down to his wrist, to check a watch that looks like it costs more than my trailer. He also seems a little disappointed when he quietly speaks, "Hey, I need to get going."

My face falls at the thought of having to part ways, which I purposefully avoid thinking about.

Avoiding my gaze, Collin continues, "I had fun today though and want to see you again... Would you maybe wanna hang out tomorrow? We could just go for a drive." His face looks hopeful when he eventually meets my eyes across the table.

My lips form a grin, in reaction to his suggestion. "I'd really like that."

His entire face lights up in a smile to my response. "How about I take you home and bring your bike around tomorrow when I pick you up?"

I hesitate for a second, rethinking my agreement to his original plan. In my mind, I compare my dingy trailer to his parent's mansion. Suddenly, I become embarrassed about being dropped off at home by the guy that owns such nice things.

I allow the feeling to linger for about seven seconds, then I shrug it off. He knows where I'm from, he's seen me there before, just the other day actually. There's no use in trying to pretend my life is anything different than what it is.

"Sounds like a plan. Thanks."

Chapter 8

C ollin and I never set a time for today and I don't have his phone number, meaning I have no idea when, or even if, we're meeting. I shot upright in bed, at six this morning, panicking he would show up while I was still asleep. In my dreams, nightmares really, I was answering the door with my hair sticking up in every direction, no pants, and a line of dried drool down my chin.

It's no surprise I couldn't fall back to sleep after a dream like that.

Instead, I use the extra time to prepare for the day. For the third time in a week, which is more than my monthly average, I take my time getting ready. I use an ancient curling iron with a sticky clip. The same one my mom left in the bathroom, still plugged in, when she abandoned me and her trailer. With an unsteady hand, I curl my thick, inky strands of hair, starting halfway down the long pieces to save time and effort.

Approximately thirty minutes later, I have successfully wrapped every piece over the iron at least once. When I finish, I turn my head right and left, inspecting the results. The curls aren't even, but they look kind of sloppy and sexy.

Perching on the closed toilet with my computer, I hack into my neighbor's Wi-Fi. Honestly, choose a better password than password1234 if you don't want freeloaders. With my clunky, old laptop and free Wi-Fi, I google "How to create a smokey eye".

When my mother left me here over two years ago, she also left half her clothes and a ton of her beauty supplies. What I no longer have in parents, I'm compensated for in stripper heels and cheap make-up, neither of which has come in handy until today.

Using my mom's old shadows, I swipe and smudge, following the tutorial's exact instructions to create the complicated look. The video finishes and I examine my face in the cracked mirror above the sink. It looks like I was given a black eye, instead of becoming a sultry goddess like the tutorial advertised. Laughing, I wiggle my eyebrows and watch the dark makeup mesh together even further to become a blob of sludgy colored make-up. Wandering out to the hall, I snag a washcloth and wipe away the horrible new look.

After scrubbing off the cheap shadow with a wet cloth, I pause and stare at my bare-faced reflection. Dark, arching brows, a pert nose, narrow face, plump lips, and chocolate eyes return my focused stare. My skin is tanned and freckled from the summer sun, making me appear more exotic than I normally do. I angle my head in each direction, critically eyeing my appearance.

My mother always used to tell me I was her "mini-me". Her skin aged before its time as excess cigarettes, alcohol, and sun, took their toll. If I wrinkle my brow and squint my eyes just so, I can see a glimmer of her. In my opinion we don't look much alike, but she used to brag about my appearance as if it made her a beauty queen.

Straightening my features, I push myself off the sink. I chalk up the shadow to a failed experiment and stalk off to my room, my curly hair swinging gently behind me as I make my way to the closet.

Dressing in a pair of cutoffs and a tank top, I rest against the edge of my bed and begin tapping my left foot impatiently. I watch three minutes tick by on my alarm clock before deciding to make some eggs. Breakfast is the most important meal of the day... and it will make the time go by faster.

While I scrape the spatula around the bottom of the pan, flipping eggs about before they burn, I convince myself I'm not nervous to see Collin. None of this is about him. It's about the con Derek and I have planned for his parent's house. That's it.

My ears perk at the sound of a knock tapping lightly against my front door. Giddy excitement bubbles up, a feeling comparable to the time my mom took me to the fair to ride my first rollercoaster. I skip to the door, yanking it open with a grin, expecting to see Collin.

Waiting on the other side is a shirtless Derek, unfortunately. He's grinning back at me as the sun reflects off his pale skin. Instinctually, my eyes trace an image of dark ink. They follow the path of a snake that starts on his left bicep, winding upwards, creating a line like a dangling necklace across his chest, and ending in a hissing mouth on his right pec. Derek flexes his chest muscles in response, causing his pecs to dance under my scrutiny.

"What do you want?" I snap out, annoyed my eyes wandered without my permission.

He leans forward, invading my space as his nose practically touches mine. I step back, prepared to slam the door on him. Sensing my immediate ire, he quickly straightens, placing one palm against the door frame and raising the other in a pacifying manner. "Woah, woah woah. Somebody's ornery in the morning. Just wanted to drop by and check on your progress."

I glare at him as he stands on my porch. "It's been one day. Are we on some type of deadline you didn't tell me 'bout?" I snap out, my hand dropping to my hip, the motion matching my sassy attitude.

Derek walks backwards down my steps, his palms still in front of him as if to calm me. "No, no. Didn't want you to forget about our arrangement is all."

"I'm not a dimwit, Derek. I'm not going to forget about something we talked about one day ago."

He smirks at me, with his hands still raised in the air before turning on his heel and sauntering away. Just before he's out of sight, he calls over his shoulder, "Don't forget the other thing we talked about Kenzie-girl. Girls alone," he pauses his words dramatically while continuing to retreat. "They find themselves in spots of trouble all the time."

I scoff in an attempt to brush him off. Derek is not a

good guy, but I doubt he's truly threatening me. As I move to close my door, I spot a glint of black paint flashing down the road. The beating of my heart speeds up with anticipation and Derek's words are immediately forgotten.

Collin.

Attempting to tame my reaction, I reason any number of people could drive a vehicle, with shiny black paint, into the trailer park, but my feet are already carrying me into my trailer to gather the rest of my things. I grab my small purse, holding a few dollars, my ancient flip phone and a house key, glancing around to check if I need anything else. Not spotting anything, I twist the tiny lock in the handle, and shut the door behind me as I move onto the yellow, patchy grass preceding my trailer.

Collin's massive SUV slides into view, inching closer as he slowly navigates the bumpy, pock-ridden road. His swanky car rolls to a stop and he hops out, jogging around the hood to meet me.

My eyes drink in his handsome face, his blonde hair flopping lightly over his forehead as he moves. His thickly muscled arms are fully visible in the loose, light-blue tank top he's wearing. When he reaches me, our eyes connect and he gives a giant, genuine smile. "Hey!"

"Hey yourself," I respond, straining to maintain my normally cool demeanor. Something about Collin makes me want to flutter my lashes and flirt, which is far from my normal behavior around guys.

Collin's eyes flash over my form, pausing briefly on my bag before returning to my face. "All ready?"

I offer a curt nod, covering my awkwardness with a tentative step towards the car. Collin snags the handle, opening the passenger side for me, and offering to help me up. I quirk a brow at his extended palm, grabbing the handle and pulling myself in instead.

Colling laughs. "Miss Independent," he quips, good-naturedly.

Once I'm tucked into my seat, he gently shuts the door, then jogs back around the car. I watch him through the windshield, then the driver's side window, keeping my head tilted down to check him out through my lashes. He's so handsome, and unexpectedly kind for some big hotshot football player. I expected him to have an ego the size of Texas, considering everyone in the county celebrates his throwing abilities, but Collin seems really sweet. He makes me wish I was the kind of girl he could fall for.

Collin buckles himself in and turns the key in the ignition, cautiously backing off my lawn, and leaving the trailer park. I watch the beat-up rectangles fade from sight in the passenger mirror, thinking the whole time how great a view it is to watch the distance grow.

The sight reminds me to keep my eye on the prize.

As much as I like Collin, I need the money Derek can get from casing his parent's place. It's not ideal, not really something I ever wanted to resort to, but it's a necessary choice, in order to leave this place.

A few miles pass in silence and I space out, mulling over how to gain access to Collin's house. I suddenly realize neither of us have spoken a word in almost fifteen minutes. Is Collin upset or is this all we're going to do, ride together in silence?

I wait through another stoplight, until we've left our small town. Then I'm incapable of holding back any longer. Breaking the silence, I ask, "Is this what people do on a drive? Just watch the scenery pass without talking?"

Without turning to discern his expression, I feel his humor permeating the air. Collin clears his throat twice prior to speaking, "Well, yeah. You lounge quietly and think, or chat, or listen to music. It's just something to do, it doesn't have to be planned out to a T. Don't you ever just drive to clear your head or escape?"

Just something to do.

Huh.

His words highlight the gap in our wealth. Growing up poor, things like wasting gas without a purpose wasn't a way to spend the time. When my mom still lived in the trailer, she saved her fuel to get groceries or go to the bar. Always entering the car with a destination in mind.

Hesitating, I finally respond, carefully selecting words that won't evoke pity of any kind. I prefer to live without Collin's pity. "I've never, uh, gone on a drive. I actually never learned how to drive."

Out of the corner of my eye I see his head whip in my direction. His voice is incredulous, "You don't know how to drive? How do you get anywhere?"

I shrug, my gaze focused out the windshield. "Bike."

His reaction has me feeling like a loser. This whole drive thing feels like a mistake.

Collin responds with an "Mmm" noise, his eyes

firmly fixed out the windshield, watching the rows of tall, golden wheat pass as we drive down the two-lane road. His silence makes me think he's also realizing his invitation was a mistake.

I sink into my seat, twisting my body to face the window, waiting for him to turn around, so he can drop me off at the trailer. Instead, he surprises me when he directs the SUV onto a small gravel path behind a large oak tree.

My curiosity is piqued as he slowly navigates down the road, stopping inside a dirt circle. We're out in the countryside, surrounded by nothing but open air and nature. I tear my gaze away from the surrounding wall, of tall green grass, topped by clear sky, to meet Collin's green gaze. His gem-colored eyes are fixated on my face, watching and waiting for my reaction.

"Where are we?" I wonder aloud.

I've noticed Collin's eyes sparkle whenever he's happy or amused. They're doing it right now, and I'm interested to know what he's thinking. My ears perk when he finally speaks. "One of my favorite places. Come on, let me show you."

He hops out, but heads to the trunk, rather than the passenger side to help me out. I debark slowly on my own, taking a few tentative strides away from the vehicle, observing as Collin grabs a woven basket. He places the handle onto his shoulder and throws a thick plaid blanket over his arm before joining me.

Our eyes meet for a second, his gaze warm and comforting. Then he holds out his hand, palm facing upwards. The action is simple, and sweet, causing a swarm of butterflies low in my belly.

Collin Franzen is Dangerous.

Ignoring the thought, I gently place my palm in his and he weaves his fingers through mine. He tugs against my hand softly, when I don't immediately start walking. I silence the part of my brain telling me this feels so natural, our hands fit together so perfectly. Instead I focus on glancing around as Collin winds us through the tall grass like he's done this a thousand times. The urge to ask where we're going builds, but before I can voice the question, we emerge into a clearing.

"It's beautiful," I say quietly, consumed by the breathtaking view. Flat, green grass separates two tall, sturdy oaks, and leads to an undisturbed lake with deep-blue water.

"I like to come here to relax and think. Or sometimes a group of us will come out here to swim. My grandpa told me about this place, he said my mom used to love coming here as a kid." His tone is wistful, punctuated by a type of sadness I empathize with. He doesn't continue, turning away from the water to shake out the blanket and lay it on the grass. I watch as he places the basket in the top corner before toeing off his shoes and settling on his side, onto the blanket.

I follow his lead, slipping out of my sandals and laying on the blanket facing Collin, my hand supporting my cheek. "I wish I brought a swimsuit," I muse, my eyes jumping to the water.

"We could always go skinny-dipping," Collin

suggests jokingly, accompanying the words with an over the top wink.

I chuckle at his antics, thankful I'm here with someone like Collin that wouldn't actually take advantage of this situation. I glance down my body to stare at the water again. "Does your mom still come here?"

My question is greeted with silence. After a few beats, I finally peek through my lashes at Collin, but he appears deep in thought. I'm unsure if he heard me from his expression and contemplate asking the question again, seconds before his eyes meet mine. The heartbroken look in the vibrant green orbs has me stifling a gasp of surprise.

He opens his mouth twice, but no words come out and he resumes facing the water. I gently rub a hand up and down his arm in what I hope is a soothing manner. "I'm sorry I asked," I say quietly, when the silence lingers and Collin refuses to look at me.

Nodding once, Collin continues staring at the lake with an expression I can't identify. It feels like an eternity in the time that passes until he faces me again.

During the silence, one of us shifted closer. My hand still rests on Collin's arm and his breath lightly fans across my cheeks with each exhalation. I force my muscles to stay relaxed as Collin slowly tilts his head down, his mouth closing in on mine. My eyes flutter shut of their own accord as Collin leans near, his breath hitting my lips from a few centimeters away.

A loud splash breaks the peaceful silence and I whip my head back, intent on discovering the source. In the process, I slam my forehead into Collin's nose.

"Oomph," he groans, while I continue transitioning to a seated position, scanning the area for the disturbance. Across the lake, I spot a group of twenty or so teenagers all jumping into the water and laughing. Someone is unloading a table from a truck and a couple of the girls are unfolding lounge chairs.

Having identified the sudden noise, my eyes return to Collin. I gasp when I see his nose held between both hands, with blood dripping from his fingers. "Oh crap! Is that from me?"

Without waiting for his response, I flip open the top of his basket and dig around until I find a wad of paper towels. I offer them to Collin, then continue searching until my hand hits something cool. Wrapping my fingers around it, I pluck out a frozen ice pack. Scooting across the blanket, I approach Collin like I would a dog that I'm not sure is friendly. "Are you okay? Can I look at it?"

"I'm fine. I don't think it's broken, just a little nosebleed," Collin responds, his voice both nasally and muffled from the hold on his nose.

His eyes meet mine, and I exhale the breath I didn't realize I was holding. A little glimmer of a sparkle glints back at me above his bloody hands.

Chapter 9

Sighing, I heave my tired body onto my small, ancient couch after another long, grueling day of cleaning disgusting rooms. If I never have to touch someone else's used condoms again, it will still be too soon.

I'm struggling to be grateful I have two shifts this week at least. It's better than nothing, but it's still not enough.

Attempting to force my body into cooperating with my idea to make something to eat, I swing my feet back onto the ground. Prior to standing, my phone pings with a text. Groaning, I elongate my body as far as possible, swiping my hand across the table until I feel the cool surface of my flip phone.

Crowing over my success, I pull the plastic blob towards me. The message is from Collin: **A bunch of us are going tubing tomorrow to celebrate the end of summer, wanna come?**

Chewing on my bottom lip, I read and reread the message, dissecting each word.

A bunch of us. Like his football and cheerleader friends?

Celebrate. Like a party on tubes?

Wanna come? Is this a date or are we friends now?

It's been almost a week since we went for a drive, and we've texted a bit, but I figured Collin felt obligated to be friendly because he's a nice guy.

After the bloody nose incident, he was surprisingly cool and gentlemanly. He dropped me and my bike off at the trailer, and gave me a warm, firm hug goodbye. We exchanged numbers, but he hasn't asked to hang out since.

I hesitate for another minute. This is what I wanted, right? To get close to Collin, gain entry to his house, and survey the layout so Derek and his buddies could steal all their valuables.

Thinking about my deal makes me feel like I've swallowed a rock that's now heavily sitting in the pit of my stomach, but it's what I need to do to survive. With another heartfelt sigh, I force my fingers to type a response: **I don't have a tube.**

Holding my ancient flip phone and my breath, I wait. Ignoring the part of my brain that wants to find out why I'm nervous about his response, I leave my screen up hoping for a quick reply. Luckily for my lungs, my phone pings again in under ten seconds.

With shaky fingers, I click on the center button to open the message. **Have an extra. All you need to bring is yourself in a suit. Pick you up at 9?**

My breath whooshes out of my chest and I drag in another deep inhale. I feel like I'm hyperventilating just having a conversation with Collin, and I'm not sure why. Typing out my response takes longer than it should. I write, edit, delete, several times, finally settling on: **You know where I live.**

A few seconds later my phone pings again: **:)**

I'm grinning to myself as I throw some frozen veggies and chicken into a skillet to make a stir fry. Moving the icy pieces with a spatula, I hum. It isn't until I'm seated at my table with a full bowl in front of me that I realize I may not own a swimsuit.

Forcing myself to stay seated, I shovel my dinner into my face aggressively. Barely chewing each bite before swallowing.

Even though I make an effort to remain calm and slowly move towards my room to search for a swimsuit —like a reasonable human being—I slam my bowl into the sink and sprint through the tiny hallway.

In my bedroom, I rip a drawer out of the built-in dresser due to my haste. Flinging it onto my bed, I pounce on top of it, like a panther ripping into its prey. Bras, underwear, and socks fly in every direction. I hit the wood at the bottom of the drawer before magically discovering a swimsuit I'd forgotten I owned.

"Well, shit."

Falling back onto my haunches, I eye the mess surrounding me, contemplating my next possible move. Reluctantly, I walk to the small storage closet and remove the tub filled with my mother's belongings. I haven't touched the plastic container in the months since my mom left. I guess a part of me was saving them in case she returned, but that seems less and less likely with each passing day.

Sighing, I peel off the green lid and delve inside. Some of my mom's clothing is much nicer than mine, gifts from her various boyfriends through the years or stuff she's stolen or bought from pawn shops, on the cheap.

I sort through all her left-overs, hoping for a decent bikini in the lot. Dragging out miscellaneous scraps of fabric, inspecting each piece before placing it on the dingy linoleum next to me if it isn't a swimsuit.

The pile in the container continues to dwindle, and still nothing. She wasn't good for much, but maybe her stuff is good for this, plays through my mind, as I continue through the tub, slowly nearing the bottom. Most of the clothing is too skimpy for my tastes, but the last three items are more modest sundresses I can't recall her ever wearing.

Surveying the room around me, I emit a frustrated groan. Why can't anything ever be as simple as just owning what I need to live my life?

Guess I'm riding my bike across town in the middle of the night, hoping Walmart still has a swimsuit in my size.

I push myself off the floor, and grab a garbage bag from under the sink. First, I'm going to get rid of some of this junk.

Back in my bedroom, I pick through my mom's belongings, leaving a few shirts, a pair of jeans my size, and the three dresses. The remaining worn pieces are shoveled into the bag. Once everything is picked up, I tie off the plastic top and drag it to my front door.

Resigned, I shove my aching feet back into my shoes and step outside, locking up as I exit. I peel my bike off the trailer, and clamber on, still holding the garbage bag.

Pointing myself in the direction of the dumpster, I cruise through the dusky, night air, riding across the patchy grass to get there on the quickest route.

I heave the bag up over my shoulder, tossing it into the open dumpster with an "oomph" from the effort. Just as I step away, preparing to climb back on my bike, I hear my name.

"Kenzzzziiiee-girl." Derek slurs, his voice sounding drunk as it drifts through the clearing between the trailers.

Twirling around, I follow the direction of his voice to seek him out. My eyes track his movements as he stumbles closer. His feet staggering across the uneven dirt and dying grass as he determinedly makes his way towards me.

I redistribute my weight, balancing on my sore left leg, and gripping my bike, as he drunkenly approaches. I wait to speak until he's close enough to hear me, not wanting to shout and alert the rest of the trailer park to our drama. "Why have I been seeing so much of you lately, Derek?"

"You know why, Kenz," he slurs sloppily, as he continues on his path towards me, staggering slightly when his shoe snags on a rock.

"I don't have anything to tell you yet," I reply,

preventing my annoyance from bleeding into my tone, in an effort to end this as quickly as possible. I have more to do tonight and my achy body is ready to climb into bed already.

Derek doesn't take the hint I want to be left alone. Instead, he continues stumbling forward until he's standing four inches away. I feel the warmth radiating off his body and smell the stench of booze emanating from his sweat and breath.

My natural reaction is to step backward, but I force myself to stay in place, not wanting to give Derek the upper hand by revealing how uncomfortable I am.

Instead, I tip my head back, meeting his dark gaze a half foot above me. A smirk falls to his lips as our eyes connect. The silence lingers until I quirk a brow at him.

"Have you forgotten our deal, Kenzie-girl?" He finally asks.

With an angry exhale, my brow furrows. "How many times do I need to tell you this, Derek? I'm not an idiot, I don't have memory loss. I'm not going to forget our arrangement, but I need time to make sure everything falls into place."

"Ooohkaay," he says, drawing the word out skeptically. "I saw Franzen drop you off the other day, Kenzie-girl. It looked pretty cozy and I didn't want you to forget about our arrangement. A week has passed since then, without any updates that will help me and Zane. I would hate to be forced to tell Collin how you plotted to rob his house with me, if things fell through." He grins, his glazed eyes roving over my body while he waits for his newest threat to register.

My whole-body tenses once the meaning of his words sink in. Not that I expected anything different from Derek, he's involved in all sorts of illegal activities and I have no doubt he would throw anyone under the bus that got in his way. Still, this is a quick reaction, for him to stoop so low after one week.

I give a stunted nod of my head, then step to my left with the intention of providing myself room to clamber on my bike.

Derek stops me, his hand gripping onto my upper arm. He leans forward, his drunken breath fanning across my face, forcing me to scrunch my nose. "Kenz, we aren't like the Franzens. You can like Collin, but he's not for you. Just remember that while you spend time with him. Keep the end game in mind; find the information you promised me, then get out. That's all you can do with guys like him. We'll never be good enough for the people from Golden Oaks and we both know it."

After another stunted nod, Derek releases me.

I angrily stride away, my fingers tightly gripping the handles of my bike, as emotion forces my feet forward. Wordlessly, I continue walking until I round the corner of the next trailer.

Only then do I allow my breathing to return to normal and relax my shoulders, releasing some of the fiery rage created by Derek's dismissal of my worth. With a clearer mind, I climb onto my bike and pedal away, leaving Derek near the dumpster, where he belongs.

The rest of my anger and irritation ebbs away the second my front tire leaves the dirt road of the trailer park. The Walmart is over an hour bike ride away, giving me plenty of time to repeat the conversation, thinking over each and every word several times. As much as I want to brush Derek's message aside, I can't. They hold too much truth for me to do that.

I can wish I was the kind of girl meant for Collin Franzen as much as I want. But no matter how much I like him and think he likes me; he'll never be anything more than a mark. He's too good for someone from the trailer park plotting to steal from his family.

Someone like me.

Chapter 10

I stand in front of my cracked bathroom mirror, turning left and right, wearing the tiny, red bikini I bought last night. The scraps of fabric that seemed like a good idea in Walmart's empty dressing room, no longer feels like the right choice in the light of day. Doubt plagues me as I see the cups barely covering the center of my modest breasts and the bottoms hanging low on my flat belly, covering half of each cheek in the back.

In the store, the suit felt sexy and daring.

Posing in the mirror, I felt alluring and mature.

Now, though… now I'm worried it might be too trashy.

Sighing, I head to my bedroom and throw on my favorite pair of cutoffs and a tight tank top. Maybe the other girl's suits will also be as small as this one?

When I was flipping through the options at the store, tiny bikini seemed to be the style that was "in". If nothing else, I can keep my clothes on during our tubing adventure, to cover more skin. The thought reassures me and motivates me to finish prepping for the day.

I return to the bathroom, now fully clothed, and use the mirror to swipe on some waterproof black mascara. A little luxury item I purchased for myself when I was at the store last night. Lastly, I twist and pull my long, black strands of hair into a tight French braid beginning at my scalp and trailing down to my lower back.

Then, I step away from the counter doing a quick sweep of my appearance. I remain objective, noting my chocolate eyes and thin face. I'm pretty, enough. In my opinion, the bare-faced look suits me, plus we're going in the water, so there's no point in caking on make-up.

I deem my appearance acceptable and exit to the living room. Swiping my small purse, containing the usual items, off the table, I sweep my gaze around the room, feeling like I'm forgetting something. Suddenly, I remember the sunglasses I purchased last night, as another small luxury.

Running to the back of the trailer, I snag the aviator-style frames. The lenses are a cool light blue, which make my dark features appear more interesting. I rip the tag off the sunglasses and throw it on top of my dresser.

Popping my new accessory into place, I stride outside. I have fifteen minutes to spare, but I'd rather bask in the early morning sun than hang out in my dark, dingy trailer. I plop onto my front steps and lounge, like a snake basking in the sun. The early Alabama summer heat slowly soaks into my skin and I begin to nod off.

The sound of tires crunching along gravel, dirt, and dried grass jolts me back into awareness sometime later.

The Con

I rise to my feet, watching as Collin drives onto my front lawn. He leaves his SUV idling, opening his door and stepping onto the runner, his head clearing the top of the door by almost a foot.

"Hey McKenzie," he drawls. His voice is warm and jolly, like he's pleased to be here and happy to see me.

My eyes rake over him, noticing his tousled blonde hair, and dark sunglasses hiding his eyes from sight. They flicker over his lips pulled back to show his teeth, and his broad shoulders, partially covered by a black muscle-tee. After inspecting him head to toe, I grin back, and yell, "Hey Franzen." The tone of my voice is almost unrecognizable to my own ears. I sound... cheery. There's a teasing, amused lilt to my words that's unfamiliar. Instead of overthinking the change, I rush towards the car, whipping open the passenger door and pulling myself in.

I tug the door closed behind me; hearing Collin's shut around the same time. Pivoting, I angle my body towards the driver's seat and see he's already facing my direction. His sunglasses hide his eyes from view, making it hard to determine his expression.

In a moment of playfulness, I surge across the console. Snatching his sunglasses off his face, I stick my tongue out then retreat back to my side of the car.

I place the sunglasses over my own, tilt my head to the side and ask, "How do I look?" Then I push my lips out into a duckface and throw my hand up to the side, near my head.

Collin laughs and leans slightly closer to my position posted by the door. "Ridiculous," he says with the

81

amused sparkle making an appearance in his green gaze. He tilts further forward and my breath catches at the look that enters his eyes.

I feel myself drawn forward, an invisible line tugging me closer to Collin. My eyes drift shut as my back leaves the safety of the door. I feel the heat of Collin's body also looming closer, then suddenly his hands are on my sides.

He digs in with his fingers, tickling his way up and down my skin, with a combination of feather light touches and prods. I shriek, giggling, and gasping while I make a futile attempt at escaping the unexpected assault.

"Stop tickling me!" I cry out in a breathless voice.

"Relinquish my sunglasses," Collin replies in a mock-serious tone. His deep, southern voice making the words gentler than he probably intended.

"Never!"

The tickling attack continues, with Collin becoming more aggressive. He leans halfway across the car to chase me with his devious fingers, deftly finding the most sensitive places to make me giggle and squirm.

"Okay, okay," I finally relent, lifting my fingers to my face and prying the sunglasses away. With a huff, I hand them across the car, then cross my arms over my still heaving chest.

"No reason to be a sore loser, McKenzie," Collin taunts, as he places his dark sunglasses onto his nose, once again hiding his mirth-filled eyes from view.

"You have freakishly long arms, it was totally an unfair battle," I protest, jokingly.

"Yeah, yeah," he agrees, his tone appeasing. "Well

these gorilla arms need to navigate us out of here to pick up some of the gang, I don't want us to be late."

He starts the ignition and I tip forward, feeling comfortable enough in his car to give myself permission to fiddle with the radio. A top forties station comes on, and I twist the dial, increasing the volume of the pop music as it floats into the car through the speakers.

Before long, we're turning into the Golden Oaks neighborhood. Spotting the sign, I turn to Collin, "Do all of your friends live here?"

He nods, wordlessly, maintaining focus on the road as he drives.

"You didn't have to drive all the way over to my house! I could've ridden my bike," I exclaim, feeling guilty I dragged Collin all the way to the trailer park when the rest of his friends are his neighbors.

His eyes flit to connect with mine briefly, then return to the road. "It was no big deal. The drive is way shorter than the bike ride would have been. Plus, I like having you ride in my passenger seat." He gestures to the radio with his right hand. "You're already a great co-captain."

His easy-going smile is visible as he reassures me. My chance to reply is stolen as Collin stops the SUV in front of a colossal home, at least as large as his, painted pale gray.

The moment the car brakes, the bright white front door pops open and four people spill out, three girls I know are cheerleaders and a guy I recognize from the football team.

They swarm the car, opening the doors and piling in with choruses of "Hey Collin!"

One of the girls was my lab partner sophomore year--a redhead named Katie--she spots me and also chimes an excited, "Hey Kenzie!"

Surprisingly, the others follow suit.

Collin shoots me a happy grin, veering back onto the road and stopping at one other house. The process repeats and a total of six girls and two guys end up crammed into the back of Collin's SUV. They're all from our school, but I've never spent any time with them outside of any classes we've had together.

Another girl, named Isabelle, suddenly shrieks, "Turn up this song, I love it!!"

I tilt my head, wondering how she was able to hear the now too-quiet music, in the boisterous car. Bending forward, I wiggle the knob to the right until some pop song I've never heard comes blasting through the speakers much louder than before. Most of the girls and one of the guys begin singing off key over the noise and I find myself giggling amidst the chaos.

Collin reaches over with his right hand and gives my thigh a gentle squeeze. One of the girls from the back yells, "Ooooh." He just waves his hand at her, in a brush off motion, and everyone else continues crooning to the radio, not paying us any mind. Collin's hand floats back down to my leg and rests there, gently gripping my skin.

The rest of the drive passes that way, making the time go by quickly.

A short while later, Collin turns the SUV into a clearing near the river, stopping on a patchy spot of land comprised of a half dirt, half rock combo. The ten of us loaded into his vehicle disembark onto the uneven ground, merging with another group of ten cheerleaders and football players, this one consisting of seven guys and three girls, as they offload from a truck.

It doesn't escape my attention that the boy to girl ratio is even; it almost feels like everyone is coupled up. I eye Collin curiously, but he's already been sucked in by the newcomers and is helping to unload supplies and inflate tubes.

My focus moves to examine the rest of the group instead. I've gone to school with these kids for years. I know their names and have seen them grow up, just like they have me, but this all feels very surreal. Two weeks ago, I wouldn't have thought I'd be with Collin Franzen and the other popular kids from our school, about to go tubing down a river together.

Life is just funny that way, I guess.

Pausing, still hovering near Collin's SUV, I move my eyes past the crowd to take in the view. The rocky, dirt littered ground covers this entire side of the river. Slightly murky, green water connects the land to the other side, which is covered in tall, thick grass. Similar to the lake Collin brought me to the other day.

Glancing further down, I see the water moving steadily, diverging around a few tree trunks popping up from the river bed. Much further down, there's a tiny island, but the river continues on for miles. Surveying our surroundings, I wonder how long we'll spend out here.

I'm tempted to ask, but at this point I'm along for the ride… so, I guess it doesn't really matter much anyways.

Stepping away from the vehicle, I join the cluster of nine other girls standing between the two cars. A consistent wave of chatter coats the clearing, but I remain somewhat off to the side. Absorbing gossip without participating in the conversation.

No one outright ignores me, but no one directly invites me to join in either. My place is unclear when it comes to this new dynamic and I'm slowly figuring it out.

After a bit of standing around, the girls begin to shed their cover-ups and I'm relieved to see the tiny bikini is definitely in. Compared to some of the suits the girls are wearing here, mine could be considered modest.

I yank my own tank up, over my head, careful to avoid mussing my braid. I tug my shorts down next, stepping out of them with my sandals still on. I've never been tubing before, but it makes sense you would want your shoes on to protect your feet from the rocky bottoms. Plus, all of the other girls left theirs on.

A catcall breaks across the clearing and I glance up to see all the guys watching us as we get undressed.

Typical.

One of the guys walks past Collin, ambling in the direction of the cooler they have set up near the truck. He slaps him on the back as he passes, loudly congratulating him. "Nice work man, she's hot."

I ignore the comment, hoping they'll drop it, as I roll my tank top and shorts into a ball. Stepping away from the group, I plan to deposit my clothes back into the SUV with my purse.

The Con

One of the girls flips her long, bright hair to capture everyone's attention, including mine. She cries, in a teasing tone, "Are you...blushing, Franzen? Be still my heart, THE Collin Franzen blushing. Never thought I would see the day." She bends backwards dramatically, placing the back of her palm over her forehead in an exaggerated fashion, like she's about to swoon.

Her antics cause our group of twenty or so to burst into laughter before they return to disrobing or prepping the tubes.

I look away from my bundle of clothes to meet Collin's gaze across the rocky clearing. He's moved his sunglasses to rest across the top of his blonde hair, leaving his green eyes visible in the bright sun.

Time stills as our eyes clash, heat sizzling through the connection despite the distance. The background fades away and I silently take a half step forward, instinctually wanting to be closer to Collin.

The sound of glass breaking on the rocks interrupts the trance.

"Fuck," one of the footballers exclaims, and I shake my head to dispel the Collin-induced fog.

My eyes shift in the direction of the noise, quickly spotting the shattered bottle scattered across the ground and the soggy, broken cardboard box the beer was in. Another guy jumps in to help him, cautiously plucking the pieces of glass from the ground and placing them into a box that's still intact.

After investigating the source of the noise, I'm immediately drawn back to Collin's form. He's in the same spot, his eyes seeking mine like heat missiles.

The second my brown gaze meets his green, he shoots a wink in my direction, then a smile takes over his face.

The sun glints off his teeth, and there's only one word that describes the look.

Predatory.

Chapter 11

The top half of my body is hot and sweaty, but the cool water drifting underneath my bottom helps to temper the sun and humid air. I lazily trail my hand across the surface next to me, as the current pulls our group of twenty down the river at a steady pace.

One of the guys, maybe it was Jeremy, was clever enough to bring ropes to connect our group together. Our tubes are knotted closely to one person on the side, with slacked rope connecting to the person ahead and behind us, forming a chain of tubes, two by ten. Trailing behind the group, are two coolers filled with beers and sodas and a couple waters, with the two guys at the back dispersing the beverages as requested.

Collin was placed beside me, of course, our connected rubber circles carrying us comfortably side by side. I'd been asked, several times, if I wanted anything to drink. Each time I declined, but somehow, ended up sharing beers with Collin anyway.

He swigs on our fourth, or maybe fifth beer, handing it across the tubes for me to drink. There's something so intimate about sharing a beer, I think as I bring the neck of the bottle closer to my mouth. Our lips have occupied this same space within seconds of each other.

I already felt a connection to Collin and every time he licks his lips after I place my mouth against our beer, I feel the heat building low in my belly burn hotter.

I return the bottle and he finishes the contents in one, long guzzle, maintaining eye contact throughout.

He reaches his long arm back behind him, calling, "Trash."

Following the progress of the bottle with my eyes, I watch as it passes through two sets of hands to reach the guys in the back. The empty bottle gets added into one of the coolers to be recycled later.

I must have it bad, because even the fact that Collin and his friends recycle their garbage instead of dumping it into the river has my attraction towards him growing.

It's not clear how long we've been out here for. All of us left our phones, and the boys their fancy watches, in the car for safe/dry keeping while we float. One of the guys said the route we plan to take is about three miles, but distance doesn't mean much when you're floating on a tube.

Before we set off down the river, Collin and Matt, the owner of the truck, drove to the end point to drop off one of the vehicles. This way we don't have to trudge all the way back to the start point in soggy shoes while carrying our tubes.

My eyes drift shut again, listening as the group ribs

at each other over various inside jokes and insider information. My lips form into a soft smile as we float, listening to their banter without input.

Some kids might feel left out, being the new kid in a group of clearly close friends, but I kind of like it.

It's nice to be a fresh face in a group of friends, getting the chance to listen and participate without any attachment. It's the first time in a really long time that I can remember having fun.

Summer, a natural blond with a sunny disposition befitting her name, cuts through the chit chat. She screams, "Who's ready for SENIOR YEAR?!"

A wave of shouts and yells ripples down the tubes and I join in, yelling "Woohoo," at the top of my lungs.

The first three times this happened, I didn't join in —but it seems like some part of the tubing ritual—to periodically scream something and have everyone cheer in response. Normally I'm not the kind to partake in stuff like this, but if I'm participating in this tubing adventure, might as well join in every part of it.

My eyes remain closed and I feel myself beginning to doze, falling into a comfortable half-sleep. The consistent motion of the river and muggy air provide a drugging affect that lulls me to a semi-conscious state.

Jeremy randomly shouts, "Hi-yah."

The noise is nearby, as he's in the set of tubes directly behind Collin and I. My eyes pop open over the weird sound effect, just in time to see him attempt some sort of ninja kick against Collin's tube.

Following the line of his leg, I realize Collin has

started to drift to sleep as well. This is probably Jeremy's way of waking him up.

Jeremy's kick creates a ripple effect, hitting Collin's tube at just the right angle to career him into me. His weight provides added momentum and causes us to create a V in the line, from our spot close to the center.

None of this probably would've mattered if we'd been in a better position on the river.

Our current location is almost a bottleneck of sorts and my bottom scrapes against the rough surface of a rock near the edge of the water. This causes me to push my weight against the sides of my tube, to pull my butt out of the water, and away from any interaction with the hazards peppering the shallow river bed.

The movement shoves the sides of the tube down into the water as it lifts me up. A loud "pop" suddenly bursts out from beneath me and my tube instantly begins to lose air.

With a cry of shock, I swiftly stand in the shallow water. The surface barely tapping the top of my ankles.

My yell alerts the entire crew there's an issue, either that, or the popping noise, or the now deflating tube I'm holding in my hands. Either way, the boys hastily jump into action leaping off their tubes and dragging the chain to a halt. Together they pull it into the center of the river, so we don't lose any more tubes.

"What a bummer," Katie exclaims, watching me hold my tube with disappointment in her eyes.

One of the guys from the back, Alex, shouts, "What do we do now?"

Collin eyes me for a second, then shrugs. "We retie

the tubes, then McKenzie can lay across me. We only have about a half mile left now anyways."

My cheeks flush hotly at the thought of laying across Collin's fit, shirtless body for...however long it takes to float half a mile.

I glance around and see the rest of the crew nodding and Jeremy wading in my direction, presumably to handle the re-tying of the tubes.

Once he reaches my spot on the rocks, I hand him my deflated yellow piece of rubber dejectedly. Then I wade the way he came from, into the center, towards Collin. I stand to his side, avoiding looking directly at him, suddenly shy at the thought of having to lay on top of him for an indeterminable amount of time.

Too soon, Jeremy calls, "All set."

Everyone settles back into their tubes, except for Jeremy who steadies ours while Collin gets in. They both turn expectant gazes to me, where I'm rooted to the ground a few feet away. Reluctantly, I trudge forward, eyeing Collin apprehensively.

Do I lay on my back or my stomach? Which would be less awkward?

Collin makes the decision for me. He tips forward and snags my wrist, yanking me towards him to fall face first into his chest. He uses his hands to cushion the blow so I don't smack my nose against his stone-like pecs.

Jeremy chuckles as he releases our tube then hops onto his own. With his feet no longer anchoring us into place, our chain resumes drifting along the river, our portion of the set awkwardly sagging to one side, due to the missing tube.

I'm sprawled across Collin's chest; my arms tucked underneath me against his body and my legs creating a stiff, straight line off the side of the tube, hovering above the water.

"Let me help you get comfortable," Collin drawls quietly, his voice sounding a bit raspy as it hits my ears.

I nod against his chest after I realize he's waiting for my permission to touch me.

Seconds later, his warm palms grip around my upper thighs. He lifts me more fully across his body, aligning our crotches in the center of the tube, with my knees curling around either side of him, dipping into the water. The backs of my feet rest against the sides of the tube near his knees.

He briefly moves his hands, tugging my arms upward to wrap around his neck. Once he's satisfied with my positioning, he moves his hands back down, to rest underneath my bottom. He supports some of my weight with his palms, presumably so we don't sink too far into the water and drag against the rocks a couple feet below the surface.

"More comfortable?" he asks, his voice more of a growl than the genteel drawl I'm used to hearing.

I contemplate his question, stretching my arms up and out, and wriggling around a bit. The motion causes my barely covered chest to scrape against his and our centers to meld even closer together.

Collin inhales sharply, his hands cupping my ass tightening with his breath.

Instead of raising me up like I expected, he pushes me slightly up, then pulls my weight back down. My eyes widen and this time, my breath catches. Collin watches me with a hooded gaze, as he repeats the motion causing heat to flare between the two of us.

"Hey, you two. Don't use this time to get frisky! We're all still here you know," Katie shouts in her peppy voice. The rest of the group joins in, chuckling at our expense and yelling their agreements.

The words, although joking, are like a bucket of ice-cold water. The flush in my cheeks instantly transitions into embarrassment and I watch as Collin's eyes open wide. He scans our surroundings suddenly, like he forgot where we were.

I know I definitely did.

Collin finally drawls out, "Jealousy isn't pretty, Katie." His warm voice, drifting gently over the river like a summer breeze, his tone showing that he's joking.

"Ugh, as if," she responds, with faux offense.

The group laughs again and the sounds of chatter slowly resume around us. Collin pushes his back against the tube, placing his mouth closer to my ear. The feeling of his breath tickling my skin makes me shiver and I almost miss his words. "At least you'll tan evenly, this way."

I laugh, appreciating his ability to joke in a slightly awkward situation, surrounded by his friends. The motion causes me to jostle against him slightly and Collin groans. He moves his hands up to my hips, squeezing them tightly to stop the movement.

We spend the rest of the float like that. My cheek resting against his chest, and his hands holding my hips in place with tense arms.

Thankfully there isn't too much of the river left. It's not long before one of the boys is hopping off their tubes and towing our chain closer to the river's edge.

Once we're in place, I hear the rest of the group begin to move out of their tubes. Their voices become harder to hear as they leave the river to head towards the truck parked on the shore.

Unfortunately, I'm in a super awkward position and can't move off Collin on my own.

Jeremy senses our dilemma and suddenly appears off the side of our tube. He walks closer and inspects the two of us settled in the center before scooping me into his arms and gently setting me onto the rocky shore, he pauses briefly, his blue eyes connecting with mine while I regain my equilibrium.

I wait for another second after he releases me, pausing before I join the others, to check if Collin needs help.

A throat clearing next to me makes me jump as I wait, lost in my own thoughts. Glancing to my side, I see Jeremy's gaze locked onto my chest.

As if he can feel my eyes on him, he hastily glances away to the other side of the river, then looks pointedly at Collin. When I follow the line of his eyes, I see Collin's green gaze is also staring intently at my chest.

What the heck?

I don't even have big boobs, so I have no idea what they're gawking at.

Following their gazes, I glance down and then gasp. I fumble to cover my left boob which, at some point, became an escapee from its tiny triangle of cloth. My small handful of a breast is just out in the wind, my nipple pointing at attention.

As quickly as I can, I conceal the offending appendage. Once it's secured, I glance around to see if anyone else caught the slip.

I'm thankful when I see everyone else has started heading to the truck parked a half a dozen feet away. Their backs are to us, meaning it's likely no one else saw anything.

Without meeting the eyes of either of the boys, I join the others, trudging up the hill at the back of the pack headed to the truck, awash in embarrassment. Their chatter floats over me as I join them in the bed, and wait the few minutes it takes to get all our supplies loaded in.

The drive back to Collin's SUV is much, much shorter than the river float and soon, we're all saying our goodbyes. Several of the guys and girls give me a hug, saying things like they can't wait to see me tomorrow and they're so glad I was able to make it.

Despite the tit slip, I'm feeling cheerful as I pile into Collin's SUV with the rest of our group. My weary body easily settles deep into the seat, ready to go home, take a shower and nap.

I stare out the window as we drive down the same road from earlier, breathing a sigh of relief when the Golden Oaks sign comes into view.

Repeating the process from this morning, Collin drops off his friends at their houses in groups, until it's just us two remaining. We continue in a comfortable silence back to my trailer, the radio softly crooning to us as the tires eat up the distance in a quarter of the time it would take me to bike.

Collin drives his SUV onto the grass in front of my trailer. He surprises me when he hops out and trails me up to the door. He stands beside me wordlessly, as I unlock the trailer and push open the thin piece of tin, revealing the inside.

"Would you like to come in?" I ask, hesitantly, nervous for him to see the rest of my home and realize the differences in how we were raised.

"Nah," He says. "I just wanted to make sure you got home safe."

"Lots of danger lurking between your car and here," I retort in a joking tone.

"Never know what could happen, even in that short distance," he replies, his voice more serious than mine.

I remain quiet and we stand on my front porch, staring each other down. I silently will him to kiss me. Not bold enough to make the move myself, I attempt to transmit the message with my eyes.

Kiss me.

He leans forward and I feel victorious, my eyelids drifting down slowly with his nearness.

Expecting the feeling of his lips brushing against mine, I'm surprised when his light scruff scrapes the skin of my cheek instead.

Hot breath fans against my ear as he whispers, "I'm not going to kiss you McKenzie Carslyle. Not yet, at least. But I will be here tomorrow at six forty-five, to drive you to school."

A shiver travels down my spine, despite the warm

air. How can he make something not sexy seem so sexual?

Collin places a quick peck against my cheek then straightens up. He retreats down the stairs, ambling backwards to his SUV.

I'm stuck standing there, rooted to the ground, strangely aroused and feeling bereft after I didn't get a goodnight kiss with everything that happened between us today.

My disappointment slowly transitions to anticipation as I replay the conversation in my head. He said "yet". Which means he plans to kiss me, eventually.

Pushing the thought aside, I ask a question that's been nagging at my conscience since the first night we interacted at the park. "Why are you so nice to me, Collin Franzen?"

I don't yell, but the words are easily carried across the still air. He pauses in the process of opening his door, swiveling on his heel. His eyes skim over me, still standing with the screen half open, the trailer a gaping pit of darkness at my back.

"My parents always taught me people shouldn't need any kind of motivation to be nice," he drawls out, like kindness is obvious and inherent and everyone acts the way he does.

I nod my head like I understand the sentiment, but I don't.

I really don't.

My parents taught me it's every person for themselves. Even the bonds of familial obligation couldn't hold them, to stay here, with me. And although they didn't say it in so many words, they treated kindness as a weakness to be exploited.

I allow Collin's words to linger in the air, releasing the screen from my grip. It drifts shut, closing me into the trailer and creating a barrier between Collin and I.

Standing in the dark, I watch him get into his car and back out of the area in front of my home. I stay there, eyes focused on his SUV until his taillights disappear from sight.

His words continue to echo in my mind, growing more insistent each time they repeat.

People shouldn't need any kind of motivation to be nice.

Chapter 12

The first day of school comes too quickly and takes too long to arrive, all at once. Every year usually feels like more of the same, but not this year. This year, senior year, is going to be different. I can sense it.

This year, instead of riding the bus or my bike, I stand outside my trailer waiting for Collin. He texted me after he got home, thanking me for spending the day with him and his friends, confirming his plan to drive me to school. He apologized for the early start, explaining he had a mandatory meeting for football.

I didn't bother to tell him he's actually picking me up later than I would have to catch the bus or start biking. Collin has probably never had to ride the bus or walk to school in his entire life; it wasn't worth the awkward conversation attempting to explain what it's like to grow up poor and essentially parentless.

Instead, I wait for him on my front porch, my midnight hair drifting down my back in a straight sheet, fluttering slightly every time a small breeze blows by. I'm wearing one of the dresses I saved from my mom's tub of discarded clothing.

I hate using the things she left behind, as if it justifies her absence in a way, but I found the dress when I was searching for a swimsuit. It's a brand-new gray maxi dress with thick straps, dipping into a round neck and almost hitting the floor, despite my height. The tags were still attached, validating that it never really belonged to my mother anyway. I also have a white sweater tucked away in my worn backpack; in case they decide to be total sticklers about the dress code today.

My attention wanders around the park while I wait for Collin, my eyes briefly pausing on Derek's trailer. The sight of it makes me queasy with guilt, reminding me of the arrangement I reluctantly agreed to; betraying my budding relationship with Collin for money.

I actually really am starting to like him, and his friends. They definitely didn't act the way I expected them to when I joined their tubing adventure, as a last-minute addition. Everyone seemed super cool and welcoming. It may be because I had the Franzen stamp of approval, but still it was refreshing to spend the day having fun with kids my age.

An image of my slim funds, nestled in the tin can in my kitchen, pops to the forefront of my mind. As if the universe is reminding me of the reason I consented to conning Collin's family in the first place. My situation is grim, and despite my best efforts, I'm left with limited options.

Exhaling deeply, I push all thoughts of the con and Collin away, tilting my face to watch the clouds instead. I focus on the fluffy white puffs drifting aimlessly by, attempting to identify any recognizable shapes in the sky above me.

"Looking for something in particular up there?" A warm voice drawls.

I startle, surprised I didn't hear Collin's SUV approaching. Until I face his voice and realize he parked further away than usual. Rather than driving all the way into the yard, he's standing a dozen feet away, with his car about twice that distance.

Maybe he wanted the chance to observe me in my natural habitat: being a little odd in the trailer park.

Grinning at Collin, I joke, "Just asking for answers on how I keep getting stuck with you." I punctuate the words by sticking my tongue out playfully, showing I'm teasing.

Collin releases a playful growl then dashes straight towards me. I pace a half step back, but before I can escape, he rushes me, scooping me into his arms. Capturing me. He twirls us around, then carries me bridal style back to his car.

"Think you're going to be stuck with me for a while yet," he says, winking as he relinquishes his grip on my knees, allowing my feet to fall to the dirt next to the passenger-side, my body sliding down his until I'm firmly on the ground.

I giggle in response as he releases me. His grin looms above my face for a few seconds, his eyes sparkling with mirth.

Without another word, he steps away and rounds the car, jumping into the driver's seat with ease.

Following his cue, I open the passenger door and climb in cautiously, to avoid dirtying my dress with the dusty exterior of his car. Once I'm settled inside, Collin turns the key and proceeds to drive to school. Music floats lightly out the speakers but we remain mostly silent, with Collin focusing on driving and me watching the scenery fly by through his tinted windows.

The trip which normally lasts almost an hour, takes a quarter of that time. The ability to get around by car versus bike or bus is no joke. I could get accustomed to the convenience of being driven to class every day.

The ride is smooth all the way through, ending as we pull into the school parking lot. Collin picks a spot close to the brick building, then waits by the hood for me. He holds my hand, intertwining our fingers as we approach the double front doors of the building.

I tug on his hand, as we hit the bottom step and he turns to look at me with a question in his eyes. "I think I'm going to wait out here. It's still a little while until school starts and I don't want to lurk in the building," I say the words with a reassuring smile, not wanting him to think I'm ungrateful for the ride.

His face instantly relaxes and he releases my hand. In a quick movement, his palm grips the back of my head, holding me in place. He slowly moves closer, softly kissing my forehead with his plump lips.

The simple affection makes my breath catch.

Collin Franzen is Dangerous.

When he reels back, I glance up at him with a question in my eyes and he smiles gently. "I just like you McKenzie Carslyle," he drawls with a shrug, already able to read me after the few days we've spent together.

He doesn't wait for my reply, climbing up the steps and entering through the right side of the double doors. "See you at lunch," he calls over his shoulder, giving a small wave before disappearing into our school.

Exhaling a sigh, I slip off my backpack and allow it slide to the ground. Crossing my legs, I relax against the peeling metal handrail, contemplating how I want to spend the time before class starts.

I slide my ancient phone out of my pocket, starting a game of snake. Jamming the keys down, I grow the snake with each little snack on the screen, but I become bored after about three minutes.

I've abandoned my phone and started picking at my cuticles when a flash of red-orange hair catches the corner of my eye. I glance up to see Katie hustling towards the building.

"Hey Kenzie!" She exclaims while she's still a half-dozen yards away.

My eyes scan her form, noting the bright blue and black cheerleading uniform the squad wears at assemblies and games. I'm assuming she's here for a mandatory team meeting, like Collin.

"Hi Katie," I reply, less excited than her overly peppy tone, but still friendly.

She stops right in front of me, plopping a huge duffle to the ground nearby. The sound it emits when it hits the pavement makes it seem like it weighs at least thirty pounds. My eyebrows raise, but I don't have a chance to ask what's inside.

Katie starts in a chipper tone, "Are you here for the cheerleading meeting? Wow, that's so cool. It would be awesome to have you on the squad; you already get along so well with everyone. We can walk together, it starts in five minutes!"

I don't think she inhales a single breath the entire time she speaks and it takes a few moments for my brain to catch up with the overload of information she supplied in approximately six seconds.

"Oh," I reply slowly. "I wasn't here for the cheer meeting…"

She interrupts, snatching her bag off the ground easily, making it appear lighter than it sounded. Her other hand grabs onto my elbow with a surprisingly firm grip and she steers me towards the school.

"Well, you're already here. Might as well come check it out, never know, you might be interested. There's nothing else to do before class starts anyways," she says in a steady stream.

"Well, sure, I guess," I reply, even though it doesn't seem like I have much choice at this point.

She's right… There really isn't anything else to do anyways.

Chapter 13

I slam my tray onto the table next to Collin, louder than intended. Glancing left, then right to check no one is around waiting to tattle on me, after my next statement, I quickly whine out, "I wish you had warned me about the cheerleading meeting this morning. Katie found me while she was on the warpath and now, I need to be here early tomorrow, to learn the routines for tryouts."

Collin wraps a comforting arm around my shoulders after I plop down on the bench next to him. "Sorry McKenzie. I really didn't know." His voice sounds genuine. I believe him, but still emit a huff of frustration.

"Weren't you a cheerleader in middle school?" Matt asks from across the table, his brow furrowed like thinking is difficult for him.

"Yeah, but now we're in high school," I point out like he's slow. "I don't have the time to be a cheerleader."

Or the money, for that matter.

"It'll be okay, I'm sure you'll figure it out," Collin drawls, the words soothing me despite the fact that they don't offer a solution to my problems at all. "We'll get you here early tomorrow too. What time do you need to meet the team?"

"At six," I reply with a frown. "That's so early though, you don't have to drive me."

"Nah, it's okay," Collin replies, giving me one more squeeze. He removes his arm to pick up the slice of pizza from the tray in front of him. "We have early practice anyways." He takes a massive chomp of the cheese covered dough, chewing quietly before he continues, "Honestly, if you made the team, it would make it easier to drive you to school every day. A lot of the practices for football and cheerleading line up, so we'd have similar schedules."

Drive me to school every day?

As in long term?

While I mull over his words, surprised by his commitment to driving me, the rest of the girls arrive at the table. Placing their trays on top of the gray surface, they slide into the empty spaces on the bench, filling in the gaps between the football players.

Isabelle flips her deep, rich auburn hair over her shoulder. The movement is incredibly sassy, but her voice is sweet when she asks, "How are you, Kenzie?"

Collin answers for me while I chew a huge bite of pizza. "She's good. McKenzie was telling us she's trying out for cheerleading." He smiles at her warmly and a flare of jealousy bubbles low in my gut.

I tamp down the unnecessary feeling, reminding myself Collin is nice and nice people smile at other people.

Isabelle grins at me, but the look lacks any of the warmth or happiness that typically accompanies the expression. "Oh, I didn't realize you were interested, Kenzie. I hope you make it." Her tone is a direct contradiction with her words, she even pauses between "you" and "make" like she silently added a "don't" in between.

I dip my head and take another large bite of pizza, in lieu of responding.

She turns her attention to Collin next. "Why do you always call her McKenzie? Doesn't she prefer to go by Kenzie?" she asks.

I continue to eat silently, even though Isabelle is now talking about me like I'm not even at the table. I'm also curious to hear Collin's response so I don't interrupt. Acting like I'm engrossed by my tray of free lunch, I watch him out of my peripherals.

He shrugs, then replies simply, "I've never met another McKenzie. It feels unique, like I should appreciate the name because it's special." He meets Isabelle's gaze directly before glancing at me while I pretend to read the label of my milk. Then, he turns back to his food, finishing the rest of his pizza in two bites.

"Well it's kind of weird. You should just call her by her nickname, since that's clearly what she prefers," Isabelle snarks out. Her jealous tone has the entire table pausing their own conversations, eager to become privy to the drama.

Thankfully, Katie intervenes. Drawing the attention

away from my newly blooming relationship with Collin by asking a question to Jeremy, who's sitting across the table at the furthest point possible. "Do we have English homework already? What kind of BS is that?" She shouts, to be heard across the distance.

Matt rolls his eyes and joins in, "I hate when teachers assign homework the first day."

Their conversation slowly takes over, the loud chatter around the table resuming as everyone becomes immersed in their complaints about homework, forgetting the conflict with Isabelle. I remain silent, thinking over Collin's words, and a small smile creeps onto my face.

I read between the lines, he calls me by my full name because he thinks I'm special and unique.

Turning, I face Collin and snag his hand off the table, intertwining my fingers with his. I use the affection to reassure him, I like him calling me McKenzie, now that I know the reason why.

He's started talking to Alex, but he shoots me a smile and pulls our connected hands to rest in his lap, on top one of his thickly muscled legs. The motion tugs me closer, making our thighs press together and I can feel his warmth radiating through his jeans.

Summer snags my attention, effectively distracting me from my imminent swoon over all things Collin. "Kenzie, do you need a ride to practice tomorrow? Katie told me you're trying out for the team. Yay!"

Her enthusiasm causes a genuine smile in response. "Nah, Collin already said he would drive me," I reply. "Thanks for offering though, I may need a ride or two in the future," I tack on, wanting her to know I appreciate her thoughtfulness, and her overall chipper demeanor which quickly overshadows Isabelle's rudeness.

"Oh, any time!" She replies, her voice as bubbly as champagne.

"How many spots are there? Open on the team that is," I address the question to the table generally, since almost all of the cheerleaders are sitting with us. Or maybe I'm sitting with them, since this is their usual table.

"Three," a beautiful dark-skinned girl named Heather replies. "I think you have a good chance; I remember your moves from middle school," she adds with a grin.

I smile at her and the conversation between the cheerleaders devolves into guessing who the other two empty spots will go to. I half-listen, knowing they're including me, but unable to participate without knowing the talent of the other girls trying out for the team.

The bell rings, trilling abruptly and slicing through the sounds in the cafeteria, including the conversations at our table. With a groan, I join the others, stepping over the bench and grabbing my backpack with my free hand, in preparation of heading to class.

I have calculus next, and as much as I would like to delay that torture, the teacher is a notorious hard ass on anyone that's late. Especially on the first day.

Collin stays seated, twirling his legs around to face my direction. He tugs on our connected hands and the motion causes me to stumble forward into him. The

NICOLE MARSH

height difference from our positions causes my modest chest to smash right into his face.

"Oops, sorry," I say, taking a half step back, so he's no longer squished against my boobs.

Collin smirks and raises a single brow. "I wasn't complaining," he drawls out.

I giggle, knowing the charming Collin Franzen is joking.

His face transitions into a warm smile as he rises from the bench. Collin releases my hand to wrap both arms low around my waist instead.

"Can I walk you to class?" he asks, a serious expression replacing his teasing one.

"Of course," I respond, ignoring the growing feelings his easy touches are nurturing, to focus on his words.

"Where are we headed?"

"Calculus," I reply, ending the word with another groan.

Collin quickly drops his arms and latches onto my hand, striding towards the door with purpose.

"We better hurry, Mr. Lutz is a total jerk. He's my first class in the morning," he throws the words over his shoulder as he propels us through the halls and across the school.

He finally slows his pace when we reach the hallway containing my class. He drags me to a stop, a few feet away from the door, out of sight from everyone inside.

"Aren't you going to be late now?" I ask, in a half-whisper, not wanting to get caught even though we aren't doing anything wrong.

"Worth it, to walk my girl to class," he drawls.

My girl.

Collin drops his head, lightly pressing his lips against my forehead. My body melts against his, over the sweet gesture of affection he's given me for the second time today. He steps away and our eyes connect, a sizzling heat traveling between us.

I could stand in the hallway all day, staring at Collin Franzen.

He seems to be more aware of himself and the time, as he slowly backs away from me. "You better get to class, the bells about to ring," the meaning of his quiet words wash over me, helping me to regain my senses.

Pacing a few steps towards the classroom, I reach the doorway then turn my head to watch Collin's retreat.

The second our gazes meet he yells, "I'll meet you at your locker at the end of the day, Kenzie." He's still retreating backwards, his eyes smoldering in my direction.

I immediately curse out Isabelle in my head, already missing my full name on his lips. "Call me McKenzie," I shout back, seconds before the bell sounds.

"Ms. Carslyle," an irate voice calls from inside the classroom.

Sighing deeply, I face the room, my eyes sweeping over the full desks until they land on the last empty one. I stride across the room to the far side, near the bay of windows, and plop down into the seat, right in front of Isabelle.

I sense movement behind me as she sways forward, closing in on my back, her breathing audible with her nearness. "So glad you could join us, McKenzie," she whispers in a mocking tone.

Keeping my eyes facing forward, I force my body not to react to her jibe, but groan internally.

Of course, the entire class heard that.

Chapter 14

The beeping of my alarm cuts into my consciousness far too early the next morning. I didn't give myself much time to get ready following the sound, wanting to milk as much sleep as possible before beginning my day. With that knowledge in mind, I force myself to shove the covers down and leave the comfort of my bed.

I quickly throw my hair into a tight pony and dress in my sports bra, a pair of work out leggings, and my tennis shoes. Throwing a long, ancient tee over my head, I scoop up an outfit for after practice and shovel it into my backpack along with the rest of my school supplies.

In under ten minutes, I'm outside the trailer locking the door. My timing is almost perfect, as I spot Collin bumping along the uneven road leading through the park, heading in my direction. He pulls onto the grassy patch in front of my trailer, which is starting to acquire permanent tire marks, from the number of times he's picked me up recently.

I rush the car, eliminating his chance to get out, not wanting to waste time standing in my yard and risk being late for practice.

At first, I wasn't sure I wanted to join the cheerleading squad, but after Isabelle's attitude yesterday, I'm confident I do. Partly out of spite, but also to prove to myself that I can have a life and make it on the team.

If I make the cut, I'll have to figure out the time and money thing later.

I open the door to Collin's SUV and move to reach for the handle to clamber inside, but stop short when I notice the passenger seat. My heart melts a little more for Collin, as I spot the goodies he brought. Two protein bars, a giant bottle of water, and a reusable thermos are nestled against the back of the seat, waiting for me.

Raising my eyes, I meet his emerald gaze. "Is all of this for me?" I ask.

A shy smile blooms and he nods. "Of course, can't have my girl dragging at practice. Anything I can do to help you make the team, I'll do it," he replies.

My girl. Again.

He gathers the food and beverages onto his lap, and I swing inside, firmly shutting the door behind me. I lean across the seat and watch his lids grow more hooded with every inch I move closer.

Hovering above his mouth I say, "I'm not going to kiss you, yet." Then slide my face to the side to gently kiss his cheek, stealing a move from the Collin Franzen playbook. My breath fans over his face and ear as I whisper, "But thanks for being my guy and looking out for me."

I hear his swallow, the noise thundering in our close proximity. I'm unable to contain my smirk, leaning back and settling against my seat, keeping my eyes locked on his heated green gaze as I latch my seatbelt into place. He maintains eye contact as he hands me the treats he brought for me.

Without seeming to realize, he slowly sways forward. My smirk grows larger as his eyes flit to my mouth. I run my tongue over my lips and watch him trace the movement with his eyes, seemingly unable to look away. I think I have him, I'm sending the same vibes I did the other night.

Kiss me.

But Collin is stronger willed than I gave him credit for. He clears his throat a couple of times then drags his eyes away from me to stare out the front windshield. He fiddles with the center console for a few seconds until I feel cool air blasting through the vents.

I stifle a laugh as I watch him redirect the closest one, to douse him in cool air, before reversing onto the dirt road.

I'm disappointed he didn't kiss me, but also thrilled with the power I hold when he's fixated on me, like he was just a few minutes ago.

Sorting through the items in my lap, I inspect the thermos, bringing it to my lips after a quick sniff of the contents. I take a sip of the coffee, emitting a small moan as the rich flavor crosses my tongue.

My Folgers has nothing on the coffee brewed by Collin Franzen.

He laughs and I realize I spoke the words aloud.

"They're coffee beans specially imported from Morocco. They're kind of expensive, but my dad has always said quality is better than quantity."

"Wise man," I mumble before taking another long swig from the thermos, containing what I would consider a delicacy. By the time this is all over, Collin will have me spoiled by all his rich gifts.

The rest of the drive passes quickly in companionable silence as I chomp through my protein bar and sip on my coffee, courtesy of my guy. My eyes remain focused out the windshield, watching as Collin pulls into the front row of the parking lot, into the same spot as yesterday.

We both get out and link hands at the hood of the car, our fingers fitting together like they were made for this. Like we've been holding hands for our entire existence.

My thoughts stray into the realm of fantasy, the one where I didn't get closer to Collin to rob his house.

We stroll to the front of the school happily ensconced in each other.

He opens the door for me, ushering me to enter before him. Together we amble towards the gym stopping a few feet short from the entrance. Collin twirls me around, wrapping his arms low around my waist and squeezing me tightly against his firm body.

"Good luck in there," he murmurs against my hair. "You're going to crush it."

Stepping backward, I lock gazes with him. "You too, kick some butt on the football field," I say with a grin.

Collin chuckles and reluctantly drops his arms to his

sides. "Oh," he tacks on like an afterthought. "My parents were asking about you… they wanted to know if you could come over for dinner in two days."

"They want me to come over?" I ask, hesitantly.

I'm nervous about spending time with Collin's parents, even though learning the layout of the Franzen house is supposed to be my ultimate goal. The whole reason behind spending time with Collin in the first place.

"Yeah," he says with a shrug. "They want to get to know the girl I've been spending so much of my time with lately," he states simply.

I guess that makes sense, for someone with parent's that actually care what their kids are up to.

"Okay, I'm free Thursday," I agree slowly.

Collin laughs, "Don't sound so reluctant. They're really cool, you'll have fun. I promise. My parents are chill and great cooks."

I chuckle, surprised by his ability to read me so well after such a short time, but I don't know why. He's consistently shown he pays attention, even when I don't realize it. He knows me already, despite the short length of our friendship.

My lips fall into an easy smile. "I've never done this whole 'meet the parents' thing… but I'm excited to do it with you," I admit.

The words are truthful, but I try not to linger on them. The more time I spend with Collin, the less and less I'm convinced my agreement with Derek is the answer to my problems. I don't have time to dwell on that now though, I need to keep my head in the game to learn the cheer for tryouts. The last few minutes before dancing and cheering is not the time for solving all my money problems.

Collin steps forward again, leaning down to brush his lips against my cheek. He hovers close by and I angle my face so our lips are mere inches apart. Heat pings between us and I slowly drift towards him.

Summer's peppy voice interrupts our daze, "Girl, we're about to get started. You better get in here and stretch." My head pops up and I connect gazes with Summer at her post near the gym entrance. She offers me a small smile before stepping back through the doorway, parting with, "Hurry up, Kenzie!"

Blushing, I shoot a remorseful grin to Collin and back away, keeping my eyes locked on his for just a little longer. Once a few feet of distance separate us, I give a quick wave, then hustle into the gym.

"Hey girl," Katie says as I walk past her. She offers a wave of her left hand while she stretches her right arm across her body, warming up to join the practice routines.

I smile and wave back, promptly joining the other potentials on the mats along the far wall. Mimicking their motions, I begin stretching my arms and legs, limbering up for the jumps and cheers I know we'll be performing.

I'm a little rusty. It's been years since I've been on a team, but I will admit to practicing my tumbling in the dry grass and packed dirt behind my trailer, on occasion. Hopefully it's been enough to help me stay in beat with the routines and make the team. Or at the very least, keep me from embarrassing myself.

I finish up my arm stretches and plop onto the mat for legs. Eyeing the other candidates as I move, I wonder if I'm even close to being on par with their skills. Watching someone stretch isn't an indication of someone's ability to cheer though, so my intel gathering mission is a bust.

Guess I'll find out soon.

Summer and Isabelle stroll to the front of the room and clap their hands together once, in sync.

Isabelle eyes the group speculatively and addresses us first, "We are the captains of this squad and will be teaching the basic routines for tryouts. We will also be part of the group that scores you to determine whether or not you make the squad on Friday. Consider this practice an audition because first impressions matter."

She looks at me pointedly during the last part of her statement and I stifle my scoff. I don't know what her deal is or how I made a bad first impression, but I'm determined not to allow her rude attitude to bother me. My talent, if I still have any, can speak for itself.

Summer chimes in from her side, "But most importantly, let's have fun!"

Isabelle rolls her eyes and continues, "Alright, first we're going to line up into three rows and learn two, short basic cheers. Words and moves." She walks into the cluster at the back and points to different spots on the mat, directing girls where she wants them.

I end up in the first of the offset rows, front and center. I try not to let nerves take over, knowing that literally every person in the room can see me if I mess up.

Gathering all my confidence to the front of my mind, I block out everyone else and focus on memorizing Summer's movements as she slowly steps through the first cheer. Then the second.

We repeat the moves ten times before she claps her hands excitedly. "That was *fantastic*! Great job everyone. Now, we're going to separate into stunt groups. We won't actually be doing stunts, just a mockup, and then we'll transition into a little light tumbling."

If Isabelle is bitchy and sarcastic, Summer is pure sunshine and happiness. It makes me wonder about the dynamics between the two as co-captains.

Are they able to get along or do they butt heads over everything?

Isabelle doesn't strike me as a generally agreeable person.

I don't have much time to continue pondering the thought before Isabelle takes the reins again. She shouts out names to form six groups with four girls in each.

I end up with two well-muscled girls that look like freshmen, and one tiny, skinny girl. It's clear from our builds I would be expected to spot due to my height, which is fine with me.

We run through several mock stunts in our groups.

Once the captains determine we are competent in faux stunting, they call out group numbers and have us practice tumbling across the mats in a diagonal, one at a time. Most of the moves they have us do are pretty basic: cartwheels, round offs, and back tucks.

Isabelle and Summer remove the girls unable to do the basic moves, asking them to sit off to the side. The group is thinned by about half.

Next, they have us work through more advanced tumbling moves: aerials, standing tucks, and back handsprings.

By the time we get through the last trick, it's only myself and four other girls on the mat, including two from my stunt group.

I receive a glare from Isabelle as I giddily return high-fives from the girls still with me. We're each other's competition, most likely, since we could complete the advanced tumbling, but until Friday, we're all on the outskirts of the team, and therefore allies.

"All right, that's it for today," Isabelle says before stalking out the exit.

"Everyone did awesome!" Summer screams excitedly. "Official tryouts will be held in three days. Practice the routines we gave you and run through your part in the stunts. We are so excited to see all of you then." She claps her hands together once to punctuate her statement and all the girls begin to gather their things, preparing to disperse.

I stride off to the corner, collecting my things and sliding on my backpack, then I face the locker room, intending to take a quick shower. Katie intercepts me when I'm halfway across the room, practically to freedom.

"Hey girl, you looked so good out there. I could barely even tell you took any time off from cheerleading, you're a total natural. I think you'll fit in so well with the rest of us, I mean you already do, but I mean like on the squad--"

I half-listen to her words, preoccupied by the memory of the conversation with Collin, now that I don't have practice to distract me. Katie's words trail off and I realize she's frowning at me.

"Is everything okay?" I ask, worried she realized I stopped paying attention part way through her stream of chatter. I thought I was doing a good job of keeping up with my non-verbal encouragement, but maybe not.

"Is everything okay with you?" She counters, "You seem a little out of it."

"Yeah," I answer, initially planning to leave it at that or maybe blame it on post-cheer exhaustion. Then I sigh and decide to spill it all, "Collin invited me over for dinner with his parents and I'm just super nervous. I don't have anything to wear and I lack the funds to buy something new. I've never done this whole meet the parent's thing either."

Katie squeals, jumping up and down, clapping her hands. Her red hair, tied in a sleek ponytail, flounces with each movement, mimicking her excitement. "Oh. Em. Gee," she finally gasps out. "A meet the parents at the Franzens? Collin doesn't date, like not really. I don't think he's ever brought someone over to meet his parents. This is so exciting. He must really like you." She links her arm through mine and drags me towards the door. "Honestly, I have like THE perfect outfit, we can go to my house and you can try it on. I have a few things you can try on actually. Oh my gosh, I am so excited your body is like perfect for fashion. The only thing that probably won't fit you are my jeans. You're like so tall..."

She keeps up a steady stream of words as she drags me along with her, out of the gym and towards the exit door down the hall. It suddenly registers that she intends to bring me to her house right now, like instead of going to class. I stop in my tracks at the realization.

As much as I'm stressed about what to wear, I can't skip class. I don't want the school attempting to call my mom and realize she's gone. Like out of this town and my life for good, gone. Or even worse, allow missing a class to impact my graduation.

"Hey," I say softly, trying not to offend her when she's being so sweet. "I appreciate your offer to help, but I can't miss class."

Katie halts and drops my arm. She appears to instantly deflate. "Oh, yeah I guess it is the second day and we need the rest of our syllabi." Her tone is disappointed and dejected.

"I know," I tack on, channeling my inner-Summer to sound enthusiastic and upbeat. "Why don't we go after school...? Maybe we can stop and grab coffee first, like make a whole afternoon out of it," I suggest.

Katie turns to face me with a serious expression that seems out of character for her. I steel myself to be shut down, but I'm surprised by the words she utters next.

"I think we are going to be great friends Kenzie Carslyle." She eyes me for a second before allowing a beaming smile to bloom across her face, then flounces away. "Meet me by the pink bug in the parking lot after school," she shouts over her shoulder.

Mystified by all that is Katie, I twirl around and head in the direction of the locker rooms attached to the gym. They're almost empty by the time I arrive and I hustle into one of the showers, not wanting to be late to the second day of classes.

I quickly rinse off, slicking the sweat from my skin but leaving my hair in its ponytail. I don't want to walk around with wet hair all day and the mass of thick strands takes forever to dry. Dressing in the extra outfit from my bag, I even swipe on a few coats of mascara to complete my look.

By the time I leave the bathroom I'm feeling refreshed and confident.

I have a friend, one who's going to help me prepare for dinner with the Franzens, I'm going to try out for the cheerleading squad, and... Collin Franzen is crushing on me, as much as I'm crushing on him.

Life is good. Surprisingly so.

Chapter 15

I swoop by my locker before chemistry, the first class on my schedule today for B-block. Golden Oaks High students have six classes, but they're split into two days: A-block and B-block. Yesterday, we started on A-block, meeting half of our teachers and receiving our first batch of homework. Today, we repeat the process for B-block.

I'm a little disappointed I don't run into Collin on my walk from the gym. Brushing the feeling aside, I chastise myself for being pathetic. It's been less than two hours since I saw him last, so the reaction is a little dramatic.

I make quick work of swapping out my textbook and shove my dirty gym clothes in my locker so I don't have to carry them with me all day. If I make the team, it might be worth it to invest in a duffle bag for the cheer stuff I'll need to carry daily.

Lingering for a few minutes longer, I move a couple notebooks from the bottom shelf to the top, dallying inside my locker even though I've accomplished everything I needed to. I stay, thinking Collin might meet me, so he can accompany me to class like he did yesterday. The first bell rings and I finally admit to myself that I'm not going to see him until lunch.

Sighing, I set off in the direction of my class, not wanting to be late. When I reach the hallway hosting the room for my chemistry class, I see a cluster of students waiting outside a door. My curiosity piques as I join the back of the group, realizing the queue is in front of my first period.

"What's going on?" I ask the dark-haired girl next to me, also waiting to go inside.

"Ms. Rigs is assigning seats alphabetically by last name. We have to wait out here until she calls us in to show us our seat," she replies with a roll of her eyes.

As soon as the words leave her lips, I hear a friendly, feminine voice call, "McKenzie Carslyle."

Well, perfect timing, I guess.

I stride inside the room. A pleasant, maternal-looking woman with chocolate colored hair, intercepts me just inside the doorway. Her navy dress sways around her as her movement stops and she consults a clipboard, then glances back at me, kind eyes connecting with mine. "McKenzie?" she asks.

"Yes, Ma'am," I reply politely.

"Third desk on the left dear," she says with a smile, pointing to an empty table at a row near the windows, behind two others that are already filled.

I amble to the small table with two stools placed behind it. I eye both before choosing the one closest to the window. I briefly watch the door, wondering who will be assigned to sit in the empty stool, innocently waiting next to mine underneath the desk.

I hope it's not a slacker.

Shrugging lightly, I busy myself with my backpack. Sliding it from my back and onto the table, to hunt for my blank notebook and the chemistry book I picked up with my class schedule a couple weeks ago. I'm making a bit of a ruckus, loud enough that I don't notice when the seat next to me fills.

At least not until a smooth, warm voice drawls out, "McKenzie."

The word startles me, causing me to bang a hip against the table, and my pen clatters to the ground. My head pops up from digging in my bag and my eyes immediately connect with a set of vibrant green orbs. The heat in Collin's eyes causes my skin to prickle and my heart begins to pound against my chest in an erratic staccato.

This time I think my eyes aren't the only ones saying, "Kiss me" as we stare at each other a mere twenty inches apart. My feet carry me a couple steps closer to him, of their own volition. My body instinctively knows being near Collin is what I crave, what I need.

Ms. Rigs' voice breaks the trance. "Collin. McKenzie. Is my class interrupting your staring contest?"

A round of laughter punctuates her words and I drag my eyes away from Collin to survey the room. All the desks are now occupied by students.

Everyone is seated with their notebooks and books out, facing the front. I realize the bell must have already rung, at some point between unpacking my bag and locking gazes with Collin.

"I'm sorry. I, uh… got distracted," I mutter lamely, apologizing to Ms. Rigs then plopping into my seat.

Way to make a great first impression, Kenzie.

I shoot a semi-serious glower at Collin and he smirks in return. He coughs into his hand, but I can see his shoulders shaking, indicating he's actually covering a laugh. I whack him against his muscular thigh underneath the table. He doesn't outwardly react besides the growing smirk on his face.

Before my hand makes a full retreat, Collin catches my fingers with his and gives them a light squeeze. I anticipate longer contact, but he quickly releases me, his attention focused on our teacher. I shoot him one more glare, trying to maintain my anger, but failing. After finishing my last, lust-filled glare, I shift my attention to the front.

Ms. Rigs is scanning the rest of the class, her eyes stopping on every face as if she's memorizing each of us. She paces across the front of the room while her gaze moves. After looking at each student, she starts speaking, "Welcome to Chemistry. I know most of you in this class are seniors and this is a momentous point in your life. You'll finish your preparations for college, make decisions that will impact your future career, partake in all of the events that come with being in your last year of high school—including prom--and most importantly graduation. I understand this year is quite the undertaking, but I also want you to know I expect you to work hard in order to succeed in this class. We will have labs one day a week, with our first lab two weeks from now. In the time between now and then, I will introduce you to the many elements that chemistry is comprised of." She pauses, as if a bunch of high schoolers are going to laugh at her pun. Maybe they did in her other classes, but they definitely don't in mine. When no one bursts into spontaneous laughter, she continues, "Alright, let's see what you already know. Show of hands, who has heard of the periodic table?"

I tune out Ms. Rigs, distracted by Collin's hand brushing against the side of my right thigh. He keeps up the movement and my eyes flash to his face. His profile shows he's smirking, but he's focusing straight ahead with his free hand raised to answer whatever question our teacher asked.

Ms. Rigs calls out, "Collin."

He lowers his hand and his warm voice responds with, "One-hundred and eighteen."

My eyes fly to the front of the room, to catch Ms. Rigs' nod. "Very good. Who can name at least five of these elements?"

I listen as another student lists their response and Ms. Rigs continues to quiz us on our knowledge. The noises of the class once again fade as Collin's hand drifts upwards, rounding the side of my thigh to rest across the top.

I startle slightly, but stifle the urge to shift. He spreads his fingers, gently gripping my upper leg, giving a firm squeeze before stilling his hand to leave it resting there.

Under my lashes, I observe Collin, as he transitions

his focus from Ms. Rigs to jot down a few notes. The warmth of his palm seeps through my jeans as I try to scan his notes, more interested in Collin than Chemistry at the present moment.

I tilt a little closer, stifling a laugh when bold letters taking up two rows of the notebook catch my attention. **"Stop being a creep and pay attention, McKenzie Carslyle."**

Collin squeezes my thigh, punctuating the statement.

I scrape my nails lightly against the back of his palm in response, catching his gulp from the corner of my eye. I can't find it in me to care about class right this second, completely captivated by all things Collin Franzen.

While I watch him, I find myself wondering about the fairness of life. How is it that Collin is handsome, athletic, intelligent, wealthy, and blessed with loving parents?

He really has everything and I wonder what it is he sees in me.

Chapter 16

After the last bell of the day finally trills across campus, I meet Katie in the parking lot, next to a hot pink Volkswagen Beetle. She's leaning against the side, pouting her lips and holding her phone up for a selfie.

Giggling, I jog the last couple feet and photo bomb her, making the same expression with my cheek pressed against hers.

"Eeek," she squeals. "That actually came out so cute! Let's do another one."

Together we pose against the car, pouting and flipping our hair until a warm voice calls out, "Work it girls."

I pause, with my tongue still sticking out of my mouth, aimed at the camera. My eyes search for the owner of the voice and I find Collin standing off to the side with Jeremy and another guy with blonde hair and green eyes.

The third guy looks familiar, almost like Collin's

mini-me. He's younger with less defined features and slightly darker blonde hair, but he has the same confident air and the same vibrant green eyes.

"Hey you," I respond, finally sliding my tongue back into my mouth, but staying leaned against the bug with Katie.

"You two have been quite entertaining," Jeremy teases us.

His words cause my cheeks to flush and I wonder how long they stood there creeping before making us aware of their presence.

Collin saves us from further mocking with a change of topic. He interjects, "This is my brother, Luke."

The name triggers my memory. I knew Collin wasn't an only child, I just kind of forgot the details about his sibling. Luke is just young enough that we haven't gone to the same school since Elementary, so he must be a freshman this year. I've met him but haven't seen or thought about him in recent years, or even since I've been spending time with Collin over the past couple weeks. The Franzen Brothers and I didn't exactly run in the same circles until recently, so there's no reason for me to really remember his brother.

"Hey Luke," I reply, giving him a quick wave and introducing myself, just in case. "I'm Kenzie."

"Hey," he calls out, his voice a similar genteel drawl to Collin's but lacking the warmth. I hold his attention for half a second, then his gaze shifts back to his brother. "We need to go, I have to study before soccer practice later," he informs Collin, sounding bored, like the other boys forced him to stand here and gawk at us when he'd rather be anywhere else.

"I'll meet you at the car," Collin says, then he jogs away from his brother without waiting for a response.

His feet carry him to the pink bug and he hesitates briefly before slinging an arm around my waist and joining Katie and I, as we lean against the car. I lilt my head, my eyes raking over his handsome face and I'm struck with the urge to plant a kiss on him, right here, even with our audience. He hovers an inch closer, causing the urge to become more persistent.

I almost miss when he asks, "Do you need a ride home, McKenzie?"

Snaking an arm behind his back, I give him a one-armed squeeze as I decline with a shake of my head. "Thanks for looking out for me, but I'm headed to Katie's to hang out for a bit."

Katie interrupts our moment and chimes in, "I can give her a ride, no big deal… unless you can't stand to be apart from her for that long." Her tone is teasing, but still causes a light layer of pink to crest Collin's cheeks.

I've always found Collin Franzen attractive, but blushing Collin Franzen is adorable.

He finally releases me and glances at Katie, then back to me. "I guess I can spare her for a little while. You two have fun." He winks at me, then steps fully away from us.

I watch as he breaks into a jog across the parking lot towards his SUV and awaiting brother. I'm momentarily lost in thought, wondering why Luke didn't ride home with us yesterday, but Katie's long sigh quickly engages my attention.

"You're lucky Kenzie," she says when my eyes land on her face. "He's one of the good ones and so fricken' hot!"

Laughing at her statement, I round the car to plop into the passenger seat. Once we're both buckled, she turns the volume of the stereo all the way up, rolls both of our windows down, then zips out of the parking lot towards the Golden Oaks neighborhood a few miles away.

The first beats of a pop song come blaring through the speakers as she whips into the driveway of an enormous, pale gray home. The same one we stopped at the other day, to pick up some of the group for tubing.

It's a block and a half away from the Franzen house, in the same lushly manicured neighborhood, but the style of the home is completely different. Where Collin's house is warm and inviting, despite its size; Katie's is intimidating and cold. The gray a lackluster color against the greenery outside.

"We have to stay for the rest of the song," Katie demands, interrupting my observations.

She bursts into some crazy dance moves, wiggling her arms around the front seat spastically, while shouting the words like she's in a competition with the car's speakers.

With a laugh I join in, crooning along with the chorus which has already become embedded in my brain and we're only two-thirds of the way through the song. When it finally concludes, we both giggle, spilling out onto the plush, grassy lawn and make our way up the paved sidewalk.

I stand to the side while Katie types into the keypad and opens the front door. The inside of her house is almost the exact opposite of the Franzen's, all sleek modern lines, in gray, white, and black.

The entryway is tiled with a dark gray stone, contrasted with stark white walls. The staircase sits inside to the right, boxy with a black, metal rail. To the left, I can see an expansive living room filled with a low, white couch and a large black console table.

Katie kicks off her shoes, pushing them to the side of the door, then drops her bag on top of them. "Come on, let's go search through my closet," she yells, then begins to rush up the stairs. I take a second to eye them, they look like they're made of cement, each step hovering a few inches above the next without a back in between.

Dragging my eyes away, I take off my shoes in the entry, then after briefly waffling, lightly place my backpack on top.

There's nothing valuable in there, but it just feels like I'm leaving a mess in the cold, pristine foyer and I don't want to upset Katie's parents. I pause for a second, but no one comes to scream at us to clean up our stuff. Shrugging, I hustle up the steps to seek out Katie's room.

It's easy to determine where she's at, I just follow the sound of her squealing. Entering her room, I stop in my tracks. Eyes wide, I survey the absolute and utter chaos unfolding before me.

Katie has a massive bedroom, about twice the size of my entire trailer. Unlike the rest of the house, it seems to have a personality much like hers. Against the far wall sits a beautiful sleigh bed with a vibrant purple and white floral comforter. Her curtains are lilac and a large, pale pink sofa sits nearby. My eyes stop on the last piece of furniture in the room, a cluttered white vanity, filled with opened jars and tubes of make-up. It looks like it's never been cleaned, a splattering of eye shadow sitting across the wooden top, fully dispelling the idea her parents are going to shout at us for being messy.

She has the door open to another room, which is also huge, but appears to be a closet. She's throwing things through the doorway, onto the floor in her bedroom.

"Yes, this one!" She exclaims, prior to another garment flying through the door and landing on the heap growing by the second.

Within minutes, she emerges, hangers folded over her arm, as she steps around the mountain of clothes thrown from her closet. It's impressive she owns so much clothing, but glancing past her, I see the room is still brimming full of items. The ones she's chosen barely making a dent in the horde.

Inhaling a loud, deep breath, she mutters, "Okay." Barely managing to fit all the clothes from her arm onto her bed. "How about we begin here and see if we find anything?" She examines the assortment of options determinedly, with her hands on her hips.

I survey the massive pile of mish mashed clothing, then turn my surprised eyes back to her. "You're worried we won't be able to find something for me to wear in all of this," I reply, flabbergasted.

Katie giggles, covering her mouth with her hand, after scanning the lot. "Okay, we'll definitely find something. Honestly, I hardly wear any of this stuff, so anything that fits well is yours to keep." She claps her hands together. "Oh, I'm so excited. Fashion show, fashion show," she chants pumping her fist into the air.

Her vibrant enthusiasm has me laughing and I move closer to the bed, intent on starting with the items placed there.

Before I reach them, I'm interrupted by a pinging noise, indicating my phone received a new text. Eagerly, I pull the clunky cell from my pocket, wondering if it's Collin already.

But it isn't his name showing on my screen.

I read over the message, absorbing the words with an angst-filled sigh. Mr. Mouchard is cutting my shift for Friday.

The fifteenth is quickly approaching and I've only worked three shifts—with one more coming up Saturday, if it doesn't get the axe next--since I last paid the other half of my lot rent.

I've made just enough to cover what I owe to the trailer park, leaving about $10 to add to my savings. At this rate I'll never save enough money to move away from this town, or even join the cheer squad, if I were to be selected.

My shoulders slump under the weight of my disappointment.

It's not that I'm upset about losing a shift, they can

be pretty disgusting, re: cleaning vile body fluids and used condoms, but I could really use the money. At this point, my tin of savings will run out within two months from groceries, lack of shifts, and expenses from school.

Part of me wishes things with Collin were real, but they can't be. Mr. Mouchard's text just serves as a reminder that I lack options and need funds, urgently. If there were another way I would do it... there just doesn't seem to be one.

"What's wrong Kenzie?"

I glance up from my ancient, bulky cell and see Katie wearing a concerned frown. She is still, and quiet while she waits for my response, which isn't normal behavior for her. In the short time I've spent with her, she's always been spastic, constantly speaking and moving.

Trying to be casual, I reply "It's nothing."

It's everything.

Her frown deepens and she appears almost... angry. "Look, I know we're still getting to know each other, but you don't have to lie. I swear I'll take your secrets to the grave and I promise I won't judge. Sometimes talking about things makes it easier to problem solve," she says in a serious, un-Katie-like tone.

Wavering, I try to sort through my thoughts to determine what is safe to disclose without outing myself and the deal with Derek. I finally settle on a half-truth, to get her off my back for now. "I'm really broke," I begin. "And my boss at the motel just cut one of the few shifts I had on the schedule. I don't know if I'm going to be able to join the cheer team…. Even if I made it, I can't afford it."

"Oh, that's it?" Katie asks.

I'm not sure whether I should be insulted or not, that a problem like not having any money received such a flippant response from her.

"Yes…" I finally reply, unsure how to continue.

Katie waves her hand in the air, as if it will clear away my struggles. "We can just get you a sponsor. I'll even ask my dad if you want. You don't have to be rich to join a team in high school, Kenzie. You just have to be good enough to make it. I'll help you figure out the rest."

I eye her, slightly suspicious. Do people really pay for other people to join things because they're talented? It seems too good to be true, but I decide to put my faith in Katie. If she says her dad can help pay, maybe…

Maybe I won't need the deal with Derek after all.

But if I told Collin the truth, would he ever forgive me?

Katie walks closer to me and bumps her hip into mine. "Tuck your phone and frown away, girlie. It's time for a fashion show."

She plucks a sultry, slinky, red dress off the bed and holds it up with a wicked grin. "Can you imagine what Collin would do, if he saw you in this?"

Chapter 17

Katie drops me off at a random house two blocks away from the trailer park, per my request. It's not that I'm ashamed of where I live or don't trust her, or anything.

Advertising my entire situation is just not something I'm ready to do, yet.

Besides, I already told Katie about my money problems from my dwindling work shifts. I think that's a big enough revelation for one day, without exposing my entire sordid past.

Outside the car on the curb, I wave with my right hand, clutching the overflowing bag of clothes with my left.

I'm silently willing Katie to hurry up and drive away before the people that actually live here come out and shout at me for loitering on their lawn.

That's an embarrassment I don't want to go through today.

My arm becomes sore as I continue waving, mentally yelling, "Hurry up."

Katie remains sitting there, completely oblivious. She turns on the overhead light, checking her appearance in the rear-view mirror. I watch, still waving, as she swipes a finger underneath each eye, then turns the light off. Breathing a sigh of relief, I assume she's going to drive away, but she picks up her phone and begins scrolling instead.

I fight hard to keep the frown off my face. I need Katie to leave, like now. My arm slowly drops, from the wave that does not seem to be giving her the hint.

Is she waiting for me to go inside?

I give one more big, dramatic wave, unsure if she notices me since her face is buried in her phone, then I tentatively begin moving across the sidewalk towards the driveway. I keep my body angled so the car is still in view and take each step slowly, gradually treading up the slightly angled drive.

At an excruciating pace, I lift each foot up then inch it back down towards the paved ground, making minimal progress towards the house with each movement. Walking this way, I traverse half the distance to the house before spotting a pink blur zipping away from the curb.

After she finally leaves, I allow my shoulders to relax and basically sprint back down to the sidewalk. I can't afford to have the cops called on me for trespassing, or loitering, or something.

Once off private property, I begin my trek home, trudging towards the park.

The sun is hanging low in the sky, casting long shadows and I try to stay aware as I return home.

Our small town isn't exactly a hotspot for crime, but Derek and his buddies are no saints either and I feel like I've garnered their attention as of late. Well, I know I have… considering the deal we made recently.

My thoughts wander, as I mentally explore my options for breaking my agreement with Derek. Technically we didn't sign anything or make our obligation binding, but that doesn't really seem like something criminals would do anyways. My biggest concerns are that Derek knows where I live AND he knows I live there alone.

There's no way of knowing how far he'd be willing to go if he felt betrayed.

He could come after me, or even call CPS.

The ramifications of breaking my word could be serious.

By the time I'm halfway down the dirt path to my trailer, the sun has completely set, bathing me in darkness, but I've come to a solution.

Avoidance.

I'm going to avoid Derek until I come up with a better plan.

I really need to tell Collin, but I'm afraid it will make him hate me. Not that I would blame him. It was a shitty thing to do, agreeing to a plan to rob someone. But maybe, maybe if I tell him everything; about my mom, Mr. Mouchard, and the raise in my lot rent… Maybe Collin could find forgiveness and understanding of my actions.

At least I hope so.

Until I figure out a time and place to have a heart-to-heart with my new crush, the easiest solution is to avoid acknowledging the problem and stay as far away from Derek as possible. Feeling more settled, I notice my steps have brought me further into the park and I'm nearing my trailer.

My newfound awareness, channels my vision onto my home and I spot a figure leaning near the door. My pace slows and I take a step off the dirt road, into the shadowy back of a trailer nearby. I squint my eyes trying to figure out who's at my house.

As if he senses my gaze on him, the hazy figure straightens into the light cast by the small bulb hanging off my porch. The light glints off Derek's dark hair as he steps closer to the battered dirt road.

Pushing myself further into the shadows, I hug my bag to my chest and shove my back against the cool tin, embracing that it may be my salvation. Not wanting to risk being seen, I remain frozen in place, my racing heart the only sound audible in the quiet night air.

I wait.

Time passes, although I'm not sure how much. I don't move a muscle, not wanting to compromise my position and alert Derek of my presence.

It's like we're in a contest, trying to prove who will outwait the other.

Although I can't see him, I feel him lingering in the murky darkness separating our forms. I wonder how long he'll stay in hopes of intercepting me before retreating, so I can access my home.

"Derek," a high-pitched voice whines out eventually, interrupting the silence. "Why did you leave to stand in the dark? Come back to the trailer."

"Yeah, yeah. Don't get your panties in a twist, I'm comin'." Derek's voice sounds closer than it should, if he were still lurking by my trailer.

Remaining motionless, I hold my breath and strain my ears, attempting to hear his footsteps back to his trailer. Of course, the distance is too far, and my hearing isn't bat-like, so nothing reaches my ears.

To be safe, I stay in my hiding spot until my muscles begin to ache. Only then do I slowly step forward, away from the trailer. My feet and legs tingle as they wake up from being locked in place for so long.

I peek around the corner tentatively. My shoulders relax when I don't see anyone lingering in the darkness between me and my trailer. As quickly as I can on my dead legs, I run to my door, fumbling with my key in my haste to unlock the door.

Once inside, I leave the lights off, readying myself for sleep in the dark. Just in case.

I don't want to risk revealing I'm home to Derek. He might return to his post by my trailer and see my lights are turned on.

After a few minutes of fumbling around in the dark, I climb into bed.

The high I was feeling earlier in the day—from shopping in Katie's closet and learning it may be possible to join the cheer team, thanks to a sponsor—has completely faded.

Instead, my mind races with thoughts of the future.

I know I can't avoid Derek forever, but I need to buy more time to figure out how to divert his attention to something else. Then, maybe, I can call off our deal, be honest with Collin, and have a normal senior year.

Chapter 18

Tonight, I'm attending dinner at the Franzen's. Just the sentence makes a swarm of butterflies take flight in my belly, the movement threatening to displace my lunch.

I take a few deep, calming breaths and rub my palms across my abdomen before facing off with my closet.

"If you map out their house this time, you'll never have to go back," I mutter. Instead of providing relief from the butterflies, my words transform them into a ball of dread in the pit of my stomach.

I have it bad.

I'm not ready to give up Collin, yet. I might never be.

The deal I made with Derek has become a thick, black cloud hanging over my head. Collin Franzen is… different than I expected him to be.

Not to be one of those girls that puts a guy on a pedestal, but he's completely out of my league.

Except… he doesn't act that way. He's so sweet and considerate and I'm falling hard.

It took half of lunch to convince him I would be fine riding the bus home today, just for some space to think about life, about everything. Also, to make sure Derek didn't intercept us outside while I made my way home.

Even after relenting, Collin made me agree that he could pick me up at five to bring me to his house for dinner, so I didn't have to ride my bike.

Thinking of Collin slightly distracts me from the thought of having to map out his house, but doesn't do much to relieve the tension in my shoulders. My deal with Derek has constantly been on my mind since school started and this dinner isn't helping.

I have dual concerns, either Collin's parents won't like me, or they will immediately see through my façade, identifying me as an imposter before I have the chance to tell Collin the truth. For once, I'm not stressed about money, I'm concerned about ruining the new life I'm slowly starting to build.

Tabling the Derek Deal/Franzen Con problem for later, I focus on the bag of clothes Katie gave me.

I left the entire overflowing mess, sitting on my tiny closet floor. The bag is filled with designer labels and beautiful fabric. Pieces I never imagined owning, that don't fit in with the rest of my wardrobe, but they're mine just the same.

Digging my hands in, I spread out a few, laying them reverently across the bed. After a couple of minutes, I successfully sort through the dozens of items, slowly sifting through the bag, admiring each new piece.

I place them into drawers or onto hangers until only four dresses that seem pretty fancy remain.

There's two that look like they could be worn to a club and I immediately rule them both out.

The other two I ponder a few minutes longer. One is a floor-length black dress with short sleeves. It has a V-neck top that cinches at the waist and flares a bit at the hips. Although I love how it looks on, it almost seems too formal.

Eliminating that option, I hang it in my closet and prepare for dinner. I take my time, curling my long dark strands and swiping mascara on each individual lash. I settle for a clear gloss, then snag the remaining dress off the bed.

I carefully pull the soft, cotton fabric over my head, reveling in the cool, silken feel of it on my heated, nervous skin.

Striding into the bathroom, I strike a pose in the mirror. Snorting a laugh, realizing Katie is already rubbing off on me, I admire my reflection.

The dress I chose is deep red, with a pattern of large, white flowers. It wraps around my body like it was made with me in mind, showing just the right amount of cleavage and ending two inches above my knees. Paired with sandals, it appears classy, yet understated. Like I tried, but not too hard.

It's perfect.

I'm ready sooner than expected and spend my spare time pouting at my reflection, wishing I had an upgraded phone to take a selfie.

A knock sounds on my front door, interrupting my

fun and I scurry out of my bathroom towards the noise. Expecting Collin to be just a few minutes early, I answer without checking out the window hanging above the kitchen sink. Upon opening the door, I'm greeted with Derek's cool, dark gaze.

"Kenzie-girl," he purrs.

My warm smile instantly falls, my lips fading to a straight line. "Derek. I don't have time for your shit right now, Collin is on his way over here to pick me up for dinner at his house."

Derek instantly smirks as he processes my words. "Things are movin' along, that's what I like to hear. What are you doing later?" Following his words, he steps forward to wrap a thick arm around my waist and yank me against him, melding our fronts together.

My body immediately stiffens, and my tone is flat when I reply, "Let me go, Derek."

"Ahh come on… loosen up. I think we could have some fun together. Give me a chance, Kenzie-girl," he replies with a smirk, tightening his grip in a way that's painful. His eyes skim the exposed skin of my chest before returning to my face.

I swat at Derek's side with my trapped hands, then resort to pushing against him in an attempt to free myself, but he doesn't even flinch. This time my voice is louder and I enunciate each word, trying to penetrate his thick skull. "I'm serious Derek. Let. Me. Go."

Next thing I know, Derek's arm is being ripped away and I stumble down my steps behind him. Before I can regain my bearings, I'm shoved behind a tall, warm body.

Collin's unique sunshine scent washes over me and my tense shoulders immediately relax. As the tension leaves my body, I feel Collin's muscles clench, and I lay a palm against his back to reassure him I'm okay.

"Just get out of here, Derek. She said to leave her alone." Collin's voice is a low growl, a sound I've never heard from him before. His tone should be menacing, but it causes a small pit of warmth low in my belly.

He's protecting me, and I like it.

After a few seconds of silence, Derek grounds out, "Whatever, Franzen." Then he strides away, his footsteps crunching across the dead grass as he leaves my trailer.

Collin remains in front of me, his broad build blocking out the scene and Derek's retreat. When he finally turns around, his gaze is laced with concern as he scans me from head to toe. "Are you okay?"

I nod, mutely.

I'm fighting the urge to wrap my arms around Collin, which is not a normal reaction for me. Clearing my throat, I finally croak out, "Yes. You arrived just in time."

I avoid meeting his gaze, embarrassed for the position he caught me in, even though it was Derek that initiated it. I feel his eyes burning into my skin, then he holds out his hand in front of me.

Hesitating, my eyes jump to Collin's face. The concern is no longer visible in his gaze, replaced with affection and a warm smile instead. I place my palm into his and he draws me in. His arms wrap around my body, low around my waist, resting gently against the backs of my hips.

The movement mimics Derek's, but the feelings it invokes is the exact opposite. Instead of feeling uncomfortable and wanting to escape, I feel warm and cared for. Comforted. He tips his head forward, keeping our gazes locked.

His eyes flit to my mouth, then return to my eyes. Chocolate brown and emerald green collide.

"You look beautiful tonight, McKenzie," he drawls quietly.

I smile at him, appreciating the warmth he always seems to offer at the right moment. My gaze roams over his body, taking in his white button up and clean, light-wash jeans. It's almost like we coordinated, with our splashes of white.

"You clean up well yourself, Franzen," I whisper back, the intimate positions of our bodies making it feel like we shouldn't talk loudly.

"Are you ready?" He asks, leaning closer and brushing his lips over mine.

I'm not sure if the movement was intentional or not. The contact is definitely not enough to label as a kiss, yet it's the closest we've ever gotten. Either way, it distracts me from my nerves, and I nod.

My eyes scream kiss me, but my lips say, "Let's do this."

His lips tip up and he drops one arm, leaving the other wrapped around my waist. He tugs me into his side, gently squeezing me, steering us in the direction of his car. We stroll to the passenger side of the SUV connected, not separating until Collin opens the door and I'm climbing inside.

Through the windshield, I watch him jog around the hood and jump in. Unashamedly, I stare at him while he starts the car and reverses from his typical spot on my lawn, the one gaining indents from how much time he spends parked there.

He meets my gaze briefly, our eyes connecting and a happy sparkle glinting back at me. His attention refocuses on the road, but mine remains on him.

The drive passes quickly, and we reach his house prior to my nerves renewing. We exit the car and enter his massive foyer with a surprising calm washing over my body in waves. Something about Collin's presence makes it hard for me to be stressed. Maybe it's his sunshine scent or his kindness. Whatever it is, I'm grateful to be around him tonight.

Inside, we find his parents, and brother standing next to the sweeping staircase, like they're welcoming the pope, instead of little, ole me.

While Collin shuts the door, his mom steps forward, her blonde hair is pulled into a tight, tidy bun at the back of her neck. She's dressed in a pale blue sheath dress with thick straps. Her heels clacking against the beautiful flooring as she approaches.

"Hello, McKenzie. It's good to see you again. I didn't have a chance to introduce myself last time, I'm Irene Franzen," she drawls, her tone polite and refined, with a hint of the warmth her son typically speaks with.

"Hi Mrs. Franzen," I respond shyly. Is everyone rich this formal? As an afterthought I tack on, "Nice to meet you."

She hovers for a minute like she wants to give me a

hug, but isn't sure I'll accept it. Instead, she steps back and gives me a warm smile, the movement an echo of the expression that seems so familiar on Collin's face.

Collin's dad doesn't move but his genteel tone fills the air, "I'm David Franzen." He leaves his introduction short and simple, punctuating the words with a nod.

My eyes take him in, noting the similarities to Collin in both height and broad shoulders. He has darker, blonde hair, and the same striking green gaze. "Nice to meet you as well, Mr. Franzen." Moving my eyes to Luke, who's dressed similarly to Collin in a pale green button-up and jeans, I say, "Hi Luke." Giving him a small wave.

As if channeling his father, he simply nods in return, non-verbally acknowledging my greeting.

We stand around in the foyer, Collin by my side and the rest of his family in a straight line beside the staircase. I resist the urge to shuffle my feet or fidget my hands, despite the slightly odd silence. Should I ask how everyone is doing?

"Why don't we get seated?" Mrs. Franzen suggests, finally ending the awkwardly formal introductions.

She turns on her heel, heading in the direction of the kitchen. Making a hard right into another room, rather than continuing to the place I had waited the last time I was here.

Their dining room is massive, hosting a large, dark-stained table already laden with food. Place settings with two forks, a spoon, a knife and two glasses are set before half the spots and my nerves begin thrumming all over again.

Collin is from money. The kind of money that has a formal dining room, and cares about what fork you use… and I'm from a trailer park.

I shouldn't be here.

Collin keeps me from fleeing by placing a hand low on my back, using it to steer me to the opposite side of the table. He pulls my chair out and settles me, then pushes it in. Thankfully, he chooses the chair beside me.

Across the table sit Luke and Mrs. Franzen, with Mr. Franzen at the head of the table, to my left.

Food is quickly dispersed, dishes passed in a clock-wise rotation, allowing us to serve ourselves. We load our plates with each dish. I try not to be greedy in my servings, but everything looks homemade and delicious.

It's been a long time since I've had someone else to cook for me and I'm not very experienced in the kitchen. Tonight, I'm eating better than I have in at least the last year, maybe my entire life.

With a full plate in front of him, Mr. Franzen raises his fancy looking goblet into the air. Afraid to commit some sort of faux pas, I observe Luke across the table, copying his every move.

I mimic the motion of raising the goblet before me, clinking my glass in the middle against everyone else's, pretending like, I too, am the kind of person that cheers when I have guests over.

After he puts down his glass, I watch Mr. Franzen as he takes a bite of his meal. Surveying the table, I see everyone focused on their plates and I finally begin to eat.

Silence lingers, like no one is quite sure how to

bridge the gap with the strange girl Collin brought for dinner. Half of me regrets accepting the invitation, the other half wants to ask to take leftovers home, especially after a succulent piece of chicken touches the tip of my tongue.

"Collin tells us you're good at math…," Mrs. Franzen finally begins, trailing off her sentence for me to pick up the string of conversation.

"Yes, it's one of my favorite subjects," I reply with a smile, then return to my plate. I trail my fork through the potatoes and gravy piled high in one corner, wanting to continue eating, but not wanting my mouth to be full if another statement is directed my way.

I glimpse Mrs. Franzen's nod from the corner of my eye. I'm no longer looking directly at her, but she continues her thoughts anyways. "Well, Luke is in need of a tutor. Math isn't one of the strong Franzen genes," she says, her laughter tinkling lightly after, sounding like a soft chorus of bells.

"Oh," I respond, trying to be polite, but not sure how one continues that statement.

Do I say, sorry your family is genetically blessed, but sucks at math?

That seems inappropriate.

"Would it be something you're interested in, Dear?"

"I…" I open my mouth to respond, then hesitate.

Is tutoring something I would be interested in? Finding a new job could mean no more Mr. Mouchard or nasty motel rooms, but what about my deal with Derek? Once Collin finds out, he could tell his parents, then his parents would ditch me faster than I can blink.

I allow myself a few seconds to organize the thoughts fighting for my attention before formulating a response.

I reply firmly, "I'll think about it. I've been working at the Breezy Motel for a couple years... I would feel awful leaving them hanging if I quit without any notice."

"Okay, Dear. Well, try to get back to me soon," she says lightly.

I nod my head and we all turn back to our plates, thankfully Collin saves me from more stinted conversations by engaging his brother. "Who else made the soccer team, Luke?"

Chapter 19

Collin drives me back to my trailer in an easy silence. The tires of his SUV eat the distance between our homes quickly.

By the time he pulls onto the dirt road of the park, I'm wishing the distance was further so the drive could last longer. I'm not ready for the night to end, to leave Collin, and return to my trailer alone.

The vehicle slows beneath me, leading me to believe the same thoughts are running through Collin's mind. He stops a ways from my trailer, just off the side of the bumpy dirt road, placing his vehicle in park and twisting to face me.

He props himself against the console to get closer, his face nearing mine before he drawls, "I think you should do it."

His closeness had me gravitating in his direction, but his words have me reeling back in surprise. I was expecting a kiss, not a cryptic statement.

"You think I should do what?" I ask, confused.

"I think you should tutor my brother," he replies, a warm grin turning up the corners of his lips.

"Oh, do you now?" I ask, wanting to hear his reasoning.

"Well, yeah. How much do you make at the Motel? Minimum wage? My parents will easily pay double that, maybe more if you negotiate," he explains, slowly. After a beat, like he's mulling over his words, he continues, "Plus we could spend more time together, if you were at my house every day helping my brother."

"But I've never tutored anyone," I protest, feebly.

Meanwhile, my brain processes the idea of being paid double my current wage to sit in the Franzen house and teach math. I could work half as many hours and still earn as much as I do at the motel. I'd lose my tips, but those are barely a pittance anyways.

First the conversation with Katie, then the offer from Mrs. Franzen, It's like the universe is screaming at me to stay a good person and earn my money honestly.

"McKenzie, you're great at math. I was in your class last year, remember? I think you can do anything you put your mind to... at least think about it, okay?"

His words fill me with warmth and I allow myself a few seconds to bask in his praise—in the brief glimpse of what Collin sees in me. I open my mouth to respond but am interrupted by a surprisingly angry explosion of words from the man next to me.

"Is that Derek, again?" he asks, his words a vicious snarl.

I follow his gaze through the car window, to my trailer just visible down the road.

Derek's dark hair is noticeable, once again glinting in the light as he waits next to my trailer under the small porch lamp, leaning against the aged tin side. I'm guessing he wants to ask how things are going, especially now that he knows I've spent time inside the Franzen house.

I can't tell Collin that though, not yet.

Instead, I hedge around the truth. "He's been coming around a lot more, since my mom's been… out of town. He's pretty harmless," I explain.

Placing one of my hands against Collin's arm, I rub up and down hoping to soothe away some of the irritation Derek brought forth.

"It didn't seem harmless earlier," Collin argues, although with a little less vitriol than before.

He captures my hand with one of his, bringing it to his mouth to lay a soft kiss against my palm, then places it against his muscled thigh. Like always, his soft acts of affection steal my breath away.

"I don't feel comfortable with you staying here alone. Especially with that guy hanging around all the time," he says, his voice almost back to his normal, warm drawl.

"I'll be okay," I respond.

I wish I could avoid Derek's more persistent advances and presence. Unfortunately, living within a half a mile of each other makes encountering him unavoidable.

"How long is your mom gone for?" Collin asks, softly.

"Err, a couple of weeks," I blatantly lie, keeping my

gaze fixed out the windshield. I'm hoping Collin can't read my shuttered face, since he's become so adept at interpreting my expressions recently.

"I want you to come stay at my house," he states abruptly, shocking me into a stunned silence.

Without a moment's pause to allow me the time to formulate a response, Collin changes gear on the SUV and conducts a three-point turn. He's driving at a much faster speed out of my neighborhood than he drove into it, his tires spitting up small rocks embedded in the dirt with quiet pings echoing as they ricochet off his tire wells. If it wasn't dark out, I'm sure we would see a plume of dust billowing up as Collin high tails it from the trailer park back towards Golden Oaks.

"Won't your parents mind?" I ask, feeling shy and awkward at the thought of sharing a room with Collin Franzen.

"We have a few spare rooms. My mom will agree with me—it's not safe for you to be in the trailer park by yourself. We have the space, so you should stay at our place."

His words ease some of my apprehension... I'd have my own room.

Maybe a few days away from the trailer park will be enough to get Derek off my case... and provide enough time for me to work up the nerve for a confession.

"Okay," I agree hesitantly.

Collin nods and captures my hand again, squeezing it tightly. He speeds away from the trailer park like the devil is on our tail, and maybe he is. It feels like only seconds pass until we're pulling into the Golden Oaks neighborhood. Shortly after, we're parked in the Franzen driveway.

Collin shuts off the ignition and faces me. "I'll explain everything to my mom, okay?"

Like I want to explain to Mrs. Franzen that her son has taken pity on me because I live in a trailer park by myself and my neighbor is harassing me to rob her house.

I silence all the thoughts in my mind and simply respond, "Alright, thank you."

Collin tugs me into his side, syncing our footsteps as we stroll to the front door. He types the digits into the keypad, and I purposefully avoid looking, wanting to circumvent any temptation that may come with the knowledge of how to gain access to his house. We step over the threshold together.

"Collin is that you?" Mrs. Franzen asks the second our shoes hit the entry floor, her soft voice sounding like it's coming from the direction of the kitchen.

"And McKenzie," he replies, not skirting the topic at all.

I hear his mom's heels tapping against the floor, warning us of her approach. She's still dressed in the same outfit she was for dinner, with the addition of a pair of yellow dishwashing gloves.

"Is everything alright?" She asks, her brow furrowing with the question, concern marring her pretty features.

"Not really," Collin replies. "McKenzie's mom has been out of town and one of her neighbors keeps coming by to harass her. He was there when I went to pick her up earlier, then waiting outside her house when I went to drop her off," His drawl sounds irritated, but nowhere near as vicious as it did either of the times, we encountered Derek today.

"Oh Dear," Mrs. Franzen replies, her gaze raking over the two of us as she removes the yellow dish washing gloves.

She steps forward and wraps her arms around my shoulders. Her embrace is unexpectedly kind and motherly and warm, defying the cold and polite image I built of her in my mind. Part of me wonders if Collin learned to hug from his mom. Maybe it's a family trait.

My arms return the embrace, clasped around the middle of her back, overlapping each other over her slender form. I relax into the hug, allowing myself to imagine, just for a second, that this is my mom hugging me, comforting me because life can be hard... being a real mom.

Mrs. Franzen continues speaking, "That's atrocious. You must have been so scared. Why don't you stay here? At least for a few days." She doesn't drop her arms until I nod against her shoulder. In her heels we're about the same height, our faces almost even with each other.

She steps back but keeps her hands resting on the tops of my shoulders, her pale gaze meeting mine. Whatever she sees in my eyes, visibly drains the tension from her body. I watch as her shoulders relax and her brow softens.

She drops her hands and switches her attention to Collin. "Can you show her to the blue guest room?" She scans my body, still clad in my wrap dress. "Also, give her something to sleep in for tonight, whatever you have that she can borrow. We can go to her house tomorrow, or just pick up a few things. Whichever is easiest."

The matter settled—I'm staying with the Franzen's for the foreseeable future—Mrs. Franzen pivots on her heel and returns down the hall in the direction she came.

"I'll show you to your room, madame," Collin drawls.

When I turn, he's dipped in a low, dramatic bow like he's a butler from the eighteen-hundreds, his arm wrapped around his middle, knees bent, and face turned downwards.

His antics cause me to giggle and he lifts his face to meet my eyes at the sound. His gaze is intense despite his upturned lips. He straightens and stalks forward.

Not wanting to get caught making googly eyes at each other in the hall, I bolt up the sweeping staircase, evading his grasp, and admiring their luxurious house as it flies by me. At the top landing, I stop to catch my breath and wait for Collin to show me to my temporary accommodations.

He's significantly less out of breath than I, when he reaches me a second or two later. He snags my hand and continues walking to the left down a split hallway, pulling me behind him until we reach the last door down the long corridor.

Collin pushes it open and I follow him in, my hand still clasped within his. Inside the room he whips the door closed, then backs me towards it.

I don't even have a chance to examine my surroundings before his bulky form looms in front of me, filling my entire view.

The look in his eyes is fierce, possessive, and it takes my breath away.

I inch backwards, retreating until my spine hits the solid wood behind me. Collin continues his advances until his chest presses against mine forcing me back even further. He tilts his head down, keeping his emerald eyes connected to mine.

My heart pounds in my chest and my eyes scream "kiss me."

For once, Collin listens.

His mouth descends on mine, claiming my lips. I gasp at the unexpected contact and he takes advantage of my open mouth, sweeping his tongue inside. Collins's hands slide down my body, gripping the underside of my butt and yanking me even closer as his lips continue their assault.

Using every tool at his disposal—lips, teeth, tongue—he delivers a first kiss beyond compare.

Every inch of our exposed skin is connected and his mouth devours mine. I release a lusty moan, but he consumes that too, his lips never leaving mine. I feel his hard length prodding my belly and wriggle in his hold wanting—no needing—to get impossibly closer. My skin feels on fire and my heart pounds a rapid staccato.

He nips at my lips one more time, then his mouth retreats without warning or reason. My eyes pop open as I pant, trying to replenish the air he's stolen with his kisses.

"McKenzie Carslyle, you are Trouble," he rasps his lips hovering above mine.

You have no idea.

Instead of replying, I close the gap between us, sealing my lips to his.

Chapter 20

"Wake up!" an excited, high-pitched voice screams too-loudly next to my ear.

My eyes fly open and I snatch the pillow from under my head, preparing to ward off someone, in case I'm being attacked. A happy guffaw reaches my ears and my sleep-bogged brain finally registers Katie's red ponytail and pale blue eyes hovering above me.

"Were you going to attack me with your pillow?" She asks between snorts of laughter.

"I thought I was under assault after someone screamed in my ear at an ungodly hour," I grumble back moodily.

Personally, I'm not a morning person, but more than that I prefer to wake up in a relatively calm silence, sans ear screaming.

She laughs again at my attitude, hopping off the bed with way too much energy so early in the morning.

Katie's out-of-control pep before sunrise doesn't honestly surprise me, it's just who she is.

"I brought over some clothes for you! Collin texted me last night and told me you were staying here while your mom was out of town. I didn't want you to be late for tryouts, so I brought you a workout set to wear, and a couple outfits for school, in case you don't end up returning home for a few days. I don't know what your plan is. Also, I'm a little bummed you didn't tell me you needed a place to stay, I totally—"

I raise my hands in the air to cut her words short. My head is already pounding with the barrage of information immediately after gaining consciousness.

"I just need a minute… to process all that."

Katie mimes locking her lips and throwing away the key, then busies herself arranging the clothes she brought on the desk across from the bed.

Swinging my feet over the edge, I stretch my arms above my head and swivel my neck back and forth. My eyes scan the pale blue walls and I'm relieved yesterday wasn't a dream. Mrs. Franzen said I should stay here and… Collin kissed me.

And boy, are Collin Franzen's kisses worth waiting for.

My thoughts are interrupted by more chatter from Katie, who is apparently no longer able to handle silence after thirty-seven seconds.

"So, I don't want to ruin your peaceful morning routine, like at all, but also we need to get going soon. Like in the next ten minutes soon."

She shoves a stack of clothing into my lap and I

slowly clasp my arms around them, still bogged down by the last vestiges of sleep and thoughts of Collin. I stand from the bed reluctantly, but Katie isn't having any of my sloth-like movements. She pushes against my shoulder, corralling me out the door and I pick up the pace, hustling towards the bathroom just to stop being jostled.

After the door shuts, I quickly brush my teeth, tie my hair into a sloppy pony, and then douse my face in cool water, eliminating the last traces of grogginess. Feeling more awake, I step out of the giant t-shirt and boxers that Collin gave me and unfold the items Katie handed to me.

Once everything is laid out on the countertop, I groan.

The only normal thing she brought for me was a regular sports bra. The rest of the pile consists of a Victoria's Secret "sports thong", according to the label on the back, a pair of spandex bike shorts, and a cropped tank top.

I'm still eyeing the pile when a bang on the door causes me to jump. Katie shouts, "Come on Kenzie!" Then bangs again before leaving a few beats of silence.

I grumble but move to get dressed under her added pressure. I don the slightly revealing workout clothes, then gather up my discards from the floor and exit. Katie is waiting in the hall holding a backpack, a messenger bag, and a duffle.

She glances up from her phone when my first sneaker-clad foot hits the carpet. She whistles, then catcalls, "Oooooh, girl. Those shorts make your legs look straight fire. Whoa nelly!"

I laugh at her antics, then dramatically strut past her, acting like I'm on a catwalk as I traverse the hall to deposit my pile of used clothes in the corner of my temporary room. I glance around wondering what to put my school outfit in, then realize I don't even have a backpack.

I literally have nothing with me.

"Already got you covered," Katie says from the hall. When I turn, she holds up the backpack, her arm extended outwards for me to grab it. "Spare pack. School clothes are in here, and a few pencils and note-books. Oh, and your little purse with your ancient celly. Now let's go, Collin's waiting downstairs."

Collin.

Little butterflies compete in my belly. An entire swarm committing tricks and flips, fighting for my attention as I hustle down the hall. Katie skips down the stairs and I follow closely behind her, barely skidding to a stop before hitting her back when we reach the foyer.

Collin.

My massive crush has grown exponentially larger since our kiss last night. I wanted to take things further, all the way to be precise, but Collin was a perfect gentleman and excused himself without progressing any further than kissing. He returned a few minutes later with a pile of clothes, pecked my forehead, and wished me goodnight.

Now, I imagine a small trickle of drool must be running down my chin as I drink in the golden-haired Adonis standing in front of the door. He's clad in a pair of gym shorts and a muscle-tee that shows off his well-developed arms to perfection. My eyes travel up his body and connect with his vibrant, green gaze.

A sparkle in his eyes, informs me that he saw me checking him out. I shrug in return, quirking a brow as if to say, "so what". He's unfairly attractive and he must know it. I'm not ashamed to take advantage of a few free looks.

Collin's face breaks into a wide smile and he joins me where I stand, wrapping an arm around my shoulders. He tilts his face down, closer to mine. I angle my head at just the right second for his lips to meet my nose.

"Oops," I say with a giggle.

He chuckles with his face near mine and whispers, "Let's try that again."

After a few beats the words process, then my attitude immediately sobers. The second my lips close, he places a brief peck against them. I feel him beginning to retreat and on instinct, I open my mouth, sliding my tongue against his sealed lips.

Collin groans, then pulls me against his chest, deepening the kiss immediately per my unspoken request. He devours my mouth like I'm his last meal and I cling onto his shoulders, reciprocating the best I can.

I move to slide my hands down his chest when Katie's loud voice breaks through my lusty haze.

"Ugh guys. Seriously? I'm still here. I'm HERE IN THE SAME ROOM AS YOU. I'm your friend that you're ignoring. Geez, you are the worst. C'mon just go get a room already."

As she speaks, I separate my face from Collin's,

intent on twisting in her direction. He keeps his arm snug around my waist, locking my body against his.

After a wicked look, he turns to Katie and drawls, "Okay, see ya."

He pushes me towards the stairs as if we're going to skip practice and tryouts, in order to listen to Katie's advice and get our freak on. I follow his lead, jokingly placing my foot on the first step and grabbing onto the handrail.

"Wait, wait," Katie yells. "Bring me to school first. Oh, and Kenzie needs to try out. Get a room later!!"

Collin and I laugh in unison, over her quick change of heart. Our mirth spills over to Katie as soon as she realizes we were teasing her, and the three of us chuckle together.

Once we collect ourselves, Collin wraps an arm around each of our shoulders. We exit the house as a unit with Collin steering us towards his SUV.

I'm grateful for Katie's fast friendship and Collin's easy-going attitude (and his uber sexy body and fantastic kissing skills). Despite the abrupt wake-up, this is one of the best mornings that I've had in awhile. And now it's time for the icing on top of the cake...

It's time for me to make the cheerleading team.

Chapter 21

"O kay!" Summer screams, her chipper voice echoing across the gymnasium. "All of you ladies showed up today with hopes of making the cheer squad, but we only have three spots. If we could take you all, we totally would…"

"But we can't," Isabelle cuts in.

Summer shoots her an annoyed glance, but Isabelle ignores it. Instead, she appears intent on taking over the instructions, apparently done with Summer's enthusiasm and general happiness to be alive. She steps in front of her to be center stage.

Behind Isabelle and Summer stand two middle-aged females, and one male, all dressed in athletic wear and holding clipboards. These must be the people choosing who makes the squad with the input from the captains and their own observations. I can't remember which one is the coach, and based on their outfits, it could be any of them.

Isabelle's words resume, cutting through my distraction, and I unwillingly drag my gaze back to her. "We'll start with a basic cheer. Pom poms are provided in a pile to your left, go grab a set. After that we'll call out the names of the girls we want to see tumble, then we'll convene to determine who we want to join the squad. Before you leave today, we will announce the three girls that made it. Any questions?"

After Isabelle's speech, I eye them curiously, wondering if they plan to interject. The adults seem content to permit the captains of the squad to conduct the tryouts and remain quietly standing in a line.

Following a brief silence where no one raises their hands, or asks a question, Summer claps her hands again. "Okay girls, grab your pom poms and line up on the mat." Her instructions are a stark contrast in tone and pep to Isabelle's.

Girls begin jogging off to the side and I hustle with the crowd to a stack of vibrant blue and deep black pom poms. Grabbing one of each, I return to the middle of the gym floor and find a decent spot, front and center.

Isabelle and Summer watch as the other girls fill in spaces on the floor, stepping in to offset a few of us. Once they're satisfied with our placement, the two take their spots at the front of the group. One of the adults presses a button on the wall panel behind them and music pounds across the auditorium through the speakers. Unlike the practice session, the captains of the squad don't join us in the cheer. Standing side by side, Summer smiles at the group and Isabelle crosses her arms over her chest, her lips turned downward.

The music picks up and Summer's peppy voice calls out, "Five, Six, Seven, Eight."

Her count off is the only instruction my body needs to fall into the easy motions and words of the short routine we learned three days ago. A smile splits my face as muscle memory takes over and I have… fun.

As a group, we shout and jump, waving our arms and moving our bodies through two cheers, in time with the music. It's easy to spot the girls that didn't practice or just weren't cut out for cheerleading. From the corner of my eye I see Isabelle looping through and removing the girls off beat or just plain bad.

I force myself to focus and ignore her eyes on me, as I finish up the last few movements. The routine portion passes quickly and afterwards, my body is limber and my adrenaline pumping.

This time when Summer claps her hands, she shouts, "Return your pom poms, it's time for tumbling!"

I hurriedly obey her instructions, attempting to discreetly survey the girls that are left. One girl from my stunt group the other day was cut, but the rest of us remain. I smile at the three familiar faces and then scan the rest. There's no one else I recognize specifically, from the other day or from my classes, probably because it's a little late in your high school career to be trying out for cheer during senior year.

"We need to pull out the mats," Isabelle demands, interrupting my wayward thoughts.

She stands with her hands on her hip, while the rest of us, including Summer, walk towards the pile of safety mats in the corner. As a team, we drag out the tumbling practice equipment, slotting the pieces into place like a puzzle. There's about fifteen of us left and we make quick work of setting everything up, then stand to the side to wait for the next set of instructions.

Isabelle saunters into the center, clearly preening under the attention of every eye in the room. She claps her hands together and begins talking without waiting for Summer to join her. "Alright ladies, we're going to call you up one at a time to have you show us your tumbling. We will instruct you to complete moves varying in difficulty. Once you've finished them, you can join the coaches off to the side to watch the rest of the girls."

Expecting to be first, per Isabelle's usual tactics, I take a half step forward towards the mat. To my surprise she calls a freshman's name. Startled, I return to the line to observe as the girl botches an aerial and a back handspring before she's asked to join the coaches.

Another freshman is quickly summoned to replace her, and the results are pretty much the same. This one places her face in her hands as she walks off to the side, clearly embarrassed by her less than stellar performance on the mats.

When half the girls have been called and I remain to the side observing, I realize Isabelle is employing a different form of torture this go around. The longer I wait, watching most girls unsuccessfully perform the tumbles requested of them, the more nervous I become. Despite knowing the moves and knowing my body can do them, my palms become clammy and my knees grow weak.

I feel like I spend an eternity waiting for the thirteen other girls to complete their turns, but it's probably only twenty minutes to a half hour. A pit of dread has formed in my stomach by the time I'm one of the last two remaining. The girl standing next to me is called to the mat first and I give an encouraging thumbs up as she shoots me a glance.

This girl is good. She seamlessly executes every move we practiced on Tuesday, with a smile. Seeing her succeed boosts my confidence and makes me think maybe, maybe, I was placed near the end as to not intimidate the other girls with my tumbling skills, like the girl flipping and jumping across the mats right now.

She's finally excused and I watch as she jogs to the far side. Waiting until she's all the way off before I step up to the front, facing the captains before my name leaves Isabelle's lips.

She shoots me a dirty look and asks, "Can you do a double toe touch back tuck?"

Despite not practicing the move on Tuesday, I know the steps, and am confident I can complete the trick. I pivot and retreat, moving to the exact middle of the mat without responding and I can hear her snickering behind me. I'm guessing she thinks I'm giving up, but I just need some more space and, if I'm going to be given the most difficult tumbles, I want everyone to see me nail them.

Once I reach my destination, I twirl to face the front, take a deep breath, and squat down lightly before executing the trick. I stick the landing and a swell of pride mixes with a massive rush of adrenaline. I barely fight off the urge to give myself a fist pump.

Glancing back at the captains, I see Summer shoot me a smile glowing with encouragement. The look is a direct contrast from the deep frown Isabelle is wearing.

The latter barks another move at me, "Kenzie, we want to see a back-handspring series into a full twist."

I frown at the request, knowing this is already much harder than the tumbling asked from the other girls and beyond the skill level we practiced on Tuesday; this is a very advanced move. Shrugging it off I walk to the opposite corner and my dormant cheerleading skills shine.

Breaking into a light run, I twirl and twist my body, contorting my way through the moves with ease. My feet hit the mat and a smile threatens to break through my calm demeanor, but I fight it down, buffing my nails against my bike shorts casually instead.

Take that, bitch.

Isabelle opens her mouth for another request, but Summer steps up to the edge of the mat and claps her hands. Without making it seem intentional, the noise effectively cuts off her co-captain. Summer's chipper voice shouts out, covering the dig with enthusiastic words, "Okay McKenzie, thank you so much." Turning to the rest of the group she goes on, "Everyone did fantastic! We need a few minutes to confer and finalize our decisions. Please grab a seat on the bleachers while we head to the coach's office. Feel free to drink your water or use the restroom if you must, but we should be back soon, so don't go too far!"

She turns on her heel and I watch the judges exit together in a line behind her. I follow the group with my eyes until they're out of sight, then scan the gym. Girls stand scattered about the room, most of them lingering to the far side where they ended their tumbling. My eyes observe their awkward stances and stunted interactions, wondering who is going to make the team.

I'm desperately hoping one of the slots belongs to me.

Girls slowly trickle to the bleachers and I tag along, stepping up to the empty front bench and plopping down onto the middle. One of the girls from my stunt group wordlessly sits beside me and I offer a smile, which she returns, but neither of us speak. The seconds tick by, while we wait with bated breath, each of us anxiously anticipating the results.

Finally, the group of coaches and captains file into the gym, followed by the rest of the cheer team dressed in uniform. A woman that appears to be the head coach steps forward ahead of the rest. She looks pretty official in a royal blue and black tracksuit, holding a clipboard, which she consults before beginning to speak, "Hello everyone, my name is Coach Everly. I'd like to thank you for coming to tryouts today, it was fantastic to see the effort every girl put forth on the mat today. Unfortunately, there are only three spots open on the team, as we mentioned earlier. We had to make a few tough decisions on who to add, based on cheer abilities as well as tumbling skills. If your name is not called today, it doesn't mean you're not welcome to try out again next year." She pauses, her eyes perusing her clipboard one last time. Her next words boom through the gym, "Please, everyone, a warm welcome for our newest Golden Oaks Cheerleaders: McKenzie C., April S., and Samantha T."

The squad, standing behind the coach, goes nuts, clapping and cheering for us. A small smattering of applause sounds from the bleachers, as girls overcome their disappointment to celebrate the three that made it, even if they didn't.

A calm elation goes through me. I did it, I'm on the squad.

I stand from the bleachers as Katie rushes me, closely followed by Summer and Heather. Katie launches herself at me and gives me a tight squeeze, grabbing my hands excitedly as she steps back. "You were awesome! I knew you'd make it," Katie half-whispers, her excitement making her voice louder than she probably intended.

Katie drops my hands, and steps away, to allow Summer and Heather to step closer. The girls nod their heads and murmur their agreement as the three of us stand in a tight circle off to the side. I'm ecstatic, but since we're surrounded by the disappointed faces of the girls that didn't make the team, I contain myself.

Summer begins asking Heather about something, but I miss her next words. My attention has been snagged by a head of blonde hair, swiftly striding in our direction. Collin pushes his way into our circle, not caring if he's interrupting us and lifts me into the air by my waist. He spins us in a slow circle and I squeal with laughter.

"Did my girl make the squad?" He drawls while he continues to spin us around.

Laughing, I swat at his arm playfully, half-joking, half-encouraging him to put me down. When my feet finally settle against the floor once more, he keeps one arm wrapped around me and rejoins the group.

His expectant gaze hits my face and I finally give in to the grin that's been straining to break free, a beaming smile gracing my lips. "I did it, I made the team!!"

Collin nods like that's the answer he expected, then his attention is quickly pulled away by a string of words from Katie. I don't immediately move my gaze from the side of Collin's handsome face, excitement and affection still thrumming through my veins.

Senior year is going to be my year.

Chapter 22

I t's a strange feeling—living in the same house as your crush. After dinner, we both filter upstairs and hover in the hallway spanning the distance between our two bedroom; my temporary guest room and his permanent residence. I fight hard to keep from shuffling my feet or staring at the wall, forcing myself to meet the intense emerald gaze focused on me, instead.

A sizzling heat flares between us and I find my body gravitating towards Collin's room without invitation. He wordlessly lifts his arm from his side and pushes the slightly ajar door open further, allowing me to walk underneath the appendage and into his domain.

This is the first time I've stepped foot into Collin's room.

Curiosity has me pausing just over the threshold to examine my surroundings. The room has cream-colored walls, contrasted by dark oak furniture covered in a smattering of framed photos and trophies. His plain navy-colored bedspread draped haphazardly over the massive bed catches my attention, and I catalogue the information, like it's of life-altering importance to know whether a person makes their bed.

I step further inside, feeling Collin's heat permeating the clothes covering my back. His sunshine-scent seems to intensify with each inhale, concentrated in this area from the amount of time he's spent here.

The door shuts behind me, the click of the latch echoing through the silent room. My feet carry me to the bed, as if triggered by the noise. I perch on the edge, bouncing a couple times to test out its texture. It must be a rich people thing... the mattresses in the Franzen house are unreal—Collin's included. It's like sitting on a grounded cloud; fluffy but supportive, all at once. I swing my feet onto the bed and lounge back, making myself at home on the luxurious piece of furniture.

"You look good in my bed," Collin drawls, his husky words causing my heart to ricochet in my chest. The beats pound harder as he steps closer, stalking towards my place on his bed like a man on a mission.

I scoot across the plush surface, expecting him to lay beside me. Instead, the bed dips next to my body when he places a leg on the outer side of my thigh. His gaze scans my face as he picks his other leg off the ground and uses it to separate my thighs before placing it in between them.

Trustingly, I meet his gaze. Collin is one of the good guys, maybe the best guy I've ever met. If I said "stop" I know he would.

But I don't want him to.

As if reading the permission in my gaze, his second

leg joins the first and I lift my heels off the bed to wrap around his lower waist. He leans forward onto his elbows, his entire body touching the length of mine, our faces hovering inches apart.

"McKenzie," he sighs my name like the word is precious and my heart melts a little more upon hearing the infliction.

Collin Franzen is Dangerous.

Now may not be the ideal timing for this huge revelation but it's imperative I tell him; he needs to know everything in order to progress this relationship. "Collin…" I utter hesitantly, unsure of where to start.

How do you tell someone, 'I really like you, but also I made a deal to rob your house before I even knew you?'

His torso shifts back while I think, our gazes remaining connected. Whatever he notices in my expression causes him to become concerned. "Are you okay, McKenzie? Is this too much?" He immediately pushes himself up, freeing himself from my legs wrapped around his waist, and moving to sit at the edge of the bed as he asks.

I decline with a shake of my head, and drag myself upright, pulling my knees to my chest. "No, it's not that. You're perfect and I would love to take this further, I just have something to tell you and it's… complicated."

"Sometimes it's just easiest to start at the beginning, then tell everything else in order," Collin drawls, his expression intense as he studies my face and responds to my vague statements.

I nod. "Okay."

Start from the beginning.

With a sigh, I allow the words to spill forth, "About a year and a half ago, my mom met this guy, Andy. For the first time in her life, she had her shit together. She cut back on drinking and actually made dinner sometimes. Even when she didn't cook, there was plenty of food in the house to make my own meals or snacks… which was kind of a rare thing for me growing up."

Collin places a hand on my knee, gently swiping his thumb up and down in wordless encouragement. I've never thought of my knee as an erogenous zone before, but his movements cause my skin to heat with desire. Ignoring it, I force myself to carry on.

He needs to hear this.

"Things were going really well, at least for a while… Then I guess Andy received a job offer for a highly sought-after position in Florida. I returned home after school one day and my mom locked herself inside the bedroom. I could still hear her heart-broken sobs through the door, but she wouldn't let me in. She said a few words between her cries and I was able to piece together what happened. Andy was leaving and he didn't think it was fair to ask her to move since I was almost finished with high school and we were "established" here. I tried to get inside to comfort her, but she kept telling me she just needed to sleep it off. I went to school the next day and when I came home, most of her stuff was gone. At first, I was concerned something happened to her, or maybe we had been robbed, but… there was a note on the counter that said she went to find Andy, because he was the love of her life."

Collin inhales sharply. "She left for Florida without you? How long ago was this?"

"Almost a year ago," I admit in a whisper, my chin tucked between my knees and chest. My eyes remain focused on the dark bedspread while I think through the past and about the mother that would rather leave me behind than lose a man she barely knew.

The warm skin of Collin's hand touches the underside of my chin and he tugs against it, forcing me to meet his gaze. "You're incredible, McKenzie Carslyle," he says fervently. "Not everyone would be able to survive on their own, but you've done it for over a year, as a teenager. You're smart and determined and resourceful. And, you're not alone anymore."

The truth of his words shines through his eyes, and a part of me wants to cry.

After I tell him the next portion of my story, of our story, will he still feel this way about me?

I open my mouth, the most important words of my confession poised on the tip of tongue, but Collin decides to speak his own truth, interrupting my big moment. "My mom killed herself when I was a baby."

A gasp escapes my lips. My hand flies to my mouth after the fact, a belated reaction attempting to keep the noise contained.

Collin nods his head slowly, as if agreeing with my unspoken sentiment. Although his gaze is focused on the far, cream-colored wall, the sadness emanating off him is palpable. I scramble to slide my body next to his, wrapping an arm around his waist and drawing us closer to each other.

Before I met Collin Franzen, I didn't understand the power of touch, or the comfort it wordlessly provides. Now that I do, I use my half, side-hug to convey the feelings coursing through my body that I'm unable to verbalize. Sadness. Empathy. Hurt—for his situation and my own.

Collin leans further into my side, resting his cheek on the top of my head, and goes on, "I never even got the chance to know her." The words are whispered, but the air in the room is still and silent, making them seem much louder than they actually are. "My grandpa used to talk about her, as much as he could, to anyone that would listen. When I was just a kid, he would spend most of our time together reminiscing about his daughter. He would tell me about her favorite flavor of ice cream, or the lake she used to visit all the time. It wasn't until I got older, that I discovered she committed suicide."

"I'm so sorry Collin," I murmur. I'm underprepared for large emotional stories, from a pure lack of experience, but I'm doing the best I can to be a sense of comfort, as I navigate this uncharted territory.

"I asked my dad about it once. He doesn't like to talk about my mom or really even me as a baby, but he let me ask questions one time. My dad said her death was caused by untreated depression, which worsened after her pregnancy and my birth. I wasn't even four months old when it happened."

I squeeze him tighter, words flitting to the forefront of my mind too rapidly for me to formulate a logical response. He doesn't seem to need any words from me now that he's started talking. He continues to unburden himself, and I listen.

"My dad remarried a few years later, Lucas is my half-brother. His mom is my mom, even if we aren't related by blood. She raised me more than my own did, but sometimes I feel like a bit of an outsider in their perfect family. Like the one piece that doesn't really fit."

Collin and I haven't known each other for long, but this moment resonates with me, like this isn't something he speaks of often and my reaction can make or break the relationship we've been building. I tentatively reach my other hand out and place it on his shoulder, pressing firmly and urging him to meet my gaze.

Earnestness fills my chocolate eyes, as I respond, "I'm sorry for your loss, but this family is lucky to have you, whether you're blood related or otherwise." The words are spoken quiet and low, but I feel Collin's tense muscles gradually relax beneath my arm. I release a slow breath while I think of ways to navigate us toward a more positive conversation without making it uncomfortable.

Collin's eyes meet mine, the jewel-toned green making my breath catch. Their brightness is startling even when dimmed with sadness, as they are now. "I just wish I had gotten to know her, and sometimes it feels like her death is my fault. Like maybe if it weren't for me, she would've been okay or would've gotten help."

I nod to signify my understanding, but not my agreement.

Gently rubbing my hand up and down his arm, I speak slowly, so each syllable can penetrate the self-doubt plaguing his words. "It's not your fault though. A baby can't be held responsible for the choices of an adult. I'm sure she knew, at least partially, that she needed help and those around her should've been able to recognize the signs. I'm sorry for your loss, but there's absolutely nothing you could've done." Collin nods slowly, disbelief warring with another emotion I can't name, in his gaze. I change the topic, and ask "Do you get along well with your step-mom?"

A light smile graces Collin's lips and he looks away again. "Yeah, she's the best. She's my mom, we don't say step or half or anything in my family."

When his eyes meet mine again, I realize we both were inching closer as we spoke. His arm is warm, wrapped low around my waist and supporting the weight of my arm tucked around his side. Only about three inches separate our faces now.

"Thanks for listening McKenzie, we're not as different as you thought, huh?" He drawls out the question like he's reading all the thoughts racing through my mind.

"I guess not, Collin," I respond lightly. I force my tone to remain positive, despite all the heavy emotions our confessions stirred, but more importantly, the secret I still hold, unable to part with the words so shortly after gaining Collin's confidence.

"Will you stay in here with me?" Collin asks, our faces still close, breaths intermingling.

"Yeah, I'd like that," I whisper, my lips practically touching his with the words.

He tilts closer and presses a soft, gentle kiss against

my lips, then he slowly rises from our seat at the edge of the bed. "Do you need something to wear?" He asks as he ambles across the room towards his dresser.

"No, I still have the stuff from yesterday," I reply and hop off the bed. Letting myself out of Collin's room, I wander down the hall, and distractedly prepare to go to sleep, my body running through the motions as my mind reflects on my conversation with Collin.

When I return to his room, he's turned off the overhead light and the room is bathed in the dim glow of the bedside lamp. My eyes search for Collin and find him already under the covers with the far side turned down, as if it's waiting for me. The tanned skin of his chest is peeking out from the navy bedding and I'm drawn forward, ready to see him shirtless again.

I stroll to the far side and slide in, after placing my clunky cell on the nightstand. Keeping the covers lifted an extra second longer than necessary, I steal a quick glance at the guy occupying the space next to me.

His abs are just as defined as I remember with a light dusting of golden hair leading into his boxers. He flexes the muscles under my watchful gaze and I chuckle, dropping the sheet. "You caught me," I admit, raising my hands in the air in mock surrender.

Collin chuckles, grabbing one of my wrists, and yanking me towards him. I roll across the bed, closing the gap of a couple inches I had originally left between us. He wraps his arm around me, pulling me against him while he stays on his back. His other hand finds the back of my thigh and tugs it across his legs so we're completely intertwined with my body laying half-atop his.

He leaves one hand resting against my thigh and the other against my side, exhaling a deep, contented sigh. The sound conveys he's happy and peaceful, which he confirms by brushing his lips lightly against my forehead and whispering, "I'm glad you're here McKenzie."

The click of the lamp punctuates the near silence and the room falls into darkness. Collin's breathing quickly evens out into long, deep inhales and exhales, his chest rising in a steady cadence indicating he's already welcomed sleep.

Despite Collin's heat seeping into my bones as we lay on the mattress created by superior life forms, I'm restless. Guilt nibbles at my intestines as I replay our conversation from this evening.

I tried to tell him; I really did.

What was I supposed to say after he told me his truth? 'I'm sorry about your mom, oh by the way I originally befriended you to rob your house, but now I don't want to because I have an enormous crush on you?' For some reason that doesn't feel like it would go over well.

I continue mulling over the issue into the early morning hours, until I eventually fall into an uneasy sleep. One where I dream up a hundred scenarios of how Collin dumps me like yesterday's garbage after he finds out what I've been hiding from him.

Chapter 23

I wake slowly, stretching my muscles and luxuriating in the amazing comfort offered by the beds in the Franzen house. My skin is cool from their air conditioning, their bedding soft against my skin, and the smell of sunshine drifts into my nostrils with each breath.

Sunshine.

My eyes fly open as the memory of falling asleep in Collin's bed rushes to the forefront of my mind. I discreetly check my face and pillow for drool before flipping over. I expect to see Collin on the other side of the bed, but it—and the entire room—is empty. Frowning slightly, I slide out from under the covers and wander to the attached bathroom.

After I check inside for Collin, I take care of my morning business, then return to the main room. Wandering to the door, I wonder where he's disappeared to and intend to continue my search downstairs. I take a couple steps past the bed, then the door leading to the hall bursts into the room. I jump back, startled and a little concerned.

What the hell?

Collin comes barreling through the doorway, his arms laden down by a tray overflowing with food. He has it precariously balanced, with his foot still lifted in the air like he kicked in the door to enter. His gaze connects with mine and he stops short.

"Well crap, I was trying to do breakfast in bed," he drawls, disappointment peppering the look of concentration on his face.

Giggling, I twirl around, retreating to the bed and sliding back under the covers. Once I'm comfortably settled, with a pillow propping up my back, my chocolate gaze meets Collin's.

"Serve me breakfast, Serf," I announce, slightly joking but also surprisingly hungry when confronted with a tray full of waffles, fruit, yogurt, and bacon.

Collin laughs, but obeys my command. He settles the tray next to me on the bed before joining me under the covers. His long legs are angled towards me, his body curved around the tray so our feet can touch. He hands me a glass of orange juice and a fork, then the two of us dig into our meal unceremoniously.

I attack the waffles first. They're crisp and fluffy at the same time, unlike the kind I usually buy from the freezer section. These are clearly homemade, or at least made with some type of mix and a waffle maker. The buttery, fluffy goodness is dripping in syrup when it touches my lips and I immediately groan at the flavorful taste.

A girl could get used to eating like this.

Collin laughs, and I realize I've spoken the words aloud.

A light flush crests my cheeks, but my embarrassment lessens when he shoots me a heated look and responds, "I'll let you sleep in my bed and make you breakfast any day of the week." His warm drawl is raspy and lustful, his gaze flitting to my lips before he takes a slow bite of the waffles himself.

Before I'm able to form a response, a loud, electronic sounding beep blares from my clunky cell on the nightstand. As I scramble to pick it up, shutting off the ancient alarm, I remember my shift at the motel today that Mr. Mouchard didn't cancel.

"Thank you so much for breakfast," I rush out as I gently slide from under the covers, careful so I don't disturb the tray still stacked with food. "But I forgot I have to be at work in forty minutes."

I sprint towards the door, already out in the hall when Collin's words reach my ears. "I'll drive you. Come downstairs when you're ready to leave."

Without responding, I run to my temporary bedroom and sift through my small pile of belongings. A curse leaves my lips when I remember I haven't been home since dinner on Thursday and I don't have my work shirt with me.

In record time, I brush my hair and tie it off into a quick French braid before donning a pair of black pants, a t-shirt, and tennis shoes, all courtesy of Katie. I scurry down the hall and fly down the steps, barely pausing for breath when I reach Collin.

"I need to go home first, for my work shirt," I wheeze out.

He nods and grabs my hand, his warm palm wrapping around mine before he tugs me through the door, his dark SUV already idling in the driveway.

I'm reminded how different our lives are by the simple fact that he left his car running in the driveway, with the key in the ignition. If he did that a few miles away in my neighborhood, he'd probably return to find his car stolen in under a minute. Brushing the thought aside, I clamber in and buckle my seat belt.

Collin drives us silently, the crooning of the radio the only noise in the car. I use the time to calm my stressed nerves. Since I'm being driven and not biking, I'll be on time for work. The thought fills me with gratitude and I look across the front seat at the handsome, kind face beside me. Emerald eyes meet mine and I offer a brief smile.

Reaching across the console, I snag Collin's large, warm hand and squeeze. He doesn't allow me to retreat, but rather intertwines our fingers while his gaze remains focused out the windshield.

I'm thankful for the ride and that Collin doesn't seem upset, even though I spoiled his thoughtful and delicious breakfast plans. I jot down a mental note: I need to find some way to make up for ruining this morning, and to pay back all the other random bits of kindness Collin is always showing me.

If my secret doesn't ruin this, I want to be the kind of girl worthy of being in a relationship with someone so selfless.

Within minutes, we're bumping along the dirt road leading to my trailer. Collin parks in his typical spot, but leaves the car running due to our time crunch.

Pushing away thoughts of future makeup kindness, I hop out of the SUV and run to the front door, quickly fitting my key in the lock and rushing inside to change my shirt.

I find it almost immediately, pulling off Katie's tee and donning my pale blue work top in one smooth movement. It takes a few seconds longer to find my clunky, ugly work shoes and toe those on as well. But once I do, I'm ready.

Not wanting to leave the nice, borrowed clothing behind, I scramble to locate a bag. Taking an extra couple of minutes, I grab the clothes I changed out of and a few extra outfits for school, work, and cheer. I leave my bedroom, stopping in the bathroom to collect my toiletries.

When I emerge in the living room, my duffle is almost full, and I have everything I need to survive for a few weeks. My gaze sweeps across the room landing on my backpack. I scoop it off the hook near the door, then try to identify anything else I'm missing.

Although I'm not permanently moving in with the Franzen's, at least not to my knowledge, I don't want to be forced to return unless absolutely necessary.

My ancient coffee tin catches my eye and I stride towards it. In a split-second decision, I count out $180.00, the rest of what I owe this month plus the lot rent for next.

Shoving the bills in my pocket, I leave the remainder

of my cash in the tin--not wanting to bring it to my shift at the motel. I hesitate momentarily, also not wanting to leave the unassuming container out in plain sight, either.

My gaze flits around the tiny kitchen, then stops on the tallest cupboard. I climb onto the counter and force the canister into the far back corner inside, closing the door gently.

Standing back, I survey the area. I'm confident the hiding spot will keep my limited funds safe, until I return.

Duffel and backpack in hand, I leave the trailer and lock the door tightly behind me. A wave of nostalgia hits prior to facing Collin's idling SUV.

I intend to pay my lot rent at the office before we leave for the motel and I know I'll probably be back soon. The trailer will remain my home, but it feels like my life as I know it, is changing.

I whisper, "Goodbye." The words a quiet message dissipating into the summer heat quickly; a wishful thought finally voiced aloud with no one else around to hear.

It might be goodbye for now, but this little trailer houses thousands of memories of being alone and feeling hopeless.

Leaving with half of my belongings today, feels like I'm closing one chapter of my life and beginning the next. Lingering just a second longer, my gaze rakes along the side of the trailer and then I turn away, ready to see what else senior year brings.

"Everything okay?" Collin drawls with his brow

quirked, as I open the door to his SUV and clamber inside with my stuff.

"Yeah," I sigh out. "It's just strange, leaving with my things," I respond, gesturing to the duffle and backpack crowded on the floor near my feet.

Collin nods, his eyes sympathetic as they scan my face. "I can understand that, but I'm also selfishly happy to have you at my house and for you to not be alone. Plus, it's not like you can't come back here whenever you want," he adds, echoing my thoughts from earlier, that this place still belongs to me.

His gaze moves from my face to scan over the ancient tin trailer settled onto a plot of dying patchy grass. When his gaze returns, he offers a wide smile and asks, "Do you have everything? Are you ready for work?"

I nod briefly. Now that I've said goodbye, I'm ready to leave the park behind. But first, I have one more task to accomplish.

"Can we stop by the Office really fast on our way out?"

He squeezes my hand briefly as a non-verbal confirmation, then places the car into gear and backs onto the bumpy road.

After a short drive, he parks in front of the tired, squat office building. Facing me, he asks "Do you need me to come in with you?"

I wordlessly decline with a shake of my head, hopping out onto the dead grass. With firm resolve, I yank open the office door, remembering the last time I was here, forced to part with an extra portion of my hard-earned money for nothing extra in return.

Now, mere weeks later, I'm back to willingly pay ahead. Pushing the thought aside, I step up to Mildred's desk, and wait for her to acknowledge me, which takes a few minutes as she's immersed in scribbling on a notepad.

Her eyes briefly flit to my face, then I watch as she does a double take before checking her desk calendar.

Instead of being insulted over her reaction to my presence in her office, prior to the last day to pay, I want to laugh.

Stifling the giggle threatening to burst free, and without waiting for her to ask why I'm here, I silently hold out the one-hundred and eighty dollars I counted from my tin.

She takes the money, counts it, then raises a brow. "For this month and next?"

"For this month and next," I confirm with a nod.

"You can't get it back once you pay," she warns.

Despite the ominous feeling her words bring, my response is confident, "I won't need to."

Her gaze lingers on my face for a long minute, before finally returning to her desk. "Let me get you a receipt."

Chapter 24

J ust take a left onto this street over here and you can drop me off at the front corner of the white building right there," I instruct.

I use my hand to reinforce my directions, indicating the ideal point for Collin to stop at the motel. The spot prevents him from seeing inside and blocks Mr. Mouchard's view of my ride, in case he happens to look outside.

"Or I could park in the lot and walk you up?" Collin offers, shooting me a charming grin.

His smile is aimed in my direction, but his eyes are focused on the road, so he thankfully misses the panicked expression that briefly flits across my face.

I definitely do not want Collin to meet Mr. Mouchard. I'm not sure how he would react to my slimy boss, but I have a strong inclination to believe it would be somewhere in the realm of "not well".

"Err, that's okay. My boss has been cutting my shifts lately, I don't want to give him any reasons to think I'm not a professional employee. Which includes my guy walking me to the door," I lie, teasingly jabbing him in the arm and covering my unease with a slight grin.

"If you're sure," he agrees reluctantly as he pulls the SUV up to the corner, as requested.

I throw out a quick, "Yes I'm sure. Thank you for the ride, I'm done at two." Then exit the car like my ass is on fire, slamming the door shut and sprinting away, without waiting for a response.

My feet pound against the paved ground as I rush toward the lobby, hoping Collin doesn't change his mind in the brief time it takes me to reach the door. Even though I'm ten minutes early--and would much rather wait in the heat than spend any extra time with Mr. Mouchard--I pry open the ancient door and enter the air-conditioned room without a backward glance.

I stop short when I spot Candy's pink hair stationed in front of the computer. She's typing something, her gaze intent on the screen while Mr. Mouchard stands right behind her. His crotch is pressing against her ass, his hands resting against either side of the counter, caging her in.

Candy doesn't seem to notice his presence, or maybe she doesn't care. She tilts her head to reference something beside the keyboard. Then a few more clicks sound across the lobby as she presses the keys in front of her, not paying him any attention as she carries on with her task.

It's unclear if I release the sound of disgust building in my throat, or if it's maybe a belated reaction to the sensor that dings when the door opens, but Mr. Mouchard's beady eyes suddenly swing in my direction.

"McKenzie?" He asks.

The confusion in his tone doesn't bode well for me and I hesitantly walk forward. "Hi, Mr. Mouchard. And Candy. I'm here for my ten o'clock shift… just a few minutes early," I state in a falsely chipper tone.

Mr. Mouchard strokes a single finger across his thin mustache and gestures me forward with his right hand. He steps away from Candy in the direction of his office situated along the back wall, striding away without pausing to ensure I follow.

A cold feeling of dread dances down my spine, but I force myself towards the office entry. I've never been called into this room and I'm not certain I want to be stuck in such close quarters with a creep, like Mr. Mouchard.

It doesn't seem like I have much choice. My mind blanks on excuses to conduct our conversation in the open, as my leaden feet make slow progress across the old stained carpet covering the lobby floor. It takes eons for me to reach the office, but I finally make it.

"Close the door, McKenzie," Mr. Mouchard practically purrs, the words activating my flight instincts, my body screaming at me to run.

I push the door shut behind me with my heel, reluctant to turn my back on Mr. Mouchard. The sound of the latch clicking has me working double time to stifle my urge to flee. The noise is a distinct signifier I should go.

Instead, my eyes survey the office I was beckoned

into. The room smells like a combination of cat litter and mothballs, making it that much harder to remain in the small space.

One cracked, black, leather couch sits against the far wall with a coffee table in front of it. In the corner is a desk hosting an ancient computer and an assortment of papers. Next to the desk sits an enormous safe, which makes me want to laugh because I doubt the Motel's income justifies such a massive piece of equipment.

Once my eyes reach him, Mr. Mouchard sits on the leather sofa and pats the space next to him, twice. "Come join me, McKenzie," he commands, noticing my feet glued to the dirty carpet near the door.

Wordlessly, I force my reluctant body to move towards him, perching on the edge of the couch at the furthest point possible. I angle my legs in his direction to provide a buffer in case he attempts to close in on me.

Mr. Mouchard eyes my spot and looks like he intends to move closer, measuring the distance between our bodies with his gaze. I angle my body more in response, making a stronger barrier of my long legs, and he decides to stay in place.

Lounging back into the couch, he finally speaks, "I'm sure you're aware of the reason I called you in here."

Thoughts whirl in my head, my brain has been on overdrive since the moment he motioned with his hand in the lobby. I'm pretty sure he called me in here to fire me, but I don't want to voice the words aloud.

Maybe if I deny the truth, it won't come to fruition.

With that thought in mind, I shake my head.

He somehow interprets my decline as an invitation and inches his way across the couch. The motion looks ridiculous, like a worm moving across the sidewalk.

His wiry frame scoots as close as possible to my knees angled in his direction. Then, he places a clammy palm on my closer knee, the dampness seeping from his hand into the fabric of my work pants.

I force myself not to kick him, fixating a furious glare on the offending appendage, instead.

He ignores the look and continues speaking, his hand a heavy weight trapping me in place. "Well, McKenzie. I'm sure you've realized the motel doesn't really need you anymore... now that Candy is working here. I'm afraid I don't have any extra shifts to hand out."

I move to get up, but Mr. Mouchard presses his hand down firmly, with a surprising amount of strength, effectively locking me into place. A smarmy smile spreads across his face and he leans closer, the stench of his coffee breath fanning over me.

Forcing myself not to panic, I remain still as a statue, not flinching away from his stinking presence, even as he moves his torso in a way that places him practically on top of me.

"I do have a different position I think you would be excellent at, though." His eyes scan my body, lingering on my chest before returning to my face.

If his words didn't make his intentions clear, his actions certainly have.

I school my face into a neutral expression "I'm only

seventeen," I reply calmly, curious to see his reaction, but not expecting him to change his tune.

Mr. Mouchard is a creep, he always has been, and now his true colors are on full display.

"Age doesn't matter between friends, beautiful McKenzie," he replies, scooting closer.

This time, I don't allow Mr. Mouchard's tight grip to stop me. I jump from the couch and square my shoulders before facing him. Surprise briefly flashes across his features, but he quickly neutralizes his reaction.

He slowly stands, occupying most of the foot of space between us despite his small stature. Mr. Mouchard is sleazy and skeevy, but not tall, so the move brings us practically nose to nose.

"Look here," I start, cutting him off as his mouth opens to speak. "I appreciate you offering me a job last year when I really needed one, but I will NEVER accept your proposition. I am not that girl. I'm leaving this town, the first chance I get, and I don't need you or your offers of *charity*."

I leave a brief pause, then spit out, "I quit."

Spinning on my heel, I storm out of the office, feeling offended but also proud of myself. I know my values and when to stick to my guns.

As I pass through the doorway, I hear Mr. Mouchard scoff, his belated reply reaching me just before I exit the lobby entirely, "You'll be back. Look at Candy, she came crawling back."

His words barely penetrate my anger or resolve, despite my surprise. Did Candy used to work here?

Pushing the thought aside, I stomp all the way to the

curb where I was dropped off, not wanting to be seen by Mr. Mouchard after his disgusting offer.

I flip open my ancient, clunky cell phone, I bought with honest, hard work. My fingers fly over the number pad as I rapidly dial Collin.

To my relief, he answers after two rings. "McKenzie are you okay?"

Am I okay? No, no I'm not.

But to Collin I reply, "Uh yeah. My shift got cut and my boss forgot to text me—"

Collin interrupts, "I'm turning around right now. I'll be there in ten to pick you up."

I didn't realize how tense my shoulders had gotten until his words cause all my tension to flee. Every muscle relaxes, dragging them down from my ears, restoring their normal position.

With a deep breath, I nod my head even though he can't see me. "Thanks," I whisper.

We hang up, but I keep my phone in both hands, cradled against my stomach, in case I need to call for help while I pace the small strip of sidewalk.

Thankfully, Mr. Mouchard stays inside and Collin arrives in under ten minutes.

His massive SUV effortlessly slides up to the curb beside me. I can see him move to put the car in park, but I spring forward and tug the door open, not wanting to spend one second more of my life near this building.

"Is everything okay?" Collin drawls, his tone and eyes peppered with concern, along with their usual warmth.

"Yeah," I reply with a sigh.

After a pause, I tell him a portion of the truth, "My boss pulled me aside and basically said he's overstaffed, and they don't need me anymore."

Collin turns his head to eye me for a beat. "What are you going to do now? Do you need to find another job?" he asks, as his gaze returns to the road.

I nod, then realize he might not catch the movement since his gaze is focused elsewhere.

"I'm fine. I don't know what I'm going to do yet... I do need to find a new job as soon as possible. I'm paid ahead on my lot rent, but I'm running a little short on emergency funds—in case anything else comes up. I haven't worked in over a week, so all I have is a small savings from the beginning of summer."

His warm palm finds my knee and gives a quick squeeze. He doesn't immediately pull away, his hand lingering against my work pants as he softly swipes his thumb up and down.

It's a mimic of Mr. Mouchard's actions, but instead of making my skin crawl, his touch erases the unpleasant memory. I focus on the contact, using the affection to replace the imprint of my disgusting boss's hand.

I'm so focused on the feelings of safety and comfort Collin's touch evokes, that I almost miss his half-whispered words. "I think you should tutor my brother, like my parents were talking about on Thursday. He could use the help; you could use the money. It's a win for everyone." His volume and tone sound like he's trying to coax a scared cat out of hiding.

I move past the infliction allowing the words to sink

in, so I can mull them over. I'm already taking advantage of the Franzen's hospitality; I have been since the very beginning, as my place in their life is all due to a scheme with my neighbor. I don't want to lose Collin, but I need to tell him the truth, especially if I plan to become further involved with his family.

My brain tries to form the words several times, unsuccessfully. I finally open my mouth, intending to delve into the conversation, my brow furrowed with focus.

Prior to voicing the words, Collin's arm bands across my chest, pushing me against the seat.

"Crap, hard stop, sorry."

His words punctuate the SUV screeching to a halt. The momentum of the large vehicle pauses just in time; barely avoiding a collision with a car stopped in the middle of the road.

My heart pounds in my chest from the sudden rush of adrenaline, and Collin keeps me locked into place with his arm as we both observe the scene on the road ahead of us. The driver door of a car is propped open, and the owner of the vehicle is rummaging in their trunk for something. Apparently whatever they're looking for is urgent enough to hold up traffic.

Collin's tense muscles slowly relax, his palm returning to my knee, as we watch the driver sort through his messy vehicle. He appears content to patiently wait for the person to finish their task before we resume driving, and my heart warms at another example of his compassion.

It makes me optimistic the discussion about my

arrangement with Derek might not go as poorly as I've been imagining it will.

"What were you going to say?" Collin asks, his warm gaze connecting with mine as his car idles on the road behind the stopped vehicle.

Deciding to table the serious conversation for a time when I have his full attention, I simply reply, "I'll do it. I'd really appreciate the opportunity to tutor your brother."

Chapter 25

Monday arrives quickly, after a weekend spent cuddling under the covers with Collin. He seemed morally offended by my lack of movie knowledge, so we spent the majority of our time watching a slew of old western movies Collin deemed "classics".

He also practically force-fed me waffles for almost every meal, upon discovering they're my all-time favorite food. Not that I'm complaining about the obscene amount of fluffy goodness I consumed in a forty-eight-hour period.

Somehow, between all the cuddles and waffles, there was never an appropriate time to come clean and tell Collin about the deal.

But I will, soon. I know I need to… it's just been surprisingly difficult to force the words past my lips. It's like fear is holding the confession inside me; my body fighting to enjoy as much time with Collin as possible before uttering the truth.

Now, with the early rays of the sun seeping into my light blue room at the Franzen's, I stand next to my borrowed bed, feeling like my new reality is too good to be true.

The royal blue and black cheerleading uniform given to me on Friday is laid out, ready to be worn in its first official capacity. Today, we have a spirit assembly in the afternoon, where we stand around and pep up the crowd for our first football game, so I have to wear it to school.

I get to wear it to school.

Donning the uniform feels surreal and I treasure the moment I pull on the blended polyester and spandex fabric. Cherishing the feelings that come with the opportunity, like pride and elation. I didn't expect a chance to cheer in high school, not with my family's tight funds, then later my absentee mother making funds practically non-existent.

Earning a place on the squad was truly a dream come true.

Once I'm fully clothed, I use the mirror hanging off the closet door to check my appearance. The uniform is perfect. The fitted top accentuates my small waist, with the flared skirt making my figure appear curvier than it actually is.

My hair hangs down in an inky sheet, which is allowed for the school assemblies. I use the black and blue ribbon scrunchie Katie gave me anyways, to tie the dark strands of my hair away from my face into a high ponytail. It makes the uniform feel more official.

As a final touch, I swipe a bright red lipstick on to my lips, adding color to my face.

I strike a pose in the mirror, watching my reflection pop its hip with the tips of my hair swishing around my lower back. My lips fall into a deep pout and I feel like I look like a stereotypical, bitchy cheerleader.

I love it.

"The uniform looks good on you, McKenzie," a familiar, warm voice drawls from the doorway.

Heat crests my cheeks, but I aim to contain my embarrassment as I twirl to face him. Collin's gem colored eyes sparkle with mirth at my expense.

His teasing manner and smug attitude suddenly have me determined to make him eat his words.

Channeling my inner seductress, I strut towards Collin, stepping forward on my tiptoes to highlight my long, toned legs. I assess his reaction, observing as his eyes fill with heat and he struggles to keep his gaze fixed on my face. I barely contain the urge to gloat over my victory.

When I reach him, I lightly trail my fingers down his chest towards his belt, but keep my eyes locked on his scorching emerald orbs.

Swaying closer, I place my mouth near his ear, my lips lightly caressing his skin as they move. "Do you like what you see, Franzen?"

His swallow is audible as I lean back, placing my hand on his shoulder for balance while my face hovers near his.

Collin waits half a second before he closes the

distance between us, his lips connecting with mine in a searing kiss.

Despite being on the receiving end of at least a dozen hot, drugging kisses from Collin this weekend, I still get lost in his lips as they graze mine.

I gasp as he devours my mouth like a man deprived; like the only thing that can sustain him is the connection between our lips. My eyes seal shut as his mouth caresses mine and I reciprocate his movements with fervor.

I lose myself in the seduction that is Collin Franzen.

"Hey guys, I need a ride today can we—"

The words break through my haze of lust and I reel away from Collin. With his eyes still shut, his face chases after mine until Luke resumes talking.

"Gross guys. Can you do that later? I want to be on time for class."

I giggle to cover the awkwardness of getting caught making out by Collin's younger brother. Then, I watch under hooded lids as Collin takes a deep breath and reluctantly opens his eyes.

When he sees my attention focused on him, he winks, and wraps an arm low around my waist, ushering me out into the hall. I grab my backpack hanging near the door as we exit, then the three of us trek to the car together.

"Do you want the front?" I offer Luke, hovering just outside the door flooded with guilt over imposing on their regular routine, and potentially stealing his seat.

"Nah," Luke says then clambers into the back of the SUV unceremoniously.

Shrugging off his reaction, I heave myself into the

passenger side. Fiddling with the radio knobs briefly, I find some music and twist the dial, allowing the crooning of the radio to fill the silence.

I turn my head to glance at Luke, eager to engage him in conversation since I'll be his new tutor soon, but his gaze is focused on his phone, fingers flying across the screen at a rapid pace.

My attention shifts briefly to Collin, and he slides a quick, small grin my way, intertwining our fingers then returning his gaze to the windshield. I interpret the motion to mean this is typical for their car rides, and allow my body to relax into the plush leather seat.

The three of us remain silent during the short drive, with pop music keeping some of the awkwardness at bay.

As soon as Collin pulls into a parking spot at school, Luke jumps out and scurries away. He joins a group of other kids that also look like freshmen on the stairs leading into the school.

"Does he always act that way?" I ask, worried I'm causing tension between the two brothers. Like maybe he feels threatened by me stealing all of Collin's attention or something.

Collin shrugs. "Yeah, he's had an attitude problem, lately. I think he's just mad mom and dad won't buy him a car."

"But he's only a freshman," I contest, confused why he would need a car already.

"Yeah, he gets his permit in December, after he turns fifteen, and he wants to have his own car to practice in. It seems like he's going to act like an unmitigated jerk until he finally gets his way," Collin says with another shrug, his eyes watching his brother through the window for a brief second.

I refrain from commenting, worried I'll say something like "he sounds like a spoiled brat". I don't want to insult Collin or his brother after their family has been so generous to me.

Instead, I jump out of the SUV and round the front of the vehicle. Collin meets me at the hood, slinging his arm around my shoulder and guiding us towards the brick building.

We stroll into the school together like we own the place. Connected by Collin's arm, we pass cheerleaders and footballers, waving and exchanging cheerful hellos as we stop by each of our lockers.

I grab my chemistry book, shoving it into my backpack with Collin leaning against the locker next to me. A flash of red hair catches my peripherals, seconds before Katie is wrapping me in a side hug. She separates quickly with a small squeal and I'm unable to reciprocate the gesture fully.

"OH MY GOSH. Our first assembly of senior year. Aren't you so excited?" She jumps up and down, punctuating each of her peppy words with a bounce. "I'm so glad you made the team. Assembly today, game Friday, and I'm having a party on Saturday. You two absolutely have to come."

She turns to face Collin, her next stream of words directed at him. "No offense, but I'm going to steal your girlfriend for most of Saturday. I need her help to get ready for the party, yay!"

Collin intertwines his fingers with mine, tugging me into his side. Tucking me under his arm, his eyes sparkle at me before he fixes his gaze on Katie and drawls out, "You can borrow her for the day, but I doubt you could steal her even if you tried. I'm pretty sure she's stuck with me for a while."

Katie releases a deep, swoony sigh as she stares at the two of us together. "I feel like I'm looking at the future Prom King and Queen. You two are the cutest." She brings her fingers up into a fake camera and mocks snapping a photo of us standing together.

Collin surprises me when he extends his hand with his cellphone in it. "Here, take a real one. I want a picture of me with my girl in uniform. I don't have any yet and I need to fix that," he drawls. "She looks like a total goddess, actually she looks that way without the uniform, but I still want a photo."

His words make my, already soupy heart melt further.

Collin Franzen is Dangerous.

The kind of guy that can weasel his way into your very soul before you even realize it. He treats me like a total queen and I feel like I don't deserve him.

Forcing the thought aside, I straighten my spine and puff up my chest, shooting a beaming smile towards Katie as she situates Collin's phone to snap a photo. The shutter noise sounds, and she claps. "Oh my gosh. Adorable. But one more. Can you two face each other?"

Collin and I move as requested and the shutter on the phone makes another audible noise, then two more in rapid succession as she bends to kneel on the floor.

"Ugh you two are so photogenic, Okay, prom pose!"

I'm not sure what prom pose is, exactly, but Collin takes the lead, turning me to face the lockers. He wraps his arms around me and uses his palm to guide my hands over top, then we hear a few more snaps of the shutter.

"Yes, vogue it. Alright, next I want you to—"

"I think that's enough. There's no way you haven't gotten a good one by now," Collin drawls, interrupting Katie with a chuckle.

She hands the phone over reluctantly and I giggle at her expression. I have a feeling if Collin didn't stop her, she would've gladly directed a photo shoot for the two of us, all morning.

Collin opens his photo album and I stand on my tiptoes to peek at his phone, watching over his shoulder as he flips through the photos.

"Oh, those are really good!" I exclaim, shooting a brief grin to Katie. "I'll need to get one printed for me."

"You still print photos?" Collin asks, his warm gaze assessing when it scans my face. "I'll just text you all of them so you can have them on your phone."

"Yeah right," Katie scoffs. "Like phones from 1989 can get photo messages." Her tone is light and joking, even though she's calling me out on the piece of ancient technology currently sitting snug in my bag.

Collin's brow furrows in reaction to her words, like he's confused.

"Oh my gosh, have you never noticed Kenzie's old-ass phone before? Not that there's anything wrong with it. It's retro and still functional," she tacks on to soften the blow of her insulting words.

The bell rings, thankfully saving me from the rest of the conversation outlining the differences in our family's wealth. Collin keeps his arm wrapped around my waist, but he's silent as we wander down the hall towards our chemistry class.

We sit at our table and Ms. Rigs immediately jumps into her lesson. I half-listen to her explain some basic concepts of chemistry, but my head isn't in it today.

My thoughts are preoccupied with Collin and the conversation before class. His silence during our walk was uncharacteristic. Our relationship doesn't require constant chatter, but it felt like he was worried about something, rather than the comfortable silence we normally share. Even now, sitting in class together, he hasn't tried to squeeze my knee like he usually does.

I spend most of first period convincing myself Collin isn't going to break up with me. Not because Katie's words made him realize I'm poor.

It can't really be a secret that I don't have any money since I'm parentless, and living in a trailer. We've discussed my situation multiple times and he's seen it first-hand.

We're not going to break up over this.

Especially since I've been keeping an actual secret from him. One that I'm certain will cause friction in our relationship, once revealed.

Chapter 26

"Miss Carslyle, will you hang back for a moment please?" Ms. Rigs asks as the bell screeches through the speaker above the door, indicating the end of her chemistry class.

I exchange a look with Collin, despite his odd silence earlier he seems concerned. His brow quirks in question, but I simply shrug.

I'm not sure what this is about. Hopefully it isn't anything negative. I've kept up with all the course work so far and received good grades on the two assignments she handed back.

As requested, I remain in my seat while the rest of the class files out, heading towards their homeroom classes, like I should be doing. All the while, I'm wracking my brain for the reason why I'm still here.

Ms. Rigs hovers near the edge of the room until everyone else has exited. She firmly closes the door after the last student and strides over to perch on the stool at the table in front of me, swinging her legs to face my direction.

Silence lingers while she gathers her thoughts, and I mentally prepare myself for the worst. "Miss Carslyle, I recently spoke with your biology teacher from last year. The school receives a copy of your score results from the AP tests and the PSAT. Additionally, your scores thus far in my class are impressive. We both agree you show a lot of promise in Science, especially biology."

Shock hits my system as the meaning of her words filter through my brain. A compliment on my hard work isn't what I expected when she asked me to stay behind, but I'll take it.

My manners overcome my surprise and I stutter out, "Thank you."

"I'd like to discuss your college applications, SAT, and whether you've applied for any STEM scholarships." She pauses briefly, but continues when I neither move nor speak, "Is everything going alright? Can I help with anything?" She asks.

"Uhm," I hesitate. "I haven't taken the SAT yet; I don't really know much about them."

Last year, my homeroom teacher practically forced the entire class to participate in the PSAT. I still vividly remember the embarrassment of asking how to pay, since I didn't have the funds or a checking account.

Honestly, I expected to register for the SAT the same way, but I've been so consumed by thoughts of Collin and my issue with Derek. My focus hasn't been on college, like it should be.

Dragging my thoughts back to the present, and Ms. Rigs' expectant expression, I add, "I also haven't submitted any college applications or scholarship applications... I haven't even looked into it, to be honest. It's all coming up so fast and college is something I'm interested in..." I trail off not sure how to proceed.

She nods, appearing contemplative. "I don't want to overstep, but would you like my help? I don't have a homeroom class this year and would be happy to have you come by on Tuesdays and Thursdays, during your normal homeroom period. We could utilize the time for your college prep work, like studying for the SAT and researching schools to apply for. I also think we should look into STEM scholarships, if science is something, you're interested in pursuing further."

I mull over her words, and suddenly feel a rush of gratitude. As often as I say I'm going to get out of this town and go to college next year, I didn't have a firm starting place in mind before this conversation.

"I could use the help, if you have the time," I admit.

"Okay, you said you haven't taken the SAT?" she asks. Her voice is calm and comforting, providing a safe environment for me to confess I have no idea what I'm doing. With any of this.

"Not yet..."

"Well, there is a test coming up soon. Let's use our time tomorrow to sign you up for the exam. We'll need to check if registration is still open. I have a few study guides from past years I can bring in and we can start from there. Then, after the SAT we can move on to applications and scholarships."

I nod in agreement, remaining silent as all the things I need to do, prior to being able to escape this town, suddenly overwhelm me. As if she can sense the reason for my silence, Ms. Rigs places her soft palm on top of my hand resting against the desk. The gesture feels like a motherly touch; the kind I haven't had in years.

"It's going to be alright, McKenzie. It's not too late. We will get everything in order for you, in time for you to gain acceptance into the college of your choice, I promise," she says in a low, soothing voice.

I nod, but stay frozen in my seat. The second bell rings, piercing the air and indicating the end of the passing period. I notice Ms. Rigs remains seated, but I don't address her, overwhelmed by the thoughts clouding my mind.

It felt like my biggest problem was confessing to Collin, but I have so much more on my plate.

Ms. Rigs' promise forces its way back to the forefront of my mind, overshadowing everything else. Focusing on her words, I choose to believe her, and feel some of my stress ebb away.

As if she can sense the second I accept her statement as the truth, Ms. Rigs stands from her perch on the stool and walks towards her desk. "I'll write you a pass, to excuse your late arrival to homeroom."

"Thank you," I respond simply. The words lack the strength to convey the extent of my gratitude for her offer, but I'm unsure what else to add.

I stand with her and move to wait patiently at the side of her desk while she scribbles down a note on a scrap of paper. Taking the pass with a smile, I repeat, "Thank you." Then, I exit into the hallway.

After the door closes behind me, I lean against the wall and take a deep breath in an attempt to calm my racing pulse. Nothing horrible happened in my conversation with Ms. Rigs, actually it was the exact opposite. This isn't a bad feeling, its pure adrenaline.

For the first time since my mom left, I feel like I'm no longer fighting to survive. Now I'm fighting to thrive, to succeed, and to move on. Hope blooms in my chest with the thought. I have the cheer squad, Collin, my temporary room at the Franzen's, and now Ms. Rigs' support for my college dreams.

Life is good.

"Is everything okay?" A voice drawls from my left.

Spinning around, I meet a familiar green gaze. "Collin? Why aren't you in homeroom?"

"I was worried about you… I wanted to make sure you were okay. When you entered the hall, you seemed like you needed a moment, but I was starting to feel creepy. What did Ms. Rigs want?" He asks, his tone low and soothing.

Even though he hasn't said the words, "we're okay", his presence and concern wash away the weirdness from earlier with Katie.

Stepping forward, I lay my head against his chest and wrap my arms around his lower waist. Without hesitation, Collin embraces me in a tight bear hug, squeezing me against his body fully. I tilt my chin to meet his eyes, happy when I see the sparkle glinting back at me.

I raise to my tiptoes and lightly brush my lips against his. Collin moves to deepen the kiss, then surprises me when he rears his head back with a small growl.

His eyes are heated as he grumbles, "You can't distract me with kisses McKenzie. What did Ms. Rigs want?"

"I think I like when you demand things from me, Collin. It's sexy," I quip back, enjoying the heat in his eyes and the small bit of power that accompanies it.

He responds with another growl and I smirk, feeling wanton and desirable. Collin lightly bites against the side of my neck, growling his next words against my skin. "Tell. Me. What. Happened," he demands, his lips sliding against my neck as he speaks, causing a small shiver.

Collin might be better at this teasing game than I am.

With a sigh, I finally relent. "Ms. Rigs offered to help me with my college applications and registering for the SAT."

"Oh. That was very considerate of her," Collin drawls, his voice lower than normal, but his expression as sincere as his words.

"Yeah, it was," I agree. "I need to think about where I want to apply for school and we're going to register me for the SAT exam coming up, so I'll probably need to start cramming soon. I might be too busy for you, Franzen," I tease.

"I'll make sure you find time for me," he jokes back. "You should consider applying for Berry College. Then we can stay together next year," he whispers the words in a serious tone, just underneath my ear.

"Berry College?" I ask, dragging my face away to examine him.

"Yeah," he drawls with a shrug, turning his head to the side like he's embarrassed he even suggested it. "It's just a thought. I know you're keen on science and they have some good programs there. You don't have to make any kind of commitment to it or anything, it was just a suggestion. I applied for early admission, so I should hear back soon—"

I lightly press my lips against Collin's, interrupting his rambling. This time he dives in, deepening the kiss, sealing his lips to mine with an unexpected fierceness.

It's almost as if he's using the movement of his lips to tell me how he feels. Branding me, communicating his desires, and I read it all loud and clear.

When we finally separate, a mere inch between our parted lips, we're both panting, hard. I use the minute to collect my breath and my thoughts.

"I'll definitely look into Berry College," I whisper, my words fanning across his lips with our continued closeness.

"You will?" He asks, quirking a brow with the question.

"I like you Collin Franzen. It wouldn't be a hardship to be where you are, for the next four years," I reply truthfully, with a small, sincere grin.

Unspoken words of more truths linger between us, at least on my end. I think about the agreement I made with Derek and the fear Collin will have no desire to be anywhere near me soon. Now is neither the time, nor place to discuss it though.

Collin searches my face, dropping one of his arms from my waist, and using the other to tuck me against his side. I happily snuggle into him and match his stride as he begins marching us down the hall towards my homeroom class.

"Wont your teacher be mad you're late?" I ask as we walk further from his class and closer to mine.

"Nah. It'll be fine. I'll just say coach needed something," he drawls, giving me another squeeze with the arm wrapped around my shoulder.

"Ahh, the almighty power of the quarterback," I tease.

"Stick around, and maybe I'll share some more of the special skills that come with being a QB," he drawls, wiggling his eyebrows salaciously.

I spot a clock past Collin's face and become momentarily distracted. Homeroom is practically over. My time with Ms. Rigs in her classroom, then with Collin in the hall quickly ate away at the short, forty-five-minute period.

Pointing to the numbers plastered against the wall, I ask, "Should we even walk to my homeroom? There's only eight minutes left."

"I can definitely think of a better way to spend eight minutes than waiting for you outside of your homeroom, but won't the school call your mom if you miss a class?" Collin asks, bringing me back to the reality of my situation.

It's so easy to forget about my problems whenever

Collin is around. He makes my past inconsequential and my reality glimmer with hope. He also turns me into a total sap, apparently.

I sigh. "Yeah, you're right. I need to go to class for the last few minutes at least… so I can hand over my note explaining why I missed class." My words are punctuated with a giggle and Collin joins with a laugh.

Together, we traverse the empty hallways, content and silent. Collin pauses near the lockers a couple dozen feet away from the door to my homeroom.

"I just want one more kiss," he drawls, answering my unasked question about our stop.

It's unclear who moves first, but within seconds his lips sear mine, claiming my soul and stealing my breath. I feel myself sagging against him as his mouth continues to devour mine.

Collin murmurs words between his kisses, but I barely catch half of them. Things like "Lucky" and "Beautiful" enter my consciousness, but they don't make any sense past the drug that is Collin Franzen's lips.

Our kiss eventually ends, and he releases me from his grasp. I immediately throw a hand out, bracing myself against the lockers next to us.

Collin laughs at my wobbly legs, as he places his hands underneath my elbows to keep me steady. All I can do in response to his teasing is wave my hand in the air, in a brush off motion. My thoughts aren't coherent enough to form a verbal response.

"Get to homeroom," he instructs, after giving me a minute to gather my wits. The second I twirl around; he swats at my butt.

"Hey!" I exclaim, not angry but pretending to be.

When my gaze meets Collin's heated emerald stare over my shoulder, he winks at me. I shoot him my sultriest look, then add an extra sway to my hips, keeping my eyes on him for my next few steps.

I catch Collin adjusting himself in his jeans and finally twist my face forward to cover my smirk. Being with Collin makes me feel powerful. A tempting seductress to my equally seductive man.

"I'll be here waiting for you," Collin drawls the moment my hand touches the door handle.

I send him a smile before I enter homeroom for the last three minutes of the class, "Okay, I'll be out in a few."

Chapter 27

Between early morning and after school cheer practices, my college prep sessions with Ms. Rigs, tutoring Luke in math in the late evenings, and using every spare second I can find to spend time with Collin, the days pass by in a blur.

Friday arrives and I wake to the loud, blaring beep of my bedside alarm, per usual. I fight the desire to fall back into sleep, as the noise interrupts an amazing dream I had of Collin and I sitting in front of Clara Hall at Berry College.

I'd like to think the thoughts were placed in my head by fate, but it's more likely they were due to staying up late last night to scroll through pictures of the campus with my guy.

When he brought the idea up on Monday, he said no pressure. Since then, he's been casually finding ways to work it into our conversations every day this week.

Forcing my groggy eyes open and thoughts of college away, I swat my hand at the alarm on my nightstand. Unlike my usual routine, I'm greeted with a rectangular box wrapped in pale pink paper with a shimmery silver ribbon tied into a bow, the second my eyes hit the bedside table. I blink twice, trying to see if I'm still dreaming, but when my eyes reopen, the present remains.

Giddily, I sit up in bed reaching for the gift. The second my hands touch it, the door to my bedroom creaks open and Collin steps inside. He walks to the bed and perches next to me, the plush material sinking under his weight, rolling me into him.

I'm not complaining though. I use the excuse to snuggle into his chest, with the pretty mystery box still resting in my lap. Collin settles an arm around my waist and when I glance up, his gem-colored gaze is focused on the gift.

"Aren't you going to open it?" Collin asks, his voice still coated in sleep.

"Is this from you?" I ask in lieu of answering.

"Of course," he replies with a laugh. "It's an early birthday present. Open it," he urges in a light, joyful tone.

He doesn't have to prod me again. I excitedly rip into the wrapping, tearing off the bow and shredding the paper to get to the box underneath. I can hear Collin laughing at my savage unwrapping, but I don't turn to acknowledge him. My gaze is fixated on the gift in my hands.

"Is this an iPhone?" I ask, finally pulling my mystified eyes away from the fancy box in my palms to look at Collin's face.

His expression is smug, and he shrugs. "I thought my girl deserved a phone from this century."

"This is way too much," I half-heartedly protest as I open the top of the box to see the clean, sleek phone nestled inside.

I've seen iPhones before, so many kids at school have them, but holding one meant for me, feels different. I'm unable to tear my eyes away.

Collin drops a kiss on my forehead. "I want you to have it. Part of it is selfish, I want our picture on your lock screen so everyone knows you're mine." He punctuates the half-joking words by moving his hands to my sides and digging into the ticklish spots he found during his last fiendish assault. "The only way to stop this is to say you'll keep it," he drawls.

I plop the box with the phone still safely nestled inside onto the soft mattress, so I don't drop it in my attempt to ward him off. I'm gasping for breath, by the time I finally surrender. I hold my hands up in front of me for the universal sign of "back off, I give up".

"Okay, okay," I say between deep inhales, attempting to regain my breath. "I relent; I'll keep your ridiculously expensive early birthday present. Just don't expect anything this big from me for your birthday," I warn, shooting him some serious side-eye.

There's no way I could afford to reciprocate a gift of this magnitude, even with my new and improved tutoring pay.

"I would never, Scout's honor" he replies, solemnly, placing a hand in front of him, with his middle three fingers up, and his thumb and pinky connected in front of them, as if it reinforces his words.

"Good," I reply, with one last side-eyed glance for good measure, then I pluck the box from the bed.

Removing the iPhone reverently, I flip it back and forth between my hands not knowing how to power it on. Holding the upgraded piece of tech makes me want to transition from my old phone immediately. I dump the rest of the gear from the box, searching for an instruction manual that doesn't seem to exist.

As if he knows exactly what I'm doing and why, Collin pauses my movements by placing a gentle kiss against my lips. The touch is a light caress, with affection and warmth lingering in his gaze as he moves away and our eyes connect.

Like the kind, thoughtful soul he is, he suggests, "Why don't we both get dressed, then I'll help you set up your iPhone before school?"

"Sounds good," I reply, giving him a lazy grin as I set my new phone and all its components onto the nightstand.

Collin returns the smile, then stands and ambles towards the door. My gaze stays fixated on his broad form as he exits the room. The second the door closes, I release a deep sigh, then pluck the box off the table, removing the phone from the thin cardboard and turning it over in my hands.

An iPhone.

The gift is extravagant. Too extravagant, but I know Collin would never accept me returning it. Guilt tries to weasel its way into my thoughts along with a whisper of, "You need to tell him the truth".

I shove the words and feelings aside, rising from my bed that feels less temporary every day and go to the closet for the distraction, and necessity of finding my clothes for the day.

Pulling open the white, wooden door, I grab my cheerleading uniform. Donning the blue and black gear still fills me with as much excitement as when I was told I made the squad, a mere seven days ago.

With extra pep, infused by my uniform and my morning interaction with Collin, I tie my dark hair back with my team-colored scrunchie, then slide into my sneakers. I add a few swipes of makeup, feeling a little extra, but loving it.

This feeling, this giddiness is how life is meant to be.

At least that's what I tell myself to assuage the last lingering tendrils of guilt.

Collin slips back into my room dressed in a pair of dark jeans and the royal blue and black jersey he'll wear in the game tonight. Like the cheerleaders with their uniforms, the footballers are expected to wear their jersey to school when there's an event happening, whether it's an assembly or a game.

He grabs my new phone while I'm fixing the lipstick I swiped on. I discreetly observe his reflection through my mirror, using the time to slyly watch his handsome face. His concentration is evident in his furrowed brow and pouted lower lip, as he clicks a button on the side of my new iPhone and presses a few things on the screen as he plugs it in.

I've never considered myself to be the kind of girl that loses all her sense over a guy, but Collin brings out a different side of me. I fight the urge to strut across the room and straddle him, as my eyes rake over his attractive features.

"I couldn't keep your old number. I hope that's okay," Collin drawls, interrupting my fantasy as his emerald gaze connects with mine in the mirror.

Transitioning to the new train of thought, I nod. I wasn't overly attached to my old phone number, so the thought doesn't bum me out.

"Are they going to mail me the bill or what?" I ask, curious how the gift of a phone works exactly.

Collin looks sheepish. "I paid for the first six months, but yeah, after that the bill will come to your trailer."

I hope the plan he chose isn't too expensive but knowing Collin he thought of everything before he purchased the gift, including cost. Since he's aware of my situation, he probably chose something reasonable and I shouldn't worry.

"I don't even know how I can thank you. It's so much," I say. Then I add, "But I love it. It's amazing, you're amazing." I punctuate the words, by twirling to face him, wearing a huge smile. I wish I knew a better way to communicate my gratitude, but this will have to do for now.

Collin grins at me, the rarely dim sparkle present in his eyes. He shoots me a quick wink, then returns his gaze to my new iPhone. I watch as he presses against the screen periodically, for another couple minutes.

When he finishes the set-up, his eyes sear into mine

and he drawls, "Okay, it's ready for you. How about we take a selfie to celebrate?"

I laugh but join him on the bed, cuddling into his side and grinning at the phone extended in his left hand. The shutter sound punctuates the first photo of both of us smiling. Before he can snap another shot, I grab his far cheek, holding him in place while I lightly kiss the one closer to me. The phone makes the shutter noise and I release him.

Not to be outdone, Collin grabs the back of my neck, using his grip to tug me closer. The shutter sounds as his lips touch mine, but I tune it out.

Deepening the kiss, I brand Collin. Using my lips to convey my appreciation for all he's done for me. More than that, I want to express how much I care about him, and consider him mine.

Even if it may not seem that way, when I finally work up the courage to tell the truth.

Chapter 28

S tands for the Golden Oaks Warriors are packed, teeming with a combination of rowdy students and proud parents. The night has gone seamlessly for Collin so far, his golden arm landing every throw in the hands of his wide receiver.

Each successful pass has amped up the crowd even further. This late in the game, it's unclear if the cheerleaders are pepping up the fans, or the crowd is feeding off its own, infectious energy.

The game has flown by as I jump up and down, chant, and cheer for my team, but also, mostly, for Collin.

Not one to be outdone by my guy's success, I'm ultra-focused on making my own night a win. I'm working extra hard, to ensure my pep-filled body lands every cheer and move required. Wanting to show the rest of the squad I deserve the opportunity I've been given.

Now, during the last few minutes of the game, the crowd's screams echo around us, anticipating a victory as our team is up fourteen points. I've never felt so alive or had so much fun.

Taking another peek at the scoreboard between chants, I realize the minutes of the game have dwindled down further than I thought. The large red digits start to countdown the final sixty seconds of the game; the numbers appearing and reappearing rapidly, as each second ticks by.

Summer rallies the squad and begins to step her feet over each other, side to side, in a grapevine-like motion. She shouts the first word to our school's fight song, "Fight."

I fall in step with the rest of the girls, mimicking Summer and together we echo the word, "Fight."

She stops her feet and yells, "Dominate." Then performs a flawless toe-touch mid-air.

The crowd joins in this time screaming, "Dominate" while the rest of us mimic her toe-touch to varying degrees of perfection.

My attention leaves Summer for a brief second, just in time to catch the Warriors run their final play. Eyes laser-focused on Collin, watching as he throws the football into a high arc towards the end zone.

The wide receiver, already in position, leaps into the air, cradling the ball in his fingers as the buzzer sounds across the stadium.

Our side of the bleachers goes nuts. Students and parents cheer, clap, and stomp, the noise thundering across the grass, making it feel like the whole stadium might collapse under the weight of their enthusiasm.

Dragging my eyes away from Collin as he celebrates in the end zone, I join the rest of the squad, jumping, shrieking and waving my pom poms in the air. Despite screaming at the top of my lungs, the words are barely audible past the sounds of the crowd.

Abandoning the fight cheer, she started, Summer shouts, "Go Golden Oak Warriors!!!"

The rest of the squad and I copy her, yelling our team's name. I add a loud "Wooo." Then I jump with all the girls in a circle, our arms wrapped around each other's shoulders.

We did it. Our team won!

Collin won!

While screeching for our victory with the squad, I slyly eye the footballers as they huddle at the sideline listening to their coach. Almost everyone in the group is wearing a massive smile, clearly stoked over their killer start to the season.

A pair of emerald eyes briefly connect with mine, and Collin shoots a wink before moving his attention back to his team.

I remain on the sidelines, loitering next to the cheer risers with the rest of the squad, as the stadium slowly empties.

Some fans also linger, as if lurking will provide them the opportunity to personally congratulate the players. The team is engrossed in their coach's words though, and eventually even the most die-hard fans file out.

When the players finally grab their bags from the team bench, the squad begins to move towards the locker rooms as well, our movements synced with the guys.

As he passes, Collin grabs my palm and gives it a brief squeeze and release. My steps slow, but Collin doesn't stop to chat, he just continues his trek to the boy's locker room. Lingering for a few seconds longer, I watch as his firm backside, clad in tight spandex, disappears from view.

Regular Collin is attractive, but Collin in football gear? He's a total jaw dropper.

Once he's completely out of sight, I glance around, surprised to find myself alone in the tunnel leading out of the stadium. I swiftly scurry towards the girl's locker room and yank open the door separating me from the squad, wary of being in the abandoned area by myself.

Katie attacks me with a hug just inside the doorway. "You were sooooo amazing!! You're a total natural, I'm so glad you're on the squad. Ahhh!"

I return her tight hug wearing a grin so huge, it's making my cheeks ache. "Thanks girl, we all did great."

"Yes! Let's grab our bags then I'll wait in the parking lot with you. For *Collin*." She sings Collin's name like she's going to break out into a chant or a song. The one that starts with "First comes love, then comes marriage…" immediately pops into my head.

I hurry across the locker room away from her to snag my gym bag, hoping if I'm far enough away, she won't start. Her giggle follows me as I sprint in the opposite direction, clearly reading my intentions of escape and finding it hilarious.

Ignoring her, I turn the combination dial on my locker. I scoop up my cheer bag from the inside, and shut the door. Spinning the lock to clear it, I complete the motions on autopilot while thoughts whirl in my head.

Her teasing honestly doesn't bother me, I'm too amped up to feel anything other than happiness. Plus, I like a good joke as much as the next girl, but I am also one hundred percent not ready to talk about my quickly manifesting feelings for Collin Franzen.

Thankfully, Katie seems to get the hint. When I return to her spot near the door she flits out, silently holding it open by the outside handle. She drops the subject entirely, becoming deep in thought.

I don't interrupt, keeping my mouth shut as we make our way to the parking lot. We reach Collin's SUV and the two of us lean against it in sync.

All the cheerleaders filter by as we wait, with varying reactions. Isabelle sneers at me, which is no surprise and Heather just waves.

"Bye, see you ladies tomorrow," Summer calls as she passes, one of the few to verbally say goodbye.

My attention shifts away from the rest of the squad without registering their parting words. Instead, my eyes focus on the exit from the locker rooms, waiting for Collin.

Soon it's just Katie and I remaining. I'm grateful for both my new friend and my new phone as we wait in the empty, dark area with shadows looming ominously in the silent night air.

Katie's words startle me as they slip out in a whisper, "Do you think Alex likes me?"

"Like Alex from tubing?" I ask, not expecting to have a sudden bout of boy talk.

Katie giggles and smacks my arm. "Oh my gosh and from the football team. You're like totally oblivious to all the other boys besides Franzen, aren't you?"

A light flush graces my cheeks at the truth of her words, but I simply shrug and divert. "Well, I haven't paid much attention to Alex, so I'm not sure," I reply, answering her original question. "Why do you ask?

"I think I'm going to text him tonight and see if he wants to be my date to my party tomorrow."

My head whips towards Katie's in surprise. It's not that I didn't expect her to date, but this is the first time she's mentioned Alex, to my knowledge.

I feel like a terrible friend for not knowing more about her love life and I'm also astonished she thinks someone wouldn't like her. Katie is rich, pretty, and nice. Girls like her are on a different level than girls like me. She's a total catch.

Katie is oblivious to my shock, she's too busy worrying her lower lip between her teeth; her eyes appearing distant as she stares across the parking lot.

Tapping her arm lightly to get her attention, I respond, "I think you should ask him. There's no reason not to. If he can't see how great you are, then he's a total idiot."

"Thank you," Katie says, immediately snapping out of her funk and jumping to her tiptoes to give me a quick hug.

She pulls out her phone, then continues, "You're so right. I'm going to text him now before I lose my nerve! Maybe he'll respond from the locker room or by the time I make it to my car."

I don't bother to reply, as her attention is completely focused on her phone screen. Her fingers fly across the glass front as she types her message to Alex and then waits for a response. I rest against Collin's SUV again, wondering what's taking the boys so long.

Collin finally emerges from the locker room ten minutes later, no longer dressed in his gear and hair still damp from a shower. He's walking swiftly, making a beeline towards his SUV where I'm posted with Katie.

The rest of his team straggles out behind him, but he pays them no mind. His intentions to reach us are clear by his long strides and determined expression.

When he reaches us, he tucks me into his side, laying a soft kiss on my forehead and whispering, "Hey, you girls did great tonight."

His gaze moves from my face to fully acknowledge Katie and he asks, "Katie, do you have a ride home?" His eyes don't move away from her, but he slowly begins inching us towards the door, his hand resting on the handle before she replies.

"Yeah, I drove myself," she responds, her tone filled with mirth.

Collin drawls, "Okay cool. Well, we're headed out

now." He punctuates the words by ripping open the passenger side door.

I find myself hiding a smile at Collin's sudden rush to get me alone. Well that, and Katie's super dramatic wink over Collin urgently wanting to get me home.

A few of the footballers finally reach the parking lot and they begin catcalling Franzen as they see me wrapped up in his arms. Collin just flips them off, taking my bag before hoisting me inside the car.

I hear the trunk open within seconds, indicating he ran to the back. Directly after, I hear the noise of Collin swiftly tossing both our bags inside before he joins me in the front.

"What's the hurry?" I ask, teasing Collin as he buckles his seatbelt and immediately turns the key, starting the ignition.

Collin's heated stare finds mine, before flitting back to the windshield as his SUV flies down the road. "The rest of my family is out of town tonight for my brother's soccer game tomorrow... I thought we could enjoy having the entire house to ourselves without having to worry about being interrupted."

"Oh." Collin is rushing us home to be alone.

Like completely alone.

In his giant house.

With a lot of empty beds.

The line of thought has a combination of heat and trepidation blooming low in my belly. Before an emotion can win the fight and take over, we pull into the driveway of the Franzen house, making record time with Collin's sudden lead foot.

I slowly prep myself to get out of the car, but Collin has no patience left. He yanks open my door and sweeps me up bridal style, carrying me into the house, and bounding up the stairs three at a time, even with my body cradled in his arms. Collin doesn't let my feet touch the ground until after I hear the click of his door latch.

The plush carpet, his heated gaze, and the slow, intense build up that's been happening since I've met Collin all combine, allowing an emotion to successfully consume me.

Stepping forward, I grab onto Collin's cheeks and tug his face towards me. The second our lips touch, he takes over, claiming me with his kiss. His mouth moves against mine in deep, drugging sweeps as his hands begin to rove over my body.

I relax against him with a sigh, my legs no longer wanting to support my weight as Collin continues his assault on my mouth, fanning the flames of desire higher with his every move.

Collin Franzen is, without a doubt, the best kisser in all of Alabama. Maybe even the world.

My mind empties of all other thoughts, every cell of my being consumed by the connection of our mouths. It isn't until Collin tugs at the side zipper to my cheer top then yanks it over my head, that my attention is diverted. I shimmy out of my skirt, feeding off his urgency and helping him undress me. My uniform quickly becomes a forgotten heap on the floor.

I force my arms to stay down at my sides. Fighting the urge to cover up as I stand next to Collin's bed in nothing but black spanks and a black sports bra, while he remains fully clothed.

Collin's eyes rake over my near naked form and he leans closer to my lips. I try to continue our kiss from earlier, but he hovers just out of reach with a sparkle in his scorching gaze.

"You are so beautiful, McKenzie. I'm a lucky guy."

After his words, he seals his lips to mine once more. He kisses me like I'm his salvation, placing his hands underneath my bottom to lift me up.

My legs wrap around him naturally as he carries me backwards to his bed and deposits me softly onto the plush mattress. He takes a step back like he's mentally photographing the image, storing the memory of me in his bed for the rest of eternity.

"Seems a little unfair, that you're so overdressed," I tease in a breathy voice that doesn't sound like it belongs to me, interrupting his slow perusal of my near naked form.

Collin smirks and tugs on the bottom of his t-shirt, yanking it over his head one-handed. I scoot backwards on the bed, settling into the pillows as I take in his defined abs. My gaze travels upwards to wander across his broad shoulders, drinking in every inch of exposed muscle before landing on his chiseled face.

It should be illegal for this man to wear a shirt.

Collin chuckles, making me realize I spoke the words out loud. Unembarrassed, I shrug and lounge back onto his fluffy pillows with a "so what" expression. It's the truth and he should know it. I would almost say the world should know it, but I'm too greedy to share Collin like that.

He winks at me then slowly pops the button of his jeans open, making a show of removing his last vestiges of clothing. He stares at me with intensity as he drags his zipper downward, each prong taking seconds to separate from its neighbor.

I've felt what Collin's hiding in his jeans, but I've never seen it. The sudden anticipation of this moment is slowly killing me, and I can tell from his smirk, he knows it.

My muscles tense as I prepare to rise and hurry Collin along, but he shoots me a look. One that says, "If you get up, you'll never see what's in these jeans." Therefore, I do what any sane girl would do and relax into the pillows to enjoy the show.

When he finally steps out of his jeans, revealing a pair of snug boxer-briefs, I feel more worked up than I did from his touches. Collin only pauses for a brief moment, allowing me a glance at his muscular thighs that isn't nearly long enough to satisfy my hungry eyes, then he stalks towards me.

Grabbing onto my ankles he drags me down to the end of the bed, causing me to release a squeal of surprise. He begins kissing up my legs, pausing on the soft, sensitive skin of my upper thigh, and digging in slightly with his teeth.

The squeal transforms into a gasp, which quickly morphs into a moan when he hovers above my center, his hot breath hitting me through my panties.

In a clash of hands, the last articles of my clothing

are removed. Collin stops, standing near the edge of the mattress, drinking in my naked body displayed on his bed.

"McKenzie, you are gorgeous," he drawls, his voice a combination of reverence and lust. Tipping forward, he kisses my abdomen. "And smart." Another kiss, this one at the center of my chest. "And determined." His mouth locks around my right nipple and he sucks on the sensitive skin, rolling the bud in his mouth before abandoning it. "And fierce."

Collin reverses directions, his breath hitting my center and I swear I hear the words "And mine" before he plunges in, licking and suckling the sensitive bundle of skin between my legs with ferocity.

My back bows off the bed at the contact and a heated frenzy builds within me. In seconds, Collin has me gasping and in minutes, I'm calling his name as my legs tense, preparing me for the inevitable fall over the edge.

It happens with unexpected intensity, my muscles locking as waves of pleasure wash over me, prolonged by Collin's tongue continuing to worship my body, devouring me like I'm his last meal.

He finally stops laving at my center as the last aftershock of my orgasm shudders through my body. He slides upwards against me, his skin gliding across mine until his tongue stops on my chest, licking and teasing my left nipple before he continues his journey to join me further up the bed.

When his face reaches mine, he hovers just above it, his breath fanning across my lips as his eyes search mine.

The blazing emerald orbs look like they're trying to read my thoughts, as if staring intensely can tell you what someone else is thinking.

I close the gap between us, licking the seam of his lips until they part, allowing me to deepen the kiss. The movement of my tongue against his, releases Collin from his trance and his hands find my breasts, kneading and rubbing until I'm aching for him all over again.

In one smooth movement, he frees himself from his last article of clothing, his boxers joining the rest of our garments scattered across the floor. Without pause, he aligns himself with my core, and connects our bodies in the most intimate of ways. I gasp, as he slides into me in one slow movement, until he's sheathed to the hilt.

Collin pauses to stare at my face, with reverence, affection, and lust all bundled into one expression. Each breath I take reminds me how deeply he's seated inside me; how full my body feels.

Realizing he's waiting for my permission to continue, ensuring I'm not uncomfortable; I shoot him a sultry smile and a small nod.

He begins to move with slow, determined strokes, his hands roaming my body, kneading and tweaking, and rubbing. It's as if Collin is touching me everywhere, all at once, kindling the fire in my lower belly into an inferno with each calculated touch.

I meet him, thrust for thrust, our bodies in sync up to the moment where I cry out, pulses of pleasure zipping through my veins. Seconds later, Collin tenses above me, his muscles locking as he groans his own release.

With one last, small thrust, he places his damp forehead against mine, eyes closed as we both pant to regain our breath.

I bask in the afterglow, my entire being feeling heavy, but sated. Lazily dragging one eyelid open, I take in Collin's face centimeters away from mine.

I'm flooded with a nameless feeling that relaxes me further into bed, my eye drifting shut again as my breathing syncs with Collin's. Our bodies are still connected and every inhale feels more intimate than the last.

After a few minutes, Collin lifts his head, placing a soft kiss on my forehead, whispering, "I'll be right back."

I watch his firm backside as he strides away, completely comfortable in his naked skin. He reappears a few moments later holding a washcloth. He uses the warm, damp fabric to swipe between my legs and I fight hard to keep my embarrassment at bay. It's a sweet, but incredibly intimate gesture, and one that no one has ever done before.

"Thank you," I whisper as he finishes.

Collin smiles down at my face with a gentle expression, then uses his golden boy quarterback arm to throw the fabric into his hamper. The cloth lands perfectly inside the bin on his first try. He turns back to face me in the bed and gathers me up in his arms, pulling my still naked back against his chest.

Leaning over me, he kisses my cheek and drawls, "Goodnight, McKenzie."

I whisper back, "Goodnight Collin."

There's more I want to say, but I'm not sure how to

voice my feelings. The click of the bedside lamp sounds, and the room is bathed in darkness.

Sated, warm, content, and comfortable, I fall asleep almost instantly wrapped in the warm luxury of his arms, before I can figure out the feelings coursing through my veins.

Chapter 29

Katie arrives to pick me up early the next morning, too early for me to feel completely human after staying up so late. She barely gives me ten minutes to get ready before shoving my tired butt down the stairs in the direction of the front door.

A hand grips the top of my shoulder, twirling me around when I'm about halfway across the Franzen's entryway. The second my spin stops, my eyes lock with an emerald gaze.

"Were you trying to escape before saying goodbye?" Collin grumbles, as he buries his face in my hair, still wet from the quick shower my warden, Katie, permitted.

"I thought you went back to sleep," I reply, the words garbled by his chest.

Feeling the shake of his head against my scalp, I reel back and tap my lips against his in a brief peck. "Sorry, I'll make it up to you later," I whisper, pulling away from his grasp.

Before I can fully escape, Collin chases after me, snatching me up in his arms and sealing his mouth to mine. I keep my mouth closed, mindful of Katie and the promise I made to help prepare for the party.

My resolve quickly flees as Collin licks and nips the seam of my lips, his determination forcing me to relent. Deepening the kiss, he continues his assault until I release a moan and sag against him.

"Oh, come on guys, did you forget I was here, again?" Katie groans, interrupting us mid-make out.

Collin chuckles against my lips, but separates his face a few inches from mine. "It's your punishment for stealing my girl so early on a Saturday," he drawls, his eyes seeking Katie's over my head.

"Ugh, you're the worst, Franzen," Katie exclaims dramatically, punctuating her words with an eye roll.

Gathering my wits, I drag myself away from Collin to end this argument before it starts, squeezing his hand one last time before stepping closer to the door to join Katie. "Sorry," I laugh. "I'm ready for real now, we can go."

She nods and pivots on her heel, tugging the door open and striding into the early morning sun. I trail behind her, shooting one last lingering glance at Collin, as he leans against the doorframe, shirtless, with his delicious abs on full display. He winks at me, staying in the open door, and my line of view, until I turn around.

The sleep-deprived and Collin-lusting fog surrounding my brain, is permeated by Katie's chipper mood, barely.

"Girl! You look exhausted. Does Collin not let you

sleep?" She asks the second my butt hits the leather seat in her hot pink bug.

My cheeks flush, as I recall the reason I didn't get much rest last night. "We were both just hyped after the game yesterday," I reply with half-honesty, working hard to tame the blush threatening to cover my cheeks, prior to Katie noticing it. "Also, I could've walked, you didn't have to drive over here," I add, redirecting the topic of conversation to something involving less naked Collin.

"It's no big deal," Katie replies. "I know how much you hate mornings and I wanted your help prepping for my party. I still have to prepare the food, we need to hang some streamers, and I want to leave enough time to get ready together. If I waited for you to come over until two or something when you woke up, it would be too late to get everything done." Her tone is matter of fact as she utters the blunt words, and honestly, her assessment is accurate.

"Fair enough," I agree with a shrug as she pulls into her driveway after the two-minute journey from the Franzen house. "Don't your parents mind that you're throwing a party for a bunch of teenagers?" I ask.

"Nah," she replies as she exits the car and ambles towards the front door of her rather intimidating house. "They're never really home. As long as I clean up the mess, they won't care."

I follow her into the entry and toe off my shoes, nodding at her words. Instead of following that line of conversation, which seems to be a sore spot, I redirect to the party. "What are we doing first?"

Katie taps her fingernails against her chin, then

shoots a finger into the air like a lightbulb has gone off. "Let's go pick our outfits, then curl our hair. I want to have enough time for the curls to fall and look more natural."

I'm not great at hair styling, so I simply agree even though it seems strange to do our hair nine hours before any guests are set to arrive. "Sounds good to me."

"Race ya," Katie exclaims before bolting past me to rush up the stairs. It takes a second for her words to register, but once they do, I sprint into action. Bounding up the steps, I reach the landing a mere half second after her.

"Cheater," I tease, while resting against the bannister to catch my breath.

She shrugs, appearing smug as she wanders down the hallway. Once in her room, she immediately enters her massive closet, rifling through some of the clothes hung on the far wall. She emerges within a few minutes, carrying an armful of dresses.

"Okay, I love all of these," she announces, as she lays the pile across her bed. "Let's see which ones you want to try on."

Flipping through the stack she holds a black, shimmery number against me. "No!" We both say at the same time. Then giggle together in sync.

She lifts three more in rapid succession: a lime green cocktail dress, a sparkly purple concoction, and then something of a vague shape made primarily of pink ruffles. The last one has horror pumping through my brain, the instant she picks it up, but thankfully, she's quick to add it to the pile of discards.

"Hmm, I just don't feel like any of these are 'The One', ya know?" Her eyes continue to scan the pile of hangers while she taps her fingers against her leg, appearing deep in thought.

"Do you need to pick a dress too?" I ask, interrupting her when the silence drags on, eating away at our time to prepare everything else in the house, while we stand here.

"No, I've had it picked out for *months*," She says, immediately breaking free of her funk. "Ooh, I know. I'll go put it on and show you, so you have an idea of the vibe, then we can search in my closet together to find your dress. This is going to be so fun," she squeals, clapping her hands together as she rushes towards the bathroom, where a garment bag is hanging off the top of the door.

Seconds after the latch clicks, my new, fancy phone makes a loud chiming noise from my back pocket. "Is that mine?" Katie shouts from the bathroom. "You can open it and read it to me, I don't have a passcode."

"It's actually mine," I reply sheepishly.

The door to her bathroom flings open and she rushes across the room with her same clothes on. "Oh my gosh, you got a new phone? Letmesee!"

I pass it to her and she immediately "oohs" over the background photo I set. It's the selfie from yesterday, when I was kissing Collin's cheek. Every time I see the picture, it makes me happy, so I set it as the display on my phone.

"Ugh, you two are so dreamy. Like the perfect couple I swear. Light and dark, wholesome and sultry…" she continues as she walks back into the bathroom and I laugh.

After thinking about her words for a second, I ask, "Wait, are you saying I'm not wholesome?"

Katie cackles as she closes the door, just in time to block the slipper I throw from the floor. "Just wait until you see my dress, all will be forgiven," she yells through the wood separating us.

"Yeah, yeah," I mutter, faking my upset more than anything else at this point. My phone dings again, as if reminding me I have an unread message. I pluck it off the bed and see the alert is from Collin.

It takes me a few clicks to remember how to unlock the screen and when I finally read his message, I giggle.

Collin: **Hey hot stuff, do you and Katie want anything from the coffee shop… thinking about heading over there.**

"Hey, Collin is going to grab coffee, do you want anything?" I yell to Katie.

At the same time, I type back: **Just admit it, you miss me already and this is an excuse to come see me.**

Three dots pop up in a bubble and I stare at the screen. I'm distracted when a loud crash comes from inside the bathroom, causing me to jump from my seat.

"I'm okay, I'm okay," Katie shouts. Her words do little to help tame my now racing heart, but I sit down anyways. "Can you ask him to get me a mocha Frappuccino?"

"Sure," I reply.

Unlocking my phone again, I see I have another

message from Collin: **Maybe... I will neither confirm nor deny.**

With a grin, I respond: **We will take 2 Mocha Frappuccino's please, Professor Plum.**

I tuck my phone into my pocket just in time to see the bathroom door fly open and smack into the wall next to it, causing a small piece of plaster to break off.

Katie doesn't acknowledge the damage, instead she yells, "Ta-da!" Throwing her arms wide open in front of her.

The dress she's chosen for her party is miniscule. It's sleeveless, black, and barely goes past her bottom. Even though I would never be comfortable in something so small, Katie is rocking it. The spandex-y fabric hugs every curve, showing off her hourglass figure and toned legs, earned from the hours she's put into cheer.

"You look fantastic," I say with honesty.

She struts forward with her hands on her hips, then does a small twirl once she's a quarter of the way into the room.

"You really think so? Do you think Alex will like it? I just really like him and I've been having such a hard time getting his attention. Although he did agree to come over early and be my date for my party." She takes another step closer and groans, "Ughh, guys are so hard to read."

"I think you look like a total bombshell. Alex would be an idiot if he didn't notice you in this dress," I respond with my earnest opinion. Katie looks like a supermodel in her black mini dress and a simple pair of black stilettos.

"Thanks girl," she replies, her voice sincere, but a little less rambunctious than usual. Shaking her arms out, she does a dramatic twirl. "So, this is the kind of look we're going for. Do you want to help me search for your outfit?"

"Of course," I respond, standing from my perch at the edge of her bed.

I follow her into the enormous closet, it's the same size or bigger than my room at the Franzen's. Crossing over the threshold, I inhale deeply, then blurt out the thought that has recently been plaguing my every moment. Since Katie asked me for advice, maybe I should ask her for advice too.

"I've been keeping a secret."

"Ookay, well are you going to tell me what it is," Katie asks after a long pause.

"Err, no," I stammer. "It's not a secret from you... It's a secret from Collin and I'm not really sure what to do. Do you think I should tell him?"

Katie taps her fingers against her thigh, wearing a frown on her normally chipper face. "Without knowing what the secret is, I don't know if I can give you solid advice," she replies.

I open my mouth to protest. I'm not ready to tell her yet, especially not before I've told Collin, but she holds both her hands out in front of her, pausing my words.

"I'm not asking you to tell me what your secret is, just trying to give full disclosure," she says in an uncharacteristically calm voice. "If I were you, I would ask myself: 'Would this information hurt Collin, if he were to find out from someone other than myself?' And if the answer to that question is yes, I think we both know what you need to do."

"Yeah, you're probably right," I admit in a quiet whisper, after a brief hesitation.

"That sounded like 'I'm going to tell him' and I approve one-hundred percent, but wait until after my party, so you don't ruin it" she says with a laugh, her tone returning to its normal spastic volume and pitch. "Now let's get you a dress for this shindig so we can get my house ready!"

Chapter 30

My phone buzzes against my side with an incoming message. The vibration rattles my rib cage, due to the position of my iPhone tucked in the side of my tight, ruby-colored sheath that Katie lent me.

I carefully manipulate the slim piece of technology out from the body-hugging fabric to check the incoming text.

Collin: **I'm downstairs, come let me in.**

I push the phone back into my dress and skip down the stairs with glee. Even though it's been less than eight hours since I saw him last—when he brought Katie and I coffee, then was promptly kicked out—I still miss him.

Upon reaching the front door, I pause to smooth down my borrowed outfit, and take a deep breath.

Grasping the handle, I swing the heavy door inward to reveal Collin, waiting on the porch with an easy smile. His blonde hair is effortlessly disheveled; the longer strands on top, slicked back in a haphazard manner, looking like maybe he tried, but not too much. My eyes run down the length of his body, soaking his black button-up with the sleeves rolled to the elbow paired with dark, form-fitting jeans.

My fingers itch to touch him and its sheer force of will that keeps them tucked to my sides while his eyes peruse my body like mine did his.

I recall the mirror in Katie's room, remembering how the ruby-colored dress emphasizes my smaller, ahem, assets with a deep-V, halter neck, dropping into a short, flared skirt. If the heat in Collin's eyes is any indication, he approves of the dress Katie and I chose.

"Get a room, you two," Katie yells from the landing at the top of the stairs. "Wait, eww. No. Don't get a room, this is my house. Attend my party and after it ends go home together and get a room at your house," she corrects, laughing at the end of her chastisement.

Collin's warm chuckle mingles with my giggle and when our eyes connect, some of the intense attraction has lifted, leaving only warm affection in its place.

He steps inside, shutting the door behind him before tugging me into his side and placing a light kiss on my mouth. I temper the urge to chase his lips as they leave mine, mindful of our audience that is, apparently, a little judgey when it comes to displays of affection.

The two of us stand at the bottom of the steps, wrapped around each other, waiting for Katie. Sensing our full attention, she makes a dramatic entrance, pointing her toes before each step, as she struts down the stairs. She does a slow twirl when she reaches the foyer, her hands pointing out to her sides with her palms arched like a prima ballerina.

"Looking good, Katie," Collin drawls, sensing her need for a compliment.

Katie giggles and preens under the small praise and my insides warm at how truly kind and thoughtful Collin is to everyone.

"Is there anything left I can help with?" He asks.

"Well, why don't you come look at our spread in the kitchen and let us know if you think we're missing anything? I'm worried we don't have enough food or drinks, but Kenzie says it looks fine," she replies as she makes her way towards the kitchen.

Collin nods and Katie leads us down the sleek, modern hallway into another enormous portion of the house. The sight past the doorway still makes my jaw drop, despite spending the better half of the day in here.

Huge, pale-gray cabinets with fancy bronze handles take up most of the space, all topped by a matte, black countertop. The walls behind the cabinets are covered in a pale cream and gray patterned tile.

It's a mix of the modern style from the rest of the home, with a slightly warmer farmhouse appearance, but mostly it just feels expensive. Like, don't touch anything in case you break it because it would take two lifetimes to pay it back, expensive.

The doorbell rings before Collin is able to inspect the food situation and Katie squeals, "Our first guest. Ahh!"

She rushes towards the door as Collin yells at her back, "What am I? Chopped Liver?"

His total dad joke causes me to giggle, the chortling sound still leaving my throat when Katie reappears at the entrance of the kitchen with Alex in tow.

"The party has arrived," he shouts the second he steps onto the tiled floor of the massive chef's kitchen. "Hey man," he says to Collin, doing one of those bro-hug-pat things. Then he turns to me and does a weird little half-bow, a hank of his dark brown hair falling over his forehead with the motion. "McKenzie."

I laugh, then reply, "Hey Alex... We were just wondering what to do to pass the time until everyone else arrives. Any suggestions?"

I'm just making things up as I go along, figuring Katie wouldn't want her date to start by asking him to review the food selection.

Alex's eyes scan the island laden with snacks before touching on the far countertop, which is covered in bottles of booze and mixers, with a keg on the floor next to it.

His eyes light up and he turns to Katie giving her a wink. "How 'bout some shots?" He asks.

"Sure," she replies with an easy smile, her star-struck eyes remaining fixated on Alex since he arrived.

The three of us make our way to the far counter and the boys start to argue about what kind of alcohol is best for shots and whether we need a chaser. Katie ignores them pulling me against her side with a giggle. "He's so hot, right?"

My eyes instantly run over Collin again, even though I'm almost positive she's talking about her date for the night, not mine.

NICOLE MARSH

I force my eyes to leave him and objectively take in Alex. He's about four inches shorter than Collin but he looks good in a pair of slim black jeans and a white V-neck. He has dark brown hair and is brawny from the amount of time he must spend working out, in order to be a starter on the defensive line for the Warriors.

"Yeah, he's hot," I whisper back after I finish my perusal. "I think you two are cute together, and I'm happy he came."

Katie squeals quietly, "Ahh, I'm glad my bestie approves." In a more conspiring tone, she tacks on, "I put a sign on the door so people know just to let themselves in, this way we can hang out without getting interrupted."

"So devious," I say with a laugh.

"Don't you know it," she replies, winking. Louder she adds, "Okay boys, what's our poison?"

Tugging me forward, we join them, standing together between the two boys at the counter in front of four shot glasses filled with a clear-colored liquid.

"Vodka," Alex says, his voice tinged with pride indicating this was his selection. "Then we have some fruit punch for a chaser," he adds, pointing at the red solo cups I had previously overlooked.

Katie scrunches her nose but accepts the plastic shot glass Alex hands to her. "Okay, to senior year!" She shouts, plugging her nose and downing the liquid in one go.

I follow her lead, swallowing the contents all at once, but unlike Katie, I barely choke back the gag at the strong alcohol taste. I quickly snatch up the red solo cup

268

waiting for me and chug half of it to rid my mouth of the disgusting taste.

This shot seems super strong compared to the small amount of vodka I've had in the past. No one else seems to be having the same reaction, so I keep my mouth shut about the flavor as I put down my chaser.

The boys pour another round as a small ruckus sounds from down the hall. "More guests," Katie exclaims, then louder, "Hey, we're down the hall in the kitchen."

A group of three people I don't recognize wander into the room and Alex quirks a brow, "Shots?" He asks, holding up the vodka to punctuate his words. The group nods their assent and we all scoot down the counter to make room for the newcomers.

"Hey," a guy says, smiling down at me as he tries to slide into the small space of counter separating Katie and I.

Collin growls low in his throat, and I smirk as he not-so-subtly squeezes me tighter against him. He glares at the guy until he takes the hint and moves further down the countertop.

I run a hand gently across Collin's arm after the guy walks away, until he finally stops staring daggers at his back and glances down at me.

"What was that?" I ask.

"Nothing, I just hate that guy," he responds, keeping his arm tightly wound around my waist while he accepts a shot glass from Katie.

She hands me one next, leaning in and stage whispering, "It's kind of hot he's so possessive."

NICOLE MARSH

Alex guffaws, but Collin ignores him, raising his little shot glass and drawling, "To the Warriors." He places the plastic against his lips, and my eyes follow the lines of his throat as he gulps the shot down.

Tearing my gaze away from my guy, I follow suit. This time the alcohol goes down much more smoothly than before. I pull the plastic away from my lips, and immediately connect with Collin's intense gaze. It sears into me as he tilts forward, placing a gentle peck against my lips.

When we separate, the kitchen is more crowded than it was seconds prior, and another guy approaches the small space between Katie and I. Expecting Collin to go all caveman again, I willingly tuck myself into his side, hoping to avoid another scene.

I'm surprised when Collin pivots us together, drawling, "Jeremy!"

Realizing it's someone we know; I detach from Collin and give Jeremy a short hug. "Hey!" I exclaim, before my arms briefly wrap around his back.

He pats me in return, but he seems to barely register who I am, as his eyes remain intent on Katie. After releasing me, he joins her at the counter, accepting a plastic shot glass while grinning down at her.

Interesting.

This time after accepting my plastic glass, I yell, "To getting fucked up."

The group around me cheers and whoops as we all down our shots together. I can feel Collin's muted laugh rumbling against my side and when I catch his eye, there's a definite sparkle there. I smirk at him and he leans down, laying another light kiss on my lips.

The next round of shots is dispersed, and Jeremy wraps an arm low around Katie's waist before he shouts, "To Katie!"

I down the clear liquid in one go, my eyes absorbing Jeremy's interaction with my best friend, wondering if there's more to the story there.

After I place my shot glass back on the counter, I suddenly find my bladder has hit its limit. Disentangling myself from Collin and dragging my gaze from the Jeremy-Katie-Alex situation next to me, I stage-whisper, "I have to pee."

As I take a slightly unsteady step away, Katie's eyes catch mine from her place between Jeremy and Alex. "Do you need me to go with?" She mouths with exaggerated movements, so I can read her lips.

Waving her off with my hand, I wind my way around the bodies filling the kitchen and down the hall to the half bath. Surprisingly, there's no line at this point, so I walk right in and click the lock.

I finish up, drying my hands and attempt to focus on my reflection. My eyes are doing a poor job of focusing after so many shots, and I struggle to check my appearance. Giving up, I unlock the door and step back into the hallway.

On unsteady legs, I amble down the hall to find Collin. I check the kitchen, scanning the swarm of bodies but he isn't there, so I move towards the living room instead.

While I walk, I pass Katie and Alex standing

wrapped around each other talking to another group of people from our school and I do an internal fist pump.

Trying to subtly inspect their body language, I notice they make a super cute couple. Then I spot Jeremy, standing to the side nursing a drink while he stares longingly at Katie.

Wavering, I wonder if I should approach him or not, but he turns away, joining a conversation with someone else. Decision made for me; I continue to the living room. When I finally reach my destination, Collin spots my wobbly knees and jumps up to help me.

"Woah, McKenzie. I think you went too hard already," he drawls, with amusement tinging his tone. "Why don't we get you home? You don't look like you're going to last another three minutes anyways," he says.

"Home sounds good," I reply with a yawn.

Collin chuckles and swoops me into his arms. I nestle my face into his neck and bask in both his warmth and sunshine smell.

I whisper quietly against his neck, "You're such a good guy, way different than I expected. I hope you still like me, once you know everything."

After I utter the words, the alcohol combined with the lulling motion of Collin's steps helps sleep to claim me.

Chapter 31

I wake slowly to Collin's fingers lazily drawing circles on my lower abdomen. My back is flush against his front, nestled perfectly against his body like we were made for each other. The combination of his heat and the calm movement of his fingers make me feel languid, similar to a cat stretching out in the sun relaxing.

Per usual, I don't want to leave the coziness of Collin or his bed, but I also want to go home and check on the trailer today. I haven't been back in over a week, and it makes sense to return occasionally, to ensure nothing happens to it while I'm staying with the Franzens.

"Hey, I wanted to go check on my trailer. Do you think you could drive me over there today?" I ask Collin, my body sinking further into his, a direct contradiction to my words.

Collin's fingers leave my belly to cup my chin and he gently tugs my face towards him. His lips press against mine in a soft caress. When he pulls his head back, his gaze is heated, but I glimpse something else there too. Something like affection, but stronger.

"Yeah, let's get dressed and go check it out right now. Then on our way back we can stop and grab some brunch downtown? I know somewhere that serves breakfast until late on Sundays," he offers, his voice as warm and relaxed as his body.

"Ooh, instead of brunch, could we go see Annabelle and grab a Frappuccino and a bagel?" I ask. My tone is giddy over the prospect of returning to the place one might consider Collin and I's first date spot.

"No waffles today?" Collin asks, his tone teasing.

"You feed me waffles almost every day, I think I can skip them just this once," I reply cheekily as I roll off the bed.

Collin reaches out a hand to swat my butt. I easily dodge the attempt, darting to the door and letting myself out with a laugh.

Down the hall, I hurriedly don a sundress and slip on a pair of sandals. Checking my reflection in the mirror, I see my hair is hanging in a mostly straight hank, despite curling it yesterday. With a couple of hasty brush strokes, it's acceptable enough to leave in a shiny sheet hanging down my back.

I leave my room and at the same second Collin's door opens a few feet away.

"Perfect timing," I say with a smile.

"Everything with you always seems to be perfect timing," Collin agrees, tugging me into his side with a light squeeze.

We stroll to the SUV together, each stride synced as if our bodies are perfectly in tune with one another. Both of us climb in, buckling our seatbelts before Collin takes off.

As he drives, he reaches over the center console to intertwine our fingers, squeezing gently before resting our connected hands on my thigh.

The drive passes quickly, with the sign to the park swiftly becoming visible through the windshield of Collin's luxurious car. I take a deep breath as the dingy, run down trailers come into sight.

After less than two weeks away, the sight startles me with its griminess, in comparison to the near mansions lining the streets of the Golden Oaks neighborhood.

The Franzen's house has spoiled me.

We bump along the dirt road, and I close my eyes in preparation of seeing the tin eyesore that has been my home for years. I feel Collin's car finally braking beneath me and my eyelids pop up, taking it in quickly, like ripping off a band-aid.

A gasp escapes when I see it.

"Well, crap," Collin drawls.

I shove open the car door, jogging across the dead grass, and up the steps to my trailer, needing to be closer to assess the scene. When I reach the top step, I see the screen hanging on one hinge, with the doorknob to the thin, tin door completely broken off, laying in a shattered pile.

Stepping over the mess, I enter, and another gasp escapes.

It's as if a tornado struck inside.

My belongings are strewn all over, with every cabinet door opened, and every cushion and pillow from the couch completely shredded. Fabric, pillows, feathers, and miscellaneous garbage lay scattered about the floor. My abrupt entry startles a bird that had taken up residence and it quickly swoops out the opening as Collin attempts to enter.

"Oh, wow," he drawls, once he makes it through the doorway, past the bird obstacle. He approaches me slowly, concern etched across his face. "Should we just continue to the coffee shop, then return to my house?"

As much as I'd like to leave this mess for someone else to take care of, it's still my home and therefore my problem.

"No, I think I need to stay and clean this up. You're welcome to leave… I can ride my bike and meet you later, if you want. I have my phone," I offer, feeling guilty for ruining our Sunday morning with an emergency trailer clean-up.

"No way," Collin protests. "I'm not leaving you on your own to clean up this mess."

"Okay," I reply, barely paying him any attention as I grab garbage bags from under the sink.

Picking my way across the room, I shovel scraps into the bag, not sparing anything a second glance. From what I can tell, nothing in here is salvageable. Almost everything I touch is damp. It's either animal pee, or water that got in the trailer, or something else. Whatever it is, I try not to think too hard about it as I continue to discard everything in sight.

Collin helps silently by my side for a few minutes before he asks, "Would you be okay if I left for just a bit to go grab you a new door handle and a deadbolt? I can install it while you finish cleaning, that way when we're done you can lock up and we can leave without the door hanging open."

"Yeah, I would appreciate that. I'm okay here by myself," I reply, thankful he thought ahead and allowing my gratitude to seep into my words.

My door no longer has a handle, so we wouldn't be able to leave until it was replaced anyways, might as well kill two birds with one stone.

He forces me to stop cleaning, pulling me into his chest and cradling me in his firm grip. He drops a brief peck to my forehead before he slowly steps back.

Collin carefully navigates his way across the room, avoiding the piles of refuse. He disappears from sight with one last glance over his shoulder. Shortly after, I hear his SUV starting outside.

With a sigh, I return to ridding my trailer of garbage. After two bags are filled, I exit into the still muggy, fall Alabama air. I drag the bags behind me, on my path to the dumpster. Focusing on my anger and determination, I heave the bags over my shoulder one by one, chucking each into the large, blue bin with everyone else's trash.

"Kenzie-Girl," a familiar voice calls, the second I turn away from the dumpster.

Great, more garbage.

"Did something happen to your trailer? I noticed

you hadn't been back in a while, then saw the door broken in. Guess you're glad all that's missing was some money," Derek shouts across the park, a smirk evident on his face even with the distance separating us.

All that's missing was some money?

I replay the words in my mind until I realize I didn't check for my coffee tin containing my small bit of savings. Breaking into a jog, I rush back to my trailer, sprinting past Derek and through the door.

I tear through my cupboards, pushing aside the few cans of food that somehow made it through the destruction. Once the cans are moved, my fingertips hit air, there's nothing else left.

The coffee tin is gone, of course.

Hearing Derek's footsteps clip against the steps of my trailer, I whirl to face him. "Did you do this Derek? Did you break in here to steal a hundred bucks from a teenage girl?" I shriek the questions, my words laced with fury over his unnecessary cruelty.

He smirks at me, his dark eyes glinting with malice. Verbal confirmation is not required, I already know it was him. I knew as soon as he mentioned my money. I should've known as soon as I stepped foot into my trailer.

"Why?" I whisper, some of my anger deflating in face of his indifference.

"Why?" Derek scoffs. "Are you serious? You entered a deal with me to rob the Franzen's, then you suddenly get cozy with Collin and ditch me to move into his mansion. What did you think, you were going to leave this place behind and become one of them?" Derek laughs, but the sound lacks joy.

"Wake up. One day Collin is going to drop you and you'll end up right here, back in this trailer park where you belong, with the people you betrayed. Now, why do you think I did this to you, Kenzie-girl?" Derek asks, his tone mocking me as much as his question is.

"What?" A familiar southern twang drawls.

A head of blonde hair attached to a muscular body becomes visible behind Derek, slowly entering the trailer. Collin's carrying coffee and a bag from the hardware store with a white-knuckled grip, his expression a mix of confusion and anger as he soaks in the scene he walked in on.

"Why the hell are you here? Get out," Collin tells Derek, fury lacing each word, his threatening intent clear.

Derek smirks at me, his eyes black as night while he utters his parting remarks, "It's a bad idea to fall for your mark, Kenzie-girl. Everyone knows that." He stomps out of the trailer, leaving me with a confused looking Collin Franzen.

Once his retreating footsteps are no longer audible, Collin asks, "What is he talking about, McKenzie?"

I exhale deeply, attempting to delay the inevitable explanation long enough to gather my thoughts. "Collin, I'm really sorry," I start.

I'm watching his face closely, and instantly see the flash of hurt before he shuts me out, his expression becoming shuttered.

Pushing past the pain of his normally heated and

happy gaze becoming completely blank, I continue, "After you saved me from that creep at Derek's party, before I knew you at all, Derek came to me with a plan to make some money." I hold my arms out and gesture around, "Obviously my situation was—is—pretty dire, but I declined his offer."

I hesitate, wanting to end the story at the point I was still a good person, but knowing Collin deserves the whole truth.

With a sigh, I proceed with my confession. "At least at first. Then I showed up at the motel and my shift was cut, I searched for another job, but nowhere downtown would hire me because of my mom's... reputation and my age. I was desperate when I said yes, Collin."

I take a step forward, towards his still form, but an icy expression aimed in my direction halts my next step. "I instantly regretted the words, as soon as they left my mouth. I've been searching for a way to back out of it, I swear. Derek is just... unpredictable. I was worried about the consequences of reneging on our deal, I figured avoiding him was the best solution until I sorted it out."

"That's why he's been bothering you? Because you agreed to rob my parents with him? What the hell, McKenzie?" Collin roars, his tone incredulous and lacking its usual warmth. More than his anger, I'm surprised by him cussing. I can't recall a single other time he's uttered a cuss word.

"I'm really sorry," I say, sincerity evident in my voice.

A part of me clings to the hope my words can

convince him to forgive me, even though my actions were unforgivable.

He turns his back and sets the coffee carrier and bag from the hardware store on the counter before he exits. It isn't until his feet clomp down my front steps that I jerk into action and chase him outside.

"Collin, wait."

He pauses but doesn't face me. Despite that, I'm still encouraged by him waiting, the action showing he's willing to listen.

Bolstering my courage, I continue walking forward. "If I could go back in time and reverse what I did, I would. I'm so sorry. I should've never said yes to Derek's offer in the first place."

"No, you shouldn't have." His voice is emotionless and distant, when he speaks, "Look Kenzie, I need some space. I think you should stay here tonight so we can both have some time to think everything over."

"Nothing has changed for me," I half-whisper.

"Everything has changed," he replies, then he climbs into his SUV and reverses out of the trailer park without a second glance.

I work hard to fight the despair threatening to drown me, to incapacitate me, and make me a total non-functioning mess. Losing the battle, I sink to my knees in the scratchy, mostly dead grass with tears streaming down my face.

It's never hurt this much when anyone else has left. Not even when my mom ditched me for a near stranger. She was unpredictable at best, but Collin has been as steady as a rock the entire time I've known him. Until now.

Thinking of my mother has me realizing, maybe this is how she felt when Andy left her. The thought is like a bucket of ice water pouring over my head. I will never be like my mother and abandon my responsibilities for my own selfish desires.

With a renewed determination, I pick myself off the ground and swipe away the lingering tears trailing down my cheeks. Squaring my shoulders, I stride inside my trailer and grab the bag that Collin brought from the hardware store.

Inside there are a few tools and a handle/deadbolt combination that are much nicer than the wimpy things originally installed on the door by the manufacturer; the ones that were so easily broken because of their cheap parts. Although, I'm sure if Derek really wanted to, he could find a way past these much sturdier ones too. Pushing the thought aside, I study the packaging.

I've never installed a lock before, but people are able to accomplish impossible things all the time; there's no way I can't conquer a hunk of metal with an instruction manual.

Opening the package, I unfold the directions and begin reading. Whenever a tool is mentioned, I check the bag and sure enough Collin purchased it. Of course, he did, Collin is the kind of guy that thinks things through and makes decisions that help people instead of hurt them.

Unlike me.

Shoving my self-hatred aside, I resume reading.

When I'm about halfway through reading each word printed inside the manual, my new, fancy phone dings with a text. I rush to answer it, hoping it's Collin. Instead it's a message from an unknown number.

Unknown: **Hi McKenzie, this is Mrs. Franzen. Thank you so much for your help tutoring Luke, but we've decided to hire a different tutor with a bit more experience.**

Sighing, I close out the messaging app, still clinging onto the hope that maybe Collin just told his parents we're having a fight, and everything can go back to the way it was.

Hopefully, he didn't mention the whole, planned robbery deal, otherwise I don't think his parents would ever forgive me. Gripping onto the idea of forgiveness in my mind like the lifeline that it is, I continue reading the manual.

It takes almost two hours, both of the coffees left by Collin, and three mini pep-talks for me to feel comfortable attempting to install the items from the bag. With a deep breath, I stand from my post near the counter and approach the door with a combination of trepidation and determination.

I can do this.

Stepping forward, I open the thin piece of tin, revealing two Warrior's branded duffel bags on my top step. One I recognize as my cheer bag and the other must be something of Collin's that he used to pack my things. I drag the bags inside, pretending like I don't know what their presence signifies.

Instead, I focus on installing my brand new, state-of-the-art lock on my ancient, beat-down trailer.

There will be time to talk to Collin tomorrow.

At least I hope there will be.

The more I say the words, the less convincing they become, even to my own ears.

Chapter 32

The few weeks I spent getting to know Collin, passed in a blur of unexpected happiness, but the short hours without him seem to drag on for an eternity.

I spend most of the night pacing my trailer, waiting for the alarm on my new, fancy cell phone to go off and notify me it's time to get ready for school; to prepare to see him again.

For the entire restless night, I attempt to create excuses and apologies for my behavior, even going as far as practicing begging in front of my bathroom mirror. None of my attempts have shaken the feeling of utter dread, that I waited too long to tell Collin the truth and the way he found out was unforgivable.

Each hour that passes, the little nagging voice in my brain becomes louder, declaring, "Collin will never forgive you for the arrangement you made with Derek". The words slowly become more insistent each time they replay.

I swear, by midnight, the voice is practically screeching accusing words, screaming, "You should have told him before he found out about the deal in the worst way possible: From Derek".

When my alarm finally chimes, I startle into consciousness. I guess at some point I sat on my bed and fell into an exhausted, dreamless sleep. Despite whatever rest I was able to get, I feel groggy and half-dead as I go through the motions of getting ready.

The trailer has been my residence for as long as I can remember. First with my mom, then later on my own, after she left. Now, for the first time, as I look over my room prior to focusing on the clothes in my closet, I'm realizing it doesn't feel like a home.

It lacks the warmth and care and happiness that come with a home. The things I had experienced while staying at the Franzen's House.

Shaking myself out of my spiral of self-pity, I tug on a pair of slim skinny jeans and an almost sheer, white button up that was a gift from Katie's closet.

I slowly run a straightener through my hair, ensuring each strand is straight as an arrow. Then I apply five coats of mascara before pulling on a snug pair of leather booties, also from Katie.

She said she accidentally bought them in the wrong size when she gifted them to me at school the other day, but I have a sneaking suspicion the expensive looking shoes were just a gift she didn't want me to decline.

With determination, I inspect my appearance in the mirror, searching for any visible flaws. I want to be irresistible today, as I beg for Collin to forgive me. He always told me I looked like a goddess, and I'm hoping playing up that angle might help my case.

I will use anything I can to make him listen to me; to forgive me.

Ignoring the heavy ball of dread in the pit of my belly, I exit my trailer to sit on the steps outside. I wish I could say I wasn't pathetic enough to wait for Collin until the last possible second, but that would be a lie. And I'm done with lying when it comes to him, it's already cost me enough.

Perching on the steps, I check my phone religiously until it's ten minutes past the time Collin normally arrives. I promise myself five more minutes, set a timer, and rise to pace the deadened, yellowed grass.

Waiting, and waiting, until the alarm chimes and Collin still hasn't appeared. I check my cell three more times in two-minute intervals before finally accepting the truth and clambering onto my bike, high tailing it towards Golden Oaks High.

Collin isn't coming.

My legs pump as hard as they can, like my body thinks if I can bike to school fast enough, everything will be okay. So what if Collin didn't show up at my trailer?

He said he needed space, and we never talked about what space entailed. Once I reach the school, I'll have the chance to talk to him. After we resolve our issues, everything will go back to the way it was between us; before Derek spoiled it with the untimely reveal of my secret.

By the time I finally arrive at Golden Oaks High, the parking lot is practically full and the outside stairs are teeming with students. I disembark from my bike at the edge of the school property, to buy me a few extra minutes to slow my racing heart and compose myself as I walk to the bike rack.

Since I'm no longer pedaling with mania, I can feel the light layer of sweat on my forehead. There's nothing that can be done about it, so I shrug it off hoping my hair still looks okay.

As I'm steering my bike forward, towards the bike rack just to the side of the stairs, a sheet of shiny, auburn hair flipping over a shoulder catches my attention. My eyes lock onto the sight and immediately recognize Collin's tall, broad form resting against the side of the building. For the first time since I've met him, his sizzling green gaze isn't focused on me.

It's focused on Isabelle's beautiful, petite form, standing mere inches away from him.

"Do you want me to go cut that bitch?"

The words startle me from my daze, and I glance to my left. I notice I've stopped walking and Katie snuck up on me, her attention fixated on the brick wall.

I start to nod my head, but force myself to stop. "No, we, Collin and I, had a…a falling out. I need to lock up my bike so I can talk to him before class."

Katie nods and syncs her footsteps with mine as I continue pushing my bike forward. "Does this have anything to do with the secret you were keeping?" She asks.

Wordlessly nodding in response, my eyes remain focused ahead, observing Collin who hasn't noticed me approaching.

It's like he purposefully used to know, at all times, where I was in a room, and now he totally doesn't care. Katie doesn't speak again as we trudge towards the school and when I sneak a glance, her facial expression is somber, like we're headed to a funeral.

Katie is a good friend. I'm not really sure that I've had a good friend, or really any good people in my life until recently, but I'm starting to realize they're the kind of people worth fighting for.

That I want to be the kind of person worth fighting for.

Resolutely, I lock my bike to the designated rack, using my rusty old chain that seems to have gotten older and harder to use in the weeks Collin was driving me to school. Then, I face the steps, immediately catching a certain emerald gaze.

Unlike before, he doesn't prolong the connection. Instead, he wraps an arm around Isabelle's shoulders and leads her into the school and out of sight.

His actions feel like a dagger through my heart and I fight against the sudden onslaught of tears building in my eyes. Katie winds her arm through mine, practically dragging me into the building as I focus on breathing normally. She's a woman on a mission and despite our height difference, she's able to effectively maneuver me through the school with ease.

My focus isn't on fighting her, it's on not hyperventilating, so I let her direct me wherever she wants to. She keeps us moving at a fast clip, until we reach a reasonable distance from Collin's locker, slowing our pace as we approach.

I spot him exchanging his books in preparation for class. We're close enough Katie can wait for me without seeming weird, but far enough he can't hear our sidebar conversation.

She halts and pulls me to a stop next to her. "Do you need me to go with you?" She asks, her concerned gaze searching mine.

"No, I need to do this by myself," I reply on a sigh.

She nods, adding, "I'll wait right here."

With leaden feet, I approach Collin. He's standing near his locker with his arm now wrapped low around Isabelle's waist. She snarls at me but I ignore her. I'm here for a reason, and it doesn't have anything to do with her.

"Can we talk?" I ask the question softly, but the silence in the hall carries my words as if I had shouted.

"About what?" Collin asks without looking at me.

"Everything."

He sighs, the sound deep, mournful, and meaningful, like he's solidifying the end of what we had with one, single exhale. Collin finally faces me, but the fire that used to sizzle in his eyes has turned to ash and the sight has my heart wilting prior to him uttering a word.

He's already moved on, he's already over me.

I barely hear his next words over the sound of my heart breaking. "There's nothing to talk about, McKenzie. What we had was built on a lie. Once that was exposed the foundation crumbled and now, we have nothing. We're nothing. Now I need to get ready for class. See ya around. Or maybe not."

Isabelle's cackle punctuates the end of the conversation. Collin confirms he's done with me by turning away, blocking me out with his broad shoulders that seem almost as familiar as my own.

Somehow, my feet carry me back to Katie while my eyes blur with unshed tears. When I reach the space in front of her, she grabs onto my biceps and halts me in place with her tight grip.

My eyes scan her face for a second before sweeping over the hall, taking in the silent faces of bystanders watching my drama unfold, lining the hallway like they're witnessing a free show. The accusing glare on my face startles some of them into motion, but most of them stay in place, waiting to see what gossip they can gather next.

"Hey," Katie says gently, distracting me from our audience. "Let's play hooky today. We can go to my house and watch chick flicks and eat popcorn. Maybe even braid each other's hair," she says jokingly, a sardonic smile gracing her lips.

I return the expression, a smile forming on my face, but my lips feel strange. Like its muscle memory causing the expression and not true happiness. Blame it on my post-Collin confrontation fog, but I find myself agreeing to Katie's plan, "Okay, yeah that sounds a lot better than being here and having to watch…"

Katie lets me pause for about two point five seconds before nodding in understanding and winding her arm through mine again. She leads us towards the front of the school, in the direction of the parking lot.

My feet move on autopilot, while I purposefully avoid thinking about what could happen if the school tries to call my mother's disconnected phone number to inform her, I skipped class.

Seems like a worry for another day.

Not to sound like a dramatic, love-sick teen, but it already feels like my life, as I know it, is kind of over anyways.

Chapter 33

Fuck Collin," Katie says, while we sit on her bed watching a rom-com and eating popcorn drizzled in chocolate, both of which were Katie's idea.

I open my mouth to protest, I was the one that fucked up, but Katie shoots me a glare and I snap my jaw shut.

"No, you don't get to defend him," she chastises. "No matter what you did, he should at least have the decency to talk to you about it, instead of acting like a child. I mean, he basically spent the last few weeks being all about you, then one bump in the road, and he drops you like last week's garbage for that bitch, Isabelle? I mean I hate talking down about another girl but she needs to have some class. She's been out for Collin since day one of high school and he never has shown any interest until now. Like get a clue, girl."

I nod my head silently, unsure how to answer. How differently would Katie feel if she knew the truth? Collin immediately jumping to Isabelle is hurtful, but I hurt him too. By lying.

She continues, not needing my words to support her tirade. "We'll go to the library tomorrow during lunch for a brainstorm session, and so we don't have to see any more of the gag worthy groping between Isabelle and He Who Shall Not Be Named."

"A brainstorming session?" I ask. "Also, are you going to continue referring to Collin like he's Voldemort?"

"If he's going to act evil, I'm going to call him out on it," she responds, her tone matter of fact. "And yes, don't you need to find a new job because you were tutoring Collin's brother? Or are they still having you tutor? Actually, it doesn't matter either way, even if they still want you to, you can't go back to their house until Collin apologizes. I forbid it," she says sternly, sticking her nose up in the air to punctuate the sentiment.

I laugh and give her a side hug before settling back against the pillows on her plush bed. Nice mattresses are definitely a rich people thing, because Katie's is just as luxurious as the Franzen's.

As I lounge on her bed, enjoying its soft comfort, I allow the silence to linger, choosing not to respond to her statements. Instead, I attempt to follow the plot of the silly movie Katie chose and shovel the sweet/salty goodness, she insisted we need, into my face.

Thankfully, Katie humors me and also focuses on the movie, occasionally picking up her phone and responding to messages when her alert chimes. When the credits finally roll, I feel marginally better. I guess Katie's post break-up plan actually does work.

"Do you need a ride home?" Katie asks, after clicking the TV off with her remote.

"Err, yeah or back to the school so I can grab my bike," I reply, feeling guilty for making her drive me around.

Katie checks her phone again before she responds, "Classes are still going on. I don't want to take you back to school, in case someone sees you and narcs. How about I drop you off at home and then pick you up in the morning? You can ride your bike home tomorrow afternoon."

"Yeah, sounds good," I agree after a brief hesitation.

Gathering my things, I follow Katie downstairs and into her hot pink car. She fiddles with the stereo until a pop song is blasting through her speakers, then rolls down all the windows and takes off. Between the music and the sound of the wind it's impossible to hear each other, so I gesture with my hand to direct her to my house. Or at least the one she dropped me off at last time.

Katie and I are closer than we were before, and I'm not worried about her seeing the trailer and spreading my secrets or ditching me. I am worried if I tell her the truth now, I might lose her just like I did Collin.

That's the thing about lies.

They're so easy to tell, but once you tell one it leads you down a slippery slope. Soon you become so entangled in your false words it's hard to know what the truth is anymore. Even if you do know, it's harder to confess the truth when it requires unweaving an entire net worth of lies.

I snap out of my thoughts as the car begins to slow beneath me. Katie maneuvers her bug to the curb as indicated. I unbuckle, placing my palm against the door handle, but she stops me, mid-pull. One of her hands rests against my arm, halting my movements, while she uses the other to turn down the volume to her stereo.

"Okay, what gives?" She asks in a stern tone.

"I'm sorry?" My voice sounds taken aback, but a light sweat has started to form on my spine, my nerves flaring over her accusatory question.

"This is not the house you had me drop you off at last time," she states.

I stare out the window to look at the house, like it will confirm her words or refute them, but the house remains mute. "And don't think I didn't notice how you refused to go inside while I was sitting at the curb last time," she continues, her tone sounding frustrated by my lack of response.

"Err," I reply, stalling as I attempt to formulate an excuse. I didn't think Katie noticed last time, but I guess she's more observant than I gave her credit for.

"Where do you really live McKenzie Bonita Carslyle?" She demands.

"My middle name isn't Bonita," I point out, avoiding the true issue in our conversation.

"I know, it just sounded better with a middle name, so I made one up," she exclaims with a smirk. "But for real, where do you live? I want to drop you off at your actual house, not just in front of some random place, in some random neighborhood."

"Okay," I respond with a deep breath, as I mentally prepare to show Katie the trailer park. "Just continue straight down this road."

She follows my instructions, driving straight for another mile, then she takes a left past the sign leading to the park. The second her tires hit the dirt road she cries out, "Oh my gosh. This road is awful!"

I keep my mouth shut because everything in the park is awful . The road may be one of the least offensive things she sees here.

When we reach my trailer, she pulls into the same spot Collin used to park his massive SUV. Thinking his name makes my heart ache, but I push the feeling aside to watch Katie's expression instead. She doesn't react, at all. Besides to unbuckle her seat belt.

"Can I see inside?" She asks, eyeing my ancient, tin trailer.

"Yeah, sure," I respond, resigned to the idea Katie probably won't want to be my friend after this.

It takes her all of ten seconds to peek her head into each room after I unlock my fancy, new deadbolt. Afterwards, she surprises me by sitting on the couch, which is being held together by some strategic pieces of duct tape after Derek shredded the cushions.

"Is this what you lied to Collin about?" She asks with a concerned expression.

"No," I say on a sigh, settling into the spot next to her. "It's kind of a long story."

Katie nods. "Okay, I'm listening."

I play with the idea of stalling or changing the topic, but Katie is my friend, my best friend. Plus, she's known Collin for years. If anyone is able to give me solid advice on how to fix the mess I made, it will be Katie.

With another sigh, I begin my story. "Well, I used to work at the Breezy Motel and my boss was a total skeezeball. He hired another girl and started giving away all my hours. My equally sketchy neighbor invited me to a party where Collin saved me from the clutches of my neighbor's strange friend. Then, the next day my neighbor came to my house and offered me a deal: if I gave him info on the Franzen house he would rob it and give me half the profit."

Katie gasps, and I avoid meeting her eyes, rushing through the rest of my words to get the story out before she can judge me too harshly. "Originally, I agreed, but after spending a few hours with Collin, I didn't think I could go through with it. The more time I spent with him, the more it became clear I needed to confess my deal with my neighbor and find a way out of it. The timing just never seemed right and I was worried what my neighbor would do if I changed my mind."

I look at Katie, with imploring eyes. "I didn't feel like I had any options, when I agreed." I gesture my hands around my trailer. "I'm broke, obviously, but as soon as I got to know Collin, I wanted to call the whole plan off, regardless. It was a stupid idea to even agree in the first place."

"How did Collin find out?" Katie asks quietly.

"From my neighbor," I confess, my eyes fixed on the floor and filled with my shame.

"Oh, Kenzie," Katie says before she swoops in to give me a hug.

I can't contain the tears flooding my eyes, forcing their way silently down my face. Her hug, like so many other things, reminds me of Collin's warm comfort and I need to release some of the feelings that have been slowly building throughout the day.

Katie keeps her arms wrapped around me until the tears slow to a stop. Then, she pulls away, gripping the tops of my arms and staring intently into my eyes as she speaks. "The deal was made before the two of you got together. It was a dumb plan, but you were desperate. He'll get over it. Eventually. Probably."

"Your pep talk was good, until about halfway through," I say on a half-laugh, half-sob, still recovering from my crying fit.

"I'll work on it," she responds, her tone sincere. "Do you want me to stay here with you tonight?" She asks. "Or you could come back to my place," she offers with a look around the tiny space, probably thinking both of us wouldn't fit in here together.

"I think I need some time by myself, to process, but I may take you up on your offer another day," I respond, feeling grateful for her suggestion, but knowing I need space right now.

She nods and we both rise from the couch. I walk her the three feet to the door and give her a brief, tight hug while we stand on my tiny front porch.

"Thank you for listening and understanding. Oh, and for dropping me off at my real house this time," I add with a laugh as we release each other.

"That house was super far, I can't believe you walked from there last time," she teases in a tone that sounds more like her usual self. "I'll see you tomorrow morning, girl," she adds, climbing down my steps to my patchy grass.

Shrugging, I agree, "See you tomorrow!"

I watch as she hops into her bug and backs out onto the pitted dirt road. With one last wave, I move to close my front door. I'm startled by a familiar voice from my left, halting my movements as my brain processes his words.

"First a rich boyfriend and now a rich friend? You really seem to be moving up in the world, Kenzie-girl. I'm surprised to find you here at the trailer park tonight," Derek taunts as he emerges from the dark shadows nearby.

By the time he's done talking, I've recovered from my initial surprise and whirl around to face him. "Why are you here? Are you stalking me now?" I ask, anger penetrating each syllable.

Technically, what happened between Collin and I isn't his fault, but it sure feels like it is. No part of me wants to talk to Derek and I wish he would get the hint and leave me alone.

"You know why I'm here Kenzie-girl. I want information on the layout of the Franzen house. You were there for weeks, I know you have intel valuable to me. So, help me out and I'll see what I can do for you," Derek demands as he sidles up the steps leading to my trailer.

"Derek, if you haven't figured it out already, you

probably never will, so I'll just tell you. I'm out. I'm not going to help you with this or anything else like it."

He shoves his foot into my door to keep me from closing it, apparently reading my intentions from my demeanor and expression. "I'm older and therefore wiser," he says, invading my space. I remain rooted in place not wanting to give him anything more than what he's already taken, but he continues, undeterred by our proximity, "People like us? We don't end up with the Franzen's of the world. Ya know, the people with money and families that love them.

We're too hard for that shit and maybe we can fool those people for a little while, pretend we're like them for just a bit, but eventually they see through the facade and realize we're fucked up. They see through our charming smiles and discover our parents didn't love us like their parents love them. They find we don't have any money to our names; that we're just a little bit less than they are. And when they do? They drop us faster than last year's Gucci slippers."

I shake my head, trying to deny the truth I think I hear in his words. Isn't that part of the reason I never hung out with Collin in my trailer and didn't want Katie to know where I lived?

Although, neither of them dropped me, once they had all the facts. Well, neither dropped me because I was poor or parentless.

Derek is wrong and he needs to leave.

With my toes, I kick the center of Derek's foot. Like I anticipated, he yelps and lifts it out of the way, giving me the space, I need to slam the door in his face.

The piece of tin closes with finality, but it doesn't shield me from hearing his next words. "You know I'm right Kenzie-girl. When you're ready to talk, you know where to find me."

I reopen the door, watching as Derek's expression rapidly transforms from smug to shocked, as he stares at me through my screen. He didn't anticipate a reply, expecting to always get the last word. Well, today he messed with the wrong girl.

"You know what Derek, you're wrong. Life is hard and messy and unfair. Some people are born with less, while others with more, but we all have the same opportunity to change our situation if we put the necessary work into it. Maybe I messed things up with Collin, but I learned my lesson. I won't lie and scheme my way into other people's lives and take advantage of them, ever again."

I pause and take a deep breath. "And THAT, Derek is what separates you and me. We aren't connected because we're from the same place. We're two completely different types of people. Of that, I'm certain." I close the door with conviction before he's able to get another word out.

Then I stride into my bedroom and crawl into bed. I'm not sure how long I stew over his words, self-righteous in my anger, until I eventually fall into a deep sleep. One where I dream of being a better person.

Chapter 34

The bell rings, punctuating the end of the longest, most strained class I've ever experienced. Eating lunch in the library all week has helped me avoid Collin, but there's nothing I can do to stay away from him during chemistry, considering he's my lab partner for the entire year.

From my seat by the window, I watch Collin and the rest of my peers file out of the room. Ms. Rigs hovers, closing the door after the last student exits. I stay behind for homeroom, even though it's Friday, for a last-minute cram session.

"Are you okay McKenzie? Are you worried about your SAT exam tomorrow?" Ms. Rigs asks as she approaches my table. "You seemed distracted during class today and I want you to feel comfortable talking about these things with me," she says, in her concerned, motherly tone.

I start to decline from responding, intending to shake

my head, then open my mouth instead. "I'm stressed out, but not about the SAT… it's about a boy actually. Well and about money."

"Do you want to talk about it?" she asks, her face wearing an expression free of judgment and full of compassion.

"I'm not sure…" I start, then change my mind.

I am sure. I could use the advice and I trust Ms. Rigs. We have become much closer since she started helping me with my college prep. Right about now having an adult weigh in on the situation could help me gain some perspective.

Inhaling deeply, I unburden my truth. "I was dating this guy and I lied to him around the time we first met. I was also tutoring his brother after I quit my job at the Breezy Motel. Then, he found out about my lie from someone else and everything blew up in my face. He won't talk to me now and his family told me they no longer need me as a tutor."

Ms. Rigs perches on the stool in front of me as she nods. "Well, your first love is always the hardest to navigate, because you lack any experience. Without knowing more of the story, I can't give you further advice other than if it's meant to be, he will find a way to forgive you. If he can't, he probably didn't love you enough and you shouldn't settle for him anyways. You have your whole life ahead of you to find the real thing."

Her words soak into my consciousness. If Collin loves me, or at least thinks the bond we were building could evolve into love, he'll find a way to forgive me.

The sentiment echoes what Katie said yesterday, and I cling on to hope that maybe they're both right.

Without allowing me much time to dwell on her words of wisdom, Ms. Rigs continues, "As for the recent loss of income, I actually do have a solution for that. I have another student that approached me, searching for a tutor. You can use your homeroom period three times a week, the days you are not with me, and her parents will pay for your time. Is that something you would be interested in?"

"Really?" I ask, surprised.

"Of course," she replies calmly. "You're one of my best students, I think she would benefit greatly from your tutelage."

"Okay, I'll do it," I agree readily, without even hearing the name of the student. It doesn't matter anyways. No matter how difficult the student is, it's infinitely better to earn money and stay in my trailer than risk becoming homeless from a lack of funds.

"Perfect," she replies. "Now I want to review a few more items in your prep book. Please turn to page 342."

A renewed sense of purpose fills me, as I bask in the feeling of being employed once more. I turn the pages of my prep book, feeling lighter than I have all week.

Bolstered by my newfound optimism, I review some of the more complex math questions that will be on the test.

Surprisingly for a chemistry teacher, Ms. Rigs is exceptional at advanced math. Maybe the two subjects are closely tied together, more than I originally thought. Either that, or she's helped her fair share of students prepare for the SAT. Neither would surprise me at this point.

Our final study session flies by as I immerse myself in the last practice exam provided by Ms. Rigs, immediately following our review. Scribbling nonsense on the scrap piece of paper she left on my table and blacking out circles on the test page, I work through the equations until only three minutes of the period remain.

"Okay, put down your pencil, McKenzie," she states from her post at the front of the room. I comply with her request and gather my belongings as she strides to my table.

Ms. Rigs makes quick work of correcting my answer sheet, handing it back at the same second the bell trills, signifying the end of homeroom and the completion of our study session. "Very good. Only three of your answers were incorrect. I expect you to do very well tomorrow, McKenzie," she says with a warm smile. "Come to my classroom on Monday for your first tutoring session, and good luck," she finishes, her expression relaxed and unconcerned, like I've already aced the test in her mind.

"Thanks," I respond, as I don my backpack and give her a small smile, moving to exit the classroom and continue to my history class. "See you next week."

"Oh, one more thing, McKenzie," Ms. Rigs says, opening a drawer in her desk. She rifles around for a second before standing and passing me a lavender colored gift bag with white tissue paper peeking out the top. "Just a little something for tomorrow," she says with a warm smile, as I accept the bag.

Unsure how to react, I hug the gift against my chest. "Thank you, Ms. Rigs," I reply, grateful for everything she's done for me and surprised by the gift.

She nods and gestures to the door, excusing me from the slightly awkward situation. I take her cue, exiting into the hall without lingering to open the present.

Distracted, I wander down the hallway, stopping to swap out my chemistry books for my history text. Gently, I place the present inside my locker to keep it safe, until I can open it in the privacy of my home. My mind swims with random math facts and curiosity over the contents of the gift, as my hands leave the smooth sides of the lavender bag.

When I absentmindedly shut the metal door and face the corridor, intent on walking to my next class, I smack into a broad chest covered in a sky-blue t-shirt. I follow the muscular pecs, up a thick neck, until my eyes hit a pair of emerald colored orbs.

The second our gazes connect, Collin parts his lips to speak, but he's interrupted before any words leave his mouth.

"Collin," Isabelle shrieks from just down the hall. She strides towards us, and awareness slowly returns to my body. Collin is standing very close, with his hands gripping my biceps.

Isabelle continues screeching, "Collin, I've been looking all over for you! Have you been avoiding me? Collin!"

Isabelle's last shout of Collin's name suddenly breaks through the last of the fog surrounding my brain. "I have to leave," I whisper, slipping out of his grasp and hurrying towards history class.

I hear him take two steps towards me, his shoes pounding against the linoleum floors, but thankfully he doesn't chase me down the hall.

Practically sprinting to escape, I slip into my class earlier than usual and slide into my seat. I focus on calming my racing heart, and by the time the bell rings again, I have it mostly under control.

My entire second period passes in a daze. I half-heartedly take notes while my brain comes up with dozens of scenarios revolving around the words Collin was about to utter, prior to Isabelle's interruption.

Should I have stayed? Was it a total chicken move to leave before he spoke?

I ponder every possible situation until a headache builds in the back of my brain from the tumultuous thoughts whipping through my mind. I've never been so grateful to hear the bell for lunch, the ringing noise relieving me from the endless loop of my thoughts.

Shoving all my belongings into my bag haphazardly, I leave in a hurry, pushing past my classmates in my haste to escape. I'm the first person in the hall, other students trickling slowly out of their classes as I rush to the cafeteria.

I irritably wait for a tray to pick out whatever the best-looking items are in the free lunch line. The students in front of me feel like they're taking eons to pick out some damn soup and I barely contain my impatience, tamping down the urge to tap my foot and hurry them along.

When I finally make it through the queue, that has grown three times in size since I got in line, I snatch up my tray and head in the direction of my new lunch place. I've been zipping through every action in a rush, wanting to find Katie as soon as possible, so I can tell her what happened with Collin.

My long legs make short work eating up the distance to the library. Bumping the handle with my hip, I push open the door and make a beeline to my usual spot. Plopping down my tray, I sit at the table with Heather, Katie, Summer, and three other girls from the cheer team.

I think the librarian likes that students are finally hanging out here. She's let our slowly growing crowd eat at one of the tables every day this week, without a single shush or request for silence.

When I drop down into my chair, Katie briefly glances up from her phone and mutters, "Hey Kenz."

She immediately turns back to the screen, her fingers moving rapidly, and her brow furrowed as she continues whatever she's doing. My brow scrunches in question, but Katie doesn't notice. She's in her own world, gaze locked on whatever her phone contains.

Looking across the table, Summer's bright eyes connect with mine and she dramatically mouths, "ALEX."

I instantly feel like a horrible friend.

I've been spending almost all my free time with Katie this week. She's listened to every single one of my complaints and thoughts about Collin, reassuring me and lifting me from my pit of despair. Not once during our conversation, did I bring up Alex, or what happened after Collin and I left her party.

It's not that I'm not interested. I've just been distracted by everything else happening. Even as I think the words, they feel like an excuse. Katie's been dealing with stuff too, and she's made time for my problems.

Barely containing my regretful sigh, I tap her shoulder. She reacts slightly, giving me only a portion of her attention. "Just one more second," she says curtly, then turns back to her phone. I don't move a muscle, wanting her to know I plan to wait until she's ready to acknowledge me again.

A few minutes later, she finally puts her phone on the table and gives me her full attention. Her eyes are watery, as if she's on the verge of bursting into tears if she spends just one more second in the conversation she was having with Alex.

I rise from my chair, abandoning my free lunch tray. "Come to the bathroom with me, Katie. I have something to tell you."

She nods and slowly stands. I watch as she hesitates, glancing at her phone and I link our arms together, practically dragging her with me before she has a chance to grab it. Katie stumbles briefly, taking a couple quick steps to catch up with my steady stride as I steer her to the closest bathroom.

Pushing through the door, I check the stalls to make sure we're alone before twirling to face her. "Okay, so what's the deal with you and Alex?" I ask, keeping my tone gentle, but firm. I don't want to scare her off, but I also want to convey that I'm serious about knowing what's going on in her life.

Katie sighs and hops up onto the countertop, her shoulders sagging with the weight of her despair. "Well, he seemed interested during my party. He even stayed to help me clean after everyone else finally cleared out. I was optimistic about it, ya know? Like he finally noticed me."

She sighs again, then continues morosely, "I asked him to stay and watch a movie when we were done cleaning, but he declined. Now he's been distant ever since." She glances away briefly, swiping a couple tears off her cheeks. "I think he's worried about starting a relationship part way through senior year, in case we end up at different colleges. I've tried reminding him Berry College is both of our first choices, but he says that doesn't mean we'll end up there, together."

I lean against the counter and wrap an arm around her shoulders in a side-hug, giving a brief squeeze. "That really sucks. I'm sorry I didn't ask earlier, and kept telling you about all my Collin drama, when you had boy trouble of your own," I respond.

She smiles at me, her eyes still watery, the tears present in her eyes are barely contained, but the expression is genuine and reassuring. "That's okay. I wasn't really ready to talk about it yet anyways."

I nod, appreciating Katie's friendship even more. Not only did she listen to me complain about the Collin situation, endlessly, but now she's attempting to comfort me when I'm supposed to be the one comforting her.

"Do you think maybe he's just not that interested

and is using college as an excuse?" I ask, while thinking over the Alex situation.

"I've thought about it," she confesses, her voice sounding small. "Maybe if I wait out this year, he'll see we're meant to be together when we end up freshmen at the same college," she says, jumping off the counter and using a scrap of paper towel to swipe at the mascara running down her face as tears overflow from her eyes.

I step forward for another hug, pulling her against my chest, and smooshing her until I finally feel her arms raise and wrap around me, returning my embrace.

When we separate, I keep my tone firm, my chocolate gaze searing into her eyes. "You are worth so much more than some... kid, that's afraid to get into a relationship because you might break up later. Katie, you're an amazing friend, beautiful, kind, cheerful, and so, so fun. Wait for Alex, if you think that's what you need to do, but don't wait so long that you miss out on something better."

Katie nods slowly a few times. Then, as I watch, her face transforms into an expression of determination. I'm not sure if it means she's giving up on Alex or if she's going to work double time to ensure he'll never forget her. What I do know, is that he better watch out. Katie is fierce and I would hate to be on the receiving end of her wrath.

She squares her shoulders and offers me a smile. It doesn't quite reach her eyes, like she's practicing the expression rather than showing joy, but it's a start.

"Oh, before I forget," she says. "Do you need a ride to the SAT tomorrow?"

Appreciation warms me from the inside out. I look at my bestie that's going through her own drama, but still anticipates my needs and tries to help.

Winding my arm through hers, I lead her to the door as I reply, "Nah, I think I've got it covered."

Chapter 35

I wake up early, before my alarm, and allow myself to lay in bed for a few minutes soaking in the peaceful, quiet morning. Today I'm taking the SAT and sending the results to Berry College, Florida State University, and The University of Alabama as part of my admissions packets.

This test is the first step in my new life; the first step in leaving this place for a fresh start.

My mind begins to gradually feel more awake and I slowly roll out of bed to prepare for my day. Opening my closet, I pull on a pair of dark jeans, courtesy of Katie, and a loose-fitting long-sleeved blouse, also from Katie.

Wandering to the bathroom, I pick up my brush and slowly tug it through my dark strands, until they're tamed into a sleek, straight sheet. I quickly throw my hair into a French braid so it's out of my face for the day.

Next, I stroll into the kitchen, reaching into the

cupboards for the box of protein pancakes that Ms. Rigs gave me. I intended to wait to open her gift, but as soon as I got home, I tore into the bag, curiosity compelling me to find out what she thought I still needed. Nestled inside the tissue paper was the mix, a bottle of real maple syrup, and a pack of freshly sharpened number two pencils. The items were accompanied by a note scrawled in Ms. Rigs' cursive script that says, "For tomorrow… protein powers the brain. Good luck!"

Heeding her advice, I prepare to cook a big breakfast to fuel my day ahead. I leisurely add water to the powder, stirring the mix with intense concentration.

It's been years since I've made pancakes. The last time I can remember, I was five or six and my mom helped me stand on a chair and stir the batter with an old wooden spoon that no longer exists in the trailer.

It's been so long in fact, that I have to look up instructions on what temperature to use and how to tell when they're done. With the information pulled up on my phone, I cautiously plop blobs of batter onto the only pan I own, aiming to create perfect circles.

Following the boxes directions to produce enough pancakes for one to two people results in a stack big enough for six.

Sitting down at my small table, I smother a portion of the fluffy discs in syrup and consume as many I can. After eating my fill, I still have a large stack left. I don't want them to go to waste, so I wrap them in plastic and stick them in the fridge for later.

Stuffed to the brim, I grab my backpack and keys, preparing to exit the trailer. With one last glance around, I spot the number two pencils and shove them into my bag as well.

You can never be too prepared.

Outside I mount my bike, pedaling hard to spur myself into motion, then letting myself glide down the bumpy dirt path as far as possible, to prevent getting dusty.

As efficient as it is to catch a ride, I've kind of missed the calm that comes with riding my bike. My legs rhythmically pumping the pedals as my brain freely wanders over everything that's happened to me in the weeks since school started.

The journey doesn't feel nearly as long as it should, as my preoccupied mind distracts me from the scenery whirring by.

It seems like mere seconds pass before the sign for Golden Oaks High, my intended destination, comes into view. With thoughts still whipping around in my brain, I screech to a halt in front of the bike rack and use my chain to secure the old hunk of metal.

Straightening from my position near the tires of my bike, I square my shoulders and stride through the entrance of the school. The double doors leading inside are propped open and just past them sits a desk for check-in manned by two women that appear to be PTA moms.

A small queue of students are waiting to be checked in. I join the line, standing behind a guy with short red hair. The entire wait, I fight hard to keep my nerves at bay. Each step I move forward, closer to the table and taking the SAT, increases the anxiety trying to break free in my mind.

"Next," the lady on the left, with a short, brown bob states.

Inhaling a deep breath, I step towards her and say, "Hi, I'm here for the SAT, McKenzie Carslyle."

She nods, barely glancing at me as her finger skims down the list placed on the table. Her finger stops a third of the way down the page, and she finally looks at me. "ID please."

Thankfully, Ms. Rigs prepared me for this. I snag my school ID from my pocket and hand it to the lady. She checks my name off on the list and returns the card, which I promptly slip back into my pocket.

"Classroom 204. Keep your ID handy, your proctor will check it again when passing out the test booklets. Next."

Her quick dismissal surprises me. I'm forced to shimmy out of the way, as the next student almost bowls me over to get to the check-in point. With a deep sigh, I move further into the hallway to locate room 204.

I hear a familiar cackle and instantly freeze, my gaze scanning left to right until I spot Isabelle. She's leaning against her locker chatting with another student, half dozen feet to my right. They hug briefly before parting ways. I watch with wary eyes, hoping we aren't in the same test room.

I'm unable to force my feet to keep moving and Isabelle's dark gaze locks with mine. She sneers, remaining rooted in place. Her stance and expression are like a challenge, daring me to approach her.

Accepting the unspoken dare, I stride towards her locker without a clear plan in place. By the time my feet stop moving, my mind is a little less crowded with nerves and anticipation.

Feeling clear-headed and channeling my resolve, I decide it's time to clear the air with one of the co-captains of the cheer squad.

"Hey Isabelle," I start.

"What do you want?" She asks, her words dripping with disdain as her dark eyes maintain a baleful expression.

I sigh. "I don't want to do this, whatever this is," I respond, gesturing between us to encompass her rude expression and tone, which appear to be upset about my general existence. "I actually just came over here to say I feel like we got off on the wrong foot. It doesn't have to be today, or even next week, but I want to get to know you at some point. We have a lot of mutual friends and mutual interests. I think we should try to end high school on a high note, instead of whatever this is." I repeat the all-encompassing gesture from before to make my point.

Isabelle narrows her eyes. "Is this about Collin? Is this some pathetic attempt to win him over or something, by being nice to me?"

Adamantly, I decline with a shake of my head. "No way. Collin doesn't want me back, and that really sucks, but this isn't about him. I just want everything to be cool between us. I'm not sure why, but there was animosity between us from the start, before we even gave each other a chance." I refrain from using the words I really want to; SHE never gave me a chance before deciding to hate me.

I'm here to make nice and accusations don't usually smooth things over.

She looks like she's about to snarl something rude in response, but clamps her lips shut at the last possible second.

Her expression isn't welcoming, but I take her silence as a positive step in the right direction and continue, "Look, I'm not saying we have to become best friends, but we're going to be on the same squad for the rest of the year, and interacting with the same group of girls. I don't want there to be any bad blood between us."

The snarl falls from Isabelle's lips and her brow scrunches like she's trying to think of a comeback, but is falling short. Seconds later her features flatten and she nods slowly. "Yeah, you're right. Maybe we can be acquaintances." She holds her hand out and I eye it briefly before taking her palm and giving it a brief shake, like we just made a deal.

Isabelle turns on her heel, striding the opposite direction down the hall. She makes it three steps before she twists her upper body to face me slightly. "For what it's worth. I think Collin is still completely infatuated with you. He only wanted to hang out with me on Monday when you could see us. Now, he's dodging me, he has been all week." She takes a deep breath and lets out a sigh. "Whatever happened between you two, maybe he's not over it, but he's definitely not over you."

"Thanks," I say quietly, the words drifting softly

down the hallway separating us, while her statement echoes on repeat in my mind.

She nods once, lingering a second longer before continuing down the hall.

I straighten my spine and square my shoulders, shutting down the thoughts of Collin before I stroll in the direction of Classroom 204.

My mind tries to drift back to Isabelle's words as I walk, but I shut that shit down. Instead, I inhale deeply, counting to ten before I exhale. Repeating the process twice more to bring myself to the present.

Right now, isn't the time to worry about Collin. First, I need to focus on the SAT, so I can pursue my dreams. Then, I'll have the time to figure out a plan to win back my guy.

With renewed determination, I locate room 204 and yank open the door. My long legs carry me to the desk at the head of the room.

The proctor glances up from a crossword puzzle with a warm smile. "Name please?"

"McKenzie Carslyle," I reply, handing over my student ID for the second time today. "I'm here to ace the SAT," I add on with a bold smile.

Chapter 36

As soon as my trailer comes into sight, I almost topple off my bike. Not from exhaustion—although biking to and from school and spending almost four hours on a test was altogether tiresome—but the fall almost occurs from shock over the small crowd standing on my porch.

After a brief pause, I continue pedaling, pumping my legs steadily to carry me down the pitted path, until I reach my girls.

Katie, Heather, and Summer stand in a semi-circle on my mostly dead grass. Three vehicles sit on my yard, slightly blocking them from view, but from what I can see, they appear to be deep in conversation.

The second they notice my bike bumping along the tired dirt road, they turn to face me as a unit. Katie squeals and jumps up and down, while Heather and Summer offer me warm smiles.

I hop off my bike, and Katie immediately envelopes me in a hug. I'm forced to cling onto my bike with one hand, as I return the hug halfway. As soon as she lets go, I prop my bike against the side of my tin home, giving the girls my full attention.

"Ahh, McKenzie. How did you do? How was the SAT?" Katie asks, ecstatically bouncing on her toes when my eyes land on her.

"They were good," I reply, hiding my confusion over their presence, not wanting it to leak into my tone.

I don't want to give the impression I'm not excited to see them. I am. I'm just not sure why they came all this way on a Saturday afternoon, waiting in the decrepit trailer park for me to return home.

"That's it, good?" Summer chimes in with a laugh.

"Well, honestly," I correct, after a chance to think. "I don't really remember it." I giggle, the sound unexpectedly emerging from my throat but relieving some of the stress from the morning. "I feel like the whole exam went by in a blur of anxiety, I couldn't tell you a single question that I answered, but I hope I did well."

I grimace at the thought of not passing and then being denied acceptance from any of the colleges I've already submitted applications to.

"I'm sure you did great," Heather chimes in, distracting me. "I barely remember anything from my test either, and I did fine. I think it's the result of switching from question to question so quickly! You don't retain any of the information, you just answer on autopilot."

"I'm sure you were fantastic and we'll all be at the same college together next year. Buuut that's not why we're here," Katie squeals excitedly, clapping and bouncing like she can't wait to surprise me with something.

"Ok, what's going on?" I ask, suddenly nervous about the reason behind the crowd gathered in the middle of my dead grass.

My eyes scan the three girls, Heather's expression is blank, and Summer smirks. The second my eyes land on Katie, she steps towards me, like it was the moment she was waiting for.

She uses a surprisingly strong grip on my upper bicep to drag me towards the trunk of her car. Popping it open with her fob, we wait as the metal slowly rises. Anticipation builds inside me during the delay, I'm anxious to see the reason for my friends' presence.

The trunk finally opens and reveals a pile of... fabric?

"What is that?" I ask, unable to hide my confusion from my expression or tone.

Katie squeals instead of answering and the rest of the girls join us, also opening their trunks to reveal a bunch of random items. My eyes take in the objects, spotting a mirror, cans of paint and what looks to be other painting supplies, a box with a picture of a dining table on its side, and a few boxes with unknown contents.

"What is all this for?" I ask as my eyes flit between the items, then move to take in each of the girls excited faces.

"It's to remodel your trailer!" Summer exclaims, her expression giddy as she waves her hand at the trunk of her large vehicle like she's Vanna White.

"This is for my trailer?" I ask, perplexed as I stare into the full trunks of their vehicles.

"Yes, girl," Katie replies happily. "We're here to spruce up the place. This," she pauses gesturing at the vehicles. "Is to outfit your trailer so it's fit for the queen that lives there."

"Wow," I respond, unsure what to add, overwhelmed by their unexpected presence and even more unexpected generosity.

"Well, we're wasting daylight," Katie drawls out, sounding like a man in an old western movie. "We need to start slinging paint before the sun sets. That way we can leave all the windows down to help it dry!"

"I also brought a fan to speed up the drying process!" Heather chimes in.

"Why don't we start unloading all the paint stuff and get to work?" Summer instructs, clearly channeling her inner cheer captain to get us organized.

The four of us make quick work unloading all of the paint and supplies, piling them into the center of my living room. Katie surveys the trailer before chiming in again, "I think we should remove the old table and all the couch cushions, then we can cover the rest in plastic while we paint."

"Okay, are you attached to this table at all?" Summer asks, dragging her eyes from the chipped and stained oak to raise a brow at me. "We brought you a new one that has a banquette so you can have more seating."

"And it's super cute! White with a pink floral cushion," Katie adds.

"I would just hate to get rid of this, if it's important to you," Summer continues, eyeing my junky table like maybe it's a family heirloom or something.

"No, I'm not attached to the table," I say with a laugh.

This whole situation feels surreal, like Katie read my mind when I thought this place seemed less like a home and more like a place to sleep and store my things. Then, in typical Katie fashion, she came up with a solution to fix the problem.

"I'll help you carry the table to the dumpster," I tack on.

"No, Heather can help her. I want to show you the paint I bought," Katie directs, dragging me to join her.

She whips a screwdriver out of her back pocket, the movement erratic and the pointed tip flailing through the air. I fight the urge to flinch, worried she's going to take my eye out, but thankfully she's able to keep her grip and my eyes remain intact.

"Okay so I made a few executive decisions on the colors. I hope you like them... This one is for the main area," she declares, prying the can open to reveal a soft, sage green.

"Oh, I love it," I reply. Green has been one of my favorite colors recently, and although this isn't the exact shade I see whenever I close my eyes, it's beautiful and calming. "This will be super nice for the main space," I state.

Katie grins under my approval, moving to the next tin. "This is for the bathroom," she says, grabbing a smaller can of paint. She pries off the top, revealing a sunshine yellow color. Without giving me a chance to voice my thoughts, she continues, "And lastly, for the bedroom." The final tin contains a beautiful sky-blue color.

"I love all of these! You did a great job, Katie. Thank you so much," I state, earnestly. "Don't we need like a primer or something though, before we paint?"

I've never painted the inside of a house before, but I remember overhearing Mr. Mouchard complaining about the expenses associated with painting.

He was trying to rejuvenate the lobby, but decided it cost too much to buy both paint and primer, which he stated was basically just double paint and the motel's money would be better spent elsewhere.

My words cause Katie to frown and critically eye the dingy, white walls in my trailer. "Honestly, this kind of looks like primer that someone put up and never painted over," she responds. "I think since it's white, we should be fine without the primer."

I shrug and nod, trusting her judgement. Honestly, I think even if we messed up the paint, it would be a real accomplishment to make the inside of the trailer uglier than it already is.

Heather and Summer return from the dumpster shortly after Katie reveals the paint colors she's chosen. The four of us use plastic and blue tape to safeguard my counters and furniture from our painting efforts.

Katie even brought white coveralls for each of us to wear. After we pull them over our clothes, she makes us pose for half a dozen photos and selfies together before allowing us to begin.

Following our mini photo shoot, Katie checks her phone several times, swiftly tapping out a few responses before joining the painting party.

I watch her as I dip my foam roller into the pan, coating it with the sage green paint. "Is everything okay?" I finally ask when the rounded sponge is covered and ready to be applied to the wall.

Her eyes drift up from her phone distractedly. "Uh, yes. Just offering some advice on how to ask for forgiveness."

"Is it Alex?" I ask, her response piquing my curiosity.

"What?" She asks, her eyebrows raising into her hairline. "No," she quickly replies. "Just an old friend, it's no big deal." She puts her phone in her back pocket and picks up her own roller.

I shrug off the strange reaction, applying paint to the wall in firm, steady strokes. Despite Katie's brush off, I notice her continuing to subtly check her phone. I don't ask about it again though, not wanting to push if she isn't ready to share.

Together, the four of us make short work of applying a layer of the sage green paint to the main room. Even though it's a bit patchy in places, it already makes the entire place feel warmer. Like a place I actually want to spend time in.

I voice these thoughts aloud and Katie turns to critically eye our work.

"I love it! I can't wait to get the rest of the décor we brought set up in here as well. Why don't we split up for the bathroom and bedroom? Then after we can take a brief break for lunch while the paint dries. We'll definitely need to do two coats," Katie directs, instructing our little crew.

"We can take the bathroom," Summer says, volunteering herself and Heather to paint the smaller room.

"Sounds good to me," I agree with a nod.

Grabbing a fresh roller and the tin with the blue paint, I wander into the bedroom at the very back of the trailer. Katie follows behind slowly and I spot her phone in her hands again, her fingers flying over the screen like she's using the piece of technology to plan world domination.

Although my curiosity is eating me alive, I ignore her, and focus on applying paint to my bedroom wall as evenly as possible. Soon after, Katie picks up her own brush and joins me.

We make it halfway across the walls, when Heather and Summer join us, already finished with the bathroom paint. Together we create an indoor sky on my walls, coating them in soft blue, the same hue as a warm summer day.

With the walls covered, I take a step back and admire our handiwork. It's not perfect, but it's already an improvement. The potential of the trailer is evident, even under a simple coat of paint. Gratitude floods me, as I imagine what it will be like to live here once we finish.

Katie is on her phone again, but the second she feels my eyes on her, she places it back into her pocket. "Let's take a quick break before we apply the second coat. I brought sandwiches," she states in her usual chipper voice.

"I'll set up the fan in the main room," Summer adds, dashing out of my bedroom.

Surveying the room one last time, I open my windows, then file out of the trailer behind the girls. The four of us clamber in Summer's massive SUV, which looks almost identical to Collin's. Heather and Summer take the front, and Katie joins me in the back seat. I stretch my legs out while she opens a bag from the deli downtown, passing out wrapped bundles containing sandwiches.

Silence fills the car as we scarf down our food, then remain for a few extra minutes to rest. Painting is hard work, and my muscles are already tired and achy after applying a single coat to the rooms in my small space.

"How long do we have to wait for the paint to dry?" I finally ask.

Summer checks her pretty, rose gold watch, rolling up the sleeve of her coveralls to inspect the shiny glass face. "It's been almost an hour for the living room already. I think we should be good to paint the next coat soon."

"I want to thank you all for doing this," I say, sincerity evident in my words.

My eyes start to tear up as I think about the fore-thought and effort necessary to plan this. I still can't believe that someone would do this for me.

"It already looks like a whole new trailer, with just a coat of paint," I add.

Katie squeezes my hand, with a warm grin before

she hops out of the SUV. The rest of us follow suit, wandering to the hood of the car, our eyes focused on the ancient, tin trailer resting on the grass before us.

"This means so much to me and I don't know how to thank you," I whisper, making eye contact with each of the girls.

"It was nothing," Summer says, shooting me a warm smile.

Heather wraps her arm around me and gives me a brief side squeeze. "Girl, this is what it means to be part of a team," she says like it's the most obvious answer in the world.

"You're welcome to stay with me any time, Kenz, but everyone should have a place that feels like home, and now you do," Katie says simply, like what she arranged wasn't magnificent. But that's just the way Katie is, she thinks of others without expecting anything in return, like Collin.

His name briefly sours my happiness. My heart turns heavy with the reminder of how much I fucked up, by simply refusing to admit the truth to Collin sooner.

Pushing aside the unwanted emotion, I focus on the future.

From this day forward, all I can do is commit to being the best person I can. To treat those around me with kindness, because it's how everyone deserves to be treated.

With Collin, or without, I know my future is somewhere far beyond the confines of this trailer park.

"I guess it's time to resume painting," I finally say, forcing some enthusiasm into my voice.

"Can we get another pic?" Katie asks, excitedly as we traipse into the trailer and create a small circle around the paint pan, watching as she pours the sage colored paint inside so we can resume.

Summer, Heather and I groan in unison, "No."

Then, the four of us giggle and pick up our roller brushes to continue reclaiming the rooms inside the trailer.

Transforming this hunk of junk into my home.

Chapter 37

Katie stops in the deadened grass in front of my trailer, her car still idling, as she brings me home from our post-painting celebratory dinner.

"Did you want to come inside and hang out?" I ask, excited to spend more time in my new, updated space.

"Uhm, I can't tonight. I actually need to get home to work on something for a little while," she replies evasively.

"Oh okay," I respond, tamping down the disappointment generated by her refusal.

Reminding myself she devoted her entire afternoon to decorating my trailer lessens the blow. She probably needs some time to focus on her own life. My thoughts also briefly touch on her mysterious text conversation that she carried on throughout the day, as I unbuckle my seatbelt.

"Well, I'll see you Monday then," I say, then add, "Thank you again, for everything."

Katie gives me a side hug, then eyes me as we separate. "Hey, you aren't going anywhere else tonight, right?"

"Uhm, no," I respond, startled by her out-of-the-blue question. "I was planning on hanging out here."

"Alright, I was just wondering," she says with a shrug. "See you Monday," she adds with a smile that's more toned down than usual.

Our eyes lock for a second and I speculate as to why she's suddenly acting so strange, but her clear blue eyes reveal nothing.

Shrugging it off, I open the door and exit her hot pink bug. She nods and gives a quick wave, immediately backing onto the dirt road and bumping away before I even make it up my steps.

"Well that was weird," I mutter to myself, unlocking my front door. I pause before crossing the threshold, flipping the light switch to admire my new living room.

It's crazy how a coat of fresh paint and some new fabric can transform a space.

Stepping forward, I beeline to my updated couch and plop onto the newly covered cushions. The fabric Katie brought to replace my old, grimy cushions, is a pale yellow with little pink flowers.

It looks similar to the fabric covering the banquette for my new table without being an exact match. My eyes flit across the space, captivated by the little details Katie incorporated into one cohesive design that fits me perfectly.

Finally, I have a real home that truly feels like mine.

A grin appears on my lips and I sit in silence,

soaking in the space, and enjoying the feeling of belonging. Not because I don't have money, but because this is where I live, a space I've paid for and maintained all on my own.

A knock on the door interrupts my moment of self-reflection and my brow furrows wondering who it could be. If it's Derek, I fully intend to slam the door in his face.

Cautiously, I unlock my new deadbolt and inch open the door, ready to smash it back shut if necessary. Instead my jaw drops and my hand falls from the thin tin.

A familiar blonde stands on my steps, a bunch of lilies grasped tightly in his hand. Butterflies run amok in my stomach at the sight of him, but I do my best to contain them as I ask, "Collin? What are you doing here?"

Collin seems like he's struggling to find his words, and he shuffles his feet for a second. It's the first time I've seen this confident, sexy guy looking awkward. I think about saying something else to try and soothe away the tension, but he replies before I get the chance.

"Can I come in?"

I nod, wordlessly standing aside to let him pass. His side brushes against me as he enters, causing the butterflies to swoop and dive at an exacerbated pace. I take an extra second to lock the deadbolt, needing the time to gather my wits before facing him.

When I twirl around to Collin again, his eyes are wide as he notices the changes to my trailer. As if he can sense my gaze focused on him, he quickly locks his eyes with mine and passes me the flowers.

"These are for you."

"Thank you," I reply simply, placing the lilies on the counter behind me.

"It looks really nice in here," he drawls.

His gaze never leaves mine, eyes searing into my soul. It's a lesson in self-restraint to keep my feet still and my hands locked against my sides.

I nod again, silently, his words floating in the air between us unaddressed.

We continue staring at each other, and I force the hope blooming in my chest back down. Taking a deep inhale to brace myself for the conversation I'm about to delve into. I need to find out why Collin is here before I break my own heart all over again with unwarranted expectations.

"What—"

"'McKenzie—"

We both start and stop our sentences at the same time. Collin gestures for me to go first.

Leaning against the counter, I begin again, "What are you doing here?" I force my tone to remain open and curious, rather than hopeful and desperate.

Collin releases a deep sigh, he motions to my newly cushioned couch then quirks a brow at me, "May I?"

I nod and he sits down, lounging back against my couch and fuck me if he doesn't look like he belongs there for all of eternity.

He releases another sigh, the noise pulling me from my reverie, where I imagined walking forward and straddling him; kissing him until neither of us can remember our own names.

"I came to apologize, McKenzie. What I did on Monday was fucked up and I'm sorry." He hangs his head, holding the sides with his hands like he's ashamed of his actions at school. He continues, without glancing up again, his gaze and words aimed at his lap. "I'm not interested in Isabelle, I never have been and it didn't go any further than a little flirting and placing my arm around her, I swear."

As the final words leave his lips, he finally looks up, his pained eyes begging me to believe him. Isabelle stated as much at the SAT, but hearing the words from him provides a strange sort of relief, the feeling flooding my veins.

"Why did you do it?" I ask, my whispered words lingering in the space between us.

Collin appears abashed and trains his gaze on his hands in his lap again. I instantly miss the sight of the emerald green orbs.

"You hurt me and I wanted to hurt you back. It was all pretty petty and I'm really sorry…" He glances up at me, his tone and eyes beseeching. "Can you forgive me?"

Can I forgive him? Does that mean… he's still interested in me?

I push away from the counter, feeling bolder and more confident. Sitting next to Collin on the couch, I grab his hand and intertwine our fingers. He doesn't resist my affection or yank from my grasp, which I interpret to mean my assumption is correct.

"No, I'm sorry. I should've been honest with you about the deal I made with Derek. It just never felt like there was a right time and you found out in the shittiest way possible."

My eyes lock with Collin's, his gaze penetrating my soul with the connection. The heat that's been missing all week slowly floods my veins making me feel like I'm burning from the inside out.

"I should've told you the truth, but I was afraid it would push you away. As a result, I waited too long and lost you anyways," I half-whisper.

Collin opens his mouth to reply, but I place a single finger over his lips. The movement silences him as intended, and I continue, the words spilling from my lips. "You're so perfect. I feel like everything good in my life ends up leaving, but I don't want you to leave... not again. I don't want to fuck this up because I think I'm falling for you, Collin Franzen."

He squeezes my hand and replies, talking past my finger. "Well that's a relief because I'm definitely falling for you McKenzie Carslyle," he drawls the words out and the heat simmering between us flares into an inferno.

We fall into each other, our mouths clashing in desperation, like it's been seven years since our last kiss, instead of a mere seven days.

His teeth and tongue nip and lick at my lips until I open to his onslaught. He uses his kisses to communicate his appreciation, sorrow, and gratitude in that order; confirming he felt the same way without me as I did without him.

When we finally separate, we're both panting, my lungs scream from the lack of oxygen, but the rest of my body aches to get closer to Collin Franzen. I lean forward to resume our kiss, but Collin evades me with a smirk.

"Before we continue this, I want to make a deal," he drawls, the words low and sexy.

I almost agree without thought, purely from the sensual appeal of his tone. With painstaking care, I slowly gather my wits in an effort to formulate a reply.

"I think I'm done making deals with dangerous guys," I quip back.

"So, you think I'm dangerous?" Collin asks, his face inching closer to mine with each word.

"Definitely," I admit. "After one month, you've imprinted yourself on my soul. I don't think I could shake you even if I wanted to, and I don't want to."

Collin chuckles, shaking his head before moving to hover over my lips. "I feel the same way, so maybe you're dangerous too, McKenzie Carslyle." He brushes his lips lightly against mine, then pulls back, preventing me from deepening our kiss. "I think this is a deal you'll like though," he whispers.

"Okay, I'm listening," I reply, staring into an emerald gaze I could never tire of.

"How about we promise to tell each other the truth moving forward? Even if it's difficult," he proposes.

I put a finger to my chin, tapping lightly like I'm contemplating his words. Collin tilts forward, nipping at the digit with a growl, halting its movement.

His silly antics help to relieve some of the tension

from our serious conversation. Giggling, I remove my hand and place it in my lap.

Clearing my throat and sobering my tone, I agree, "I think I would like to accept your deal, with one amendment."

"Go on," he drawls.

"I think we need to promise to accept each other's truth without judgment, even when it's difficult," I respond.

Collin nods slowly, once. Then he repeats the motion again after a few beats, but he remains silent.

"I think it's the only way this will work," I whisper, trying to sway him to my side, not realizing the nod was his answer.

"Of course, I agree to your amendment," Collin replies. "Now tell me, when did you become so wise, McKenzie Carslyle?"

"This deal was your idea."

"So maybe I'm the wise one," he quips with a smirk.

"Well, oh wise Collin Franzen, how would you like to spend the rest of our night?" My voice becomes a little shy as I add, "Together, right?"

Collin slips his fingers into mine and gives them a tight squeeze. "Do you want to head back to my house? We can spend the night there. You can stay as long as you want…" He offers.

I pause, surveying my new, clean walls, the fresh, vibrant curtains, and the succulent that Katie gifted me. Turning to Collin, I confess, "I think I'd like to stay here, if that's okay. It finally feels like home."

His eyes search mine, and whatever he sees causes a

warm smile to bloom on his face. "I'd like that very much," he drawls and tucks my head against his chest, under his chin.

We sit there for a while, his steady breathing lulling me into a state of calm. This moment, this absolutely perfect moment, imprints itself on my brain. I want a hundred simple moments like this with my guy.

Collin's hands brush a soothing, circular motion across my upper biceps and I nestle in further, embracing the peace and warmth that he offers with his silent presence.

Soon, his hands start roving upwards, cradling my neck and guiding my face to meet his. He brushes his lips across mine softly, and I release a small, contented sigh.

The sound emboldens him and he deepens the kiss, his lips searing mine with their ardent passion. In under sixty seconds, he works me into a frenzy.

My calm state has fled, my chest heaving with my impassioned breaths as I match his kisses with fervor. Our teeth, tongues, and lips smash together, in a sloppy cadence, desperate to get as close to each other as possible.

When he finally pulls away, escaping my lips as they pursue his, he stares down at me with a smirk. "I think I could easily spend the rest of my life kissing you," he drawls.

"Would you like to see the rest of the updates to my trailer?" I ask with a smirk of my own, offering a hand intent on leading him to my bedroom.

"I would like that very much, Wise McKenzie," he

drawls, placing his warm palm in mine. He uses the grip to pull me up to my toes as he rises, sweeping me into his arms bridal style, carrying me back towards my bed. My feet never touch the ground as he places me directly onto my mattress.

He takes a step back, as if he's taking a mental snapshot of this moment to keep the memory of the day we got back together, forever.

And I would be lying if I said I wasn't doing the same.

Chapter 38

I wake up sprawled across Collin's chest, our legs intertwined, and his arms clasped around my waist, holding me in place. My eyes drink in his sleeping form, still wearing his clothes from yesterday.

I fight the urge to pinch the skin on my forearm, to ensure I'm not dreaming and imagining the handsome guy laying in my bed. His plump lips are relaxed as his chest moves with each deep breath.

Last night was surreal.

Never in a million years would I predict that Collin would show up on my porch with flowers, not after the way he dismissed me in the hall on Monday. I'm not complaining; I'm both grateful for his forgiveness and determined to approach this second chance with complete honesty.

Collin isn't slipping through my fingers again.

He lazily lifts one lid and a single emerald eye connects with mine. "Hello, beautiful," he grumbles, his voice coated in sleep.

"Hi," I respond, nerves heightening the pitch of my words.

Collin tightens his grip, squeezing me closer to his chest and dragging me with him. He scoots up, to rest against the wall behind the bed.

As an effect, I end up straddling his lap, my knees pressing into the mattress on either side of his legs. My center aligns with an erection that grows impossibly harder and thicker by the second.

His arousal triggers my own, my core flooding with heat as our eyes connect. Maintaining eye contact, I drift forward and close the gap between our mouths, stopping just shy of our lips connecting. Hovering above him, I grip his sides, rubbing my aching core across his cock.

Collin groans, sealing his lips to mine in one swift movement. He claims my mouth, taking over as his hands grip my hips, sliding my center across him in a consistent motion. The delicious friction builds, and I yearn to undress.

As if reading my thoughts, Collin slips his hands underneath my shirt. Tugging it over my head in one smooth movement, breaking our lips apart as it crosses my face. Collin leans back, his heated gaze raking over my torso.

The look in his eyes causes me to feel like I'm burning alive from the inside out, my blood heating and thrumming against my skin. With increased urgency, I tug at the bottom of Collin's shirt. Feeding off my desperation, he rips it over his head, then lifts me up and we tear off the rest of our clothing in a frenzy.

We stare at each other, a million unspoken words pinging back and forth in the connection, until I close my eyes and claim Collin's lips once more. His hands graze against my back as he pulls me closer, crushing me to his chest. My liquid heat soaks his erection as it prods against me, in a preview of what's to come.

I rock against him as our lips compete for dominance. Delicious heat continues to build with each pass of my center against his. Collin's hands wind to the front of my chest and he cups a breast in each hand, kneading and tweaking as his tongue sweeps across mine. I moan into his mouth, feeling his smug smirk against my lips as he adds to the friction at my core, two fingers sliding against my clit, lubricated by my desire.

He drives me to the edge and my muscles tense, preparing for the orgasm Collin is orchestrating with his hands and mouth. As my core tightens, his name leaves my lips, pleasure zipping through every cell as my release rips through me.

Without giving me a chance to regain my breath, Collin lifts me, sliding me slowly onto his cock. Each inch driving into me, reignites my desire, and extends the pleasure that had begun to ebb. With steady movements, he grips my hips and guides me as I ride him. His eyes lock on mine and the intensity of his gaze leaves me breathless.

This feels less like sex and more like making love.

He groans as I tighten my legs around his hips and take control, increasing my tempo. Sliding to the tip of his thick length, then slamming back down, I bring both of us to the edge. Our chests rapidly rise and fall in sync as the rest of the world fades away.

Together, we fall over the edge, giving in to our pleasure.

My second orgasm tears through me, every inch of my body tightening against Collin as he thrusts into me, groaning his own release. His arms catch my body as I sag against him, feeling weak but sated.

We stay in bed, wrapped around each other intimately as we gather our breath. Collin pecks my forehead and nuzzles his face against my sweat-drenched neck. His lips lightly graze the skin, as he lays a soft kiss there.

"Thank you," he whispers, so quietly, I almost miss his words.

"For what?"

Collin pulls back, his gaze searching mine, then he drawls, "For forgiving me. I'm so sorry."

My expression is incredulous as I process his words. "We both have made mistakes, but I think we were made for each other, Collin Franzen," I finally reply. Laying a soft kiss against his cheek, I whisper, "We have the rest of our lives to prove it to each other."

I smile at his soft expression, and heave my body off his, stumbling slightly when my over-pleasured legs touch my bedroom floor. Collin shoots up steadying me, but I slip from his grasp and exit the room.

Wandering from my bedroom, I enter the bathroom, bringing my phone with me to shoot a text to Katie. While I take care of business, I think of what to say, finally opening my messaging app after I wash my hands.

Collin came over yesterday with flowers. We stayed up half the night talking through everything…

Three dots appear on the screen immediately, showing Katie's typing a response. Seconds later, my phone dings, alerting me to her message.

Katie: **Yay! I'm glad his plan worked out!! I'm so happy for you two.**

Her words give me pause. Recalling her weirdness from yesterday, it suddenly dawns on me that Collin and Katie were texting the entire time she was at my trailer. It's probably the reason she was acting so strangely when she dropped me off. She knew Collin was on his way over.

That sneaky girl!

A grin blooms across my face, my appreciation growing for my meddling best friend.

I reply quickly: **Thank you, Katie. You're the best.**

Then I open the door to reveal a shirtless Collin waiting in the cramped hallway. He smirks at me, sliding his body against my still, drooling form as he passes and enters the bathroom. Forcing myself to snap out of it, I exit to give him space.

He lounges against the door frame, his gaze raking over my body. "Wanna get waffles?" He asks, the words infused with warmth and happiness.

Yeah, big guy. I'd love to go anywhere with you.

Collin laughs, and I realize I've spoken the words out

loud. Maybe it was unintentional, but either way, the sentiment remains the same.

I shoot him a quick wink as he slowly closes the door, milking the moment of staring at his handsome face before he disappears from sight.

Then, I skip into my bedroom, ready to start the next chapter of my life.

I clutch my packet of papers, containing all the information I'll need for the next year of my life, against my chest as Collin navigates the busy streets onto campus. Despite having all the directions memorized, I glance down at the map one more time and remind Collin, "My dorm is in Clara Hall."

He nods distractedly, as he carefully maneuvers his SUV around a crowd of students carrying boxes into a large, ornate, brick building.

"I think we need to take this right up here," I instruct, eyeing the street sign as it slowly approaches, giving us plenty of time to prepare for the turn.

"Mhmm," he agrees his brow furrowed in concentration, while our vehicle continues moving forward at a snail's pace to avoid hitting the swarms of students and parents milling about.

By the time we make it to the intersection, I'm bouncing up and down on the firm leather seat. My giddiness is filling me to the brim but I'm focusing on keeping it contained so I don't annoy Collin with the seven-hundredth conversation about how excited I am today.

It's extremely difficult to keep it to myself because I am so excited.

In my head, I run through my classes again, then transition to mentally checking off the dormitory move-in list. Reaffirming I purchased everything I need to start college off on the right foot when classes begin in three days.

My distraction works so well, it takes me a few extra seconds to realize that Collin turned left at the road, not right like I had asked.

"Hey, we missed our turn!" I exclaim.

"There's actually been a change of plans," Collin admits, appearing a little sheepish. "I was trying to figure out the best time to tell you, but I thought maybe you would like the surprise."

"What change in plans?" I ask, frantically.

I've planned everything about this day for months. Reading and rereading the guides on Berry College's website to make sure that I was enrolled in the best courses and placed in the best dorm for a female freshman.

I even stayed up until midnight with Katie on the day of dorm assignments so we could request each other, instead of being assigned some random that might smell like cheese. I've literally prepared for everything except a change in plans.

I tamp down the panic rising in my chest. This is Collin, he thinks of everything. He knows how important today is; how hard I worked to get here. He was by my side all of the late nights.

He even held onto me when I cried before opening my admissions letter, maintaining his grasp when joyful tears continued to flow after I read the word "accepted".

There's no way my sweet, thoughtful guy would do anything to mess this up. The thought reassures me slightly, but my heart is still racing in my chest when the SUV slowly rolls to a stop in the driveway of a two-story, brick townhouse.

"What is this?" I ask.

Collin just smirks, hopping out of his car and rounding the hood. He reaches the passenger side before I've moved a muscle. Opening my door for me, he grabs my hand, tugging me up the driveway and inside the townhouse.

I drag my feet to a stop, just past the threshold, taking in the clean hardwood floors and pale gray walls of a spacious living room. Off to the side, I can see a moderately sized, square kitchen that looks like it belongs in a farmhouse. A hall runs between the two rooms, disappearing past a set of stairs.

"What is this place?" I ask, turning to Collin to find his emerald gaze drinking in my every expression.

"It's our new residence," he drawls, flashing his teeth at me in a grin before tugging me into his side and walking us the rest of the way into the room.

"What about my dorm? And what about Katie? We were supposed to room togeth—"

Collin silences me with a soft kiss, placed gently against my lips. Removing his mouth from mine, he hovers just out of reach, his warm breath fanning across my face.

"I've got you. Everything has been handled. Just trust me, McKenzie Carslyle."

My tense shoulders slowly relax and I lean forward, chasing his lips with mine. He chuckles, but doesn't hold back, quickly taking over and claiming me in a searing kiss.

He walks me backwards, pressing me against the wall and I have no complaints as he turns up the heat, devouring me with his kisses. I arch into him as my pulse races and my insides become a raging inferno, encouraging me to get as much of our skin touching as possible.

"Oh, yuck," a familiar, chipper voice calls out, interrupting my make out session as the sound echoes across the empty space.

I peek around Collin's shoulder and find Katie standing on the stairs, at the edge of the room.

"We definitely need to set some ground rules against PDA if this is going to work. First on the list is definitely: 'No Sex against the Living Room Wall'." She tugs her phone from her pocket and continues, "You know what? I'm actually going to start that list, on my phone, like right now."

A dry voice adds, "I second that." Then Isabelle steps into sight, halting on the step just above Katie.

I squeal, pushing past Collin to rush over. The two girls finish descending the stairs and return my excited hugs. Although Isabelle lacks a little bit of our enthusiasm.

Over the past year, I've learned not to take it too personally, it's just who she is. The acceptance of each other's quirks is part of the reason we've become close friends after our rocky beginning.

"What are you guys doing here?" I ask. "Where are you living now? I'm sorry, I didn't know," I say, turning to address Katie.

She giggles, and throws an arm around my shoulders, steering me to the front door. "Do you think Collin was able to arrange this without the help of your besties? No way!" She exclaims. "We're all living here!"

My eyes seek out Collin's across the room and the heat continues to sizzle between us, but stronger than that is a thread of love.

I love this guy and his thoughtful caring nature. The way he always thinks of me, even when he's doing something like moving us in together for freshman year.

"Collin gets the room downstairs, and us girls will stay upstairs," Katie continues, undeterred by my silence. "There's even three bathrooms in this place which is like AMAZING."

My guy strides across the room and grabs my hand, tugging me towards him and away from Katie's endless chatter. "Do you like it?" He asks quietly, his confident gaze peppered with a little concern.

"I love it and you," I confirm, laying a quick peck on his lips before turning back to my girls.

"I love you too," he murmurs, eyeing Katie briefly before swiping his tongue across my lips.

I'm still laughing when Katie claps once, then spews her first set of instructions. "Let's bring all your things in, ASAP," she squeals. "That's the last of the stuff we need to carry, before movers arrive with actual furniture tomorrow. I want to get a picture with the 'Berry College' sign before it gets dark, so we need to move quickly!"

Isabelle, Collin, and I groan in unison, already anticipating the two-hour photo shoot in our future, but we trail out of the house behind her anyways.

Pausing in the doorway, I watch as my boyfriend and two of my best friends walk to the SUV, opening the trunk and snagging some of the boxes nestled inside.

I take the extra seconds to appreciate how far I've come since this time last year, and all the gifts that I've been given—in the form of love.

"Stop being a sentimental sap and come grab your shit," Isabelle shouts, breaking through my thoughts.

I laugh, but jog down the steps to join the group at the back of the SUV. Collin pulls me against his side, laying a soft kiss against my forehead before handing me a box with his signature sparkle-eyed grin.

Returning the look, I saunter inside, swaying my hips for his benefit, as I carry the cardboard.

It's time to start my next adventure.

The End.

Books by Nicole Marsh

The Curse Trilogy (Paranormal Romance)

Cursed

Bound

Shattered

Standalone

The Con

Interested in news about Nicole
Marsh books?

Join her Mailing List.

instagram.com/nicolemarshbooks

bookbub.com/authors/nicole-marsh

Reviews

If you enjoyed this book, please consider leaving an honest review. Reviews truly are the lifeblood of any book and your opinion matters.

Made in the USA
Middletown, DE
15 June 2021

42344933R00205